MATT JENSEN:

THE LAST MOUNTAIN MAN

MATT JENSEN:
THE LAST MOUNTAIN MAN

William W. Johnstone
with J. A. Johnstone

PINNACLE BOOKS
Kensington Publishing Corp.
www.kensingtonbooks.com

PINNACLE BOOKS are published by

Kensington Publishing Corp.
119 West 40th Street
New York, NY 10018

All Kensington titles, imprints, and distributed lines are available at special
quantity discounts for bulk purchases for sales promotions, premiums, fund-
raising, educational, or institutional use. Special book excerpts or customized
printings can also be created to fit specific needs. For details, write or phone
the office of the Kensington special sales manager: Kensington Publishing
Corp., 119 West 40th Street, New York, NY 10018, attn: Special Sales Department; phone 1-800-221-2647.

ISBN-13: 978-0-7860-3410-9
ISBN-10: 0-7860-3410-6

First printing: September 2007
Eighth printing: May 2013

16 15 14 13 12 11 10 9 8

Printed in the United States of America

Chapter One

Pettis County, Missouri, May 1865

Martin Cavanaugh shifted his position on the saddle to try and find some relief from the bone-deep tired of four long years of war. Although Cavanaugh was mustered out at Jefferson Barracks in St. Louis, he was still wearing the uniform of a captain of the Union Cavalry as he made the long ride back home to Kansas.

Just ahead was an old, weather-beaten building. For a moment, he thought it might be deserted; then he saw a hand-lettered sign nailed to the side.

FOOD——WHISKEY——TERBACKY——GOODS——BEDS

He didn't plan to waste any of his mustering-out money on a bed, but he thought a meal might be good. Also, he could use a drink, and a little tobacco for the trail, so he rode up to the building, dismounting at the hitching rail.

There were two men sitting on the porch. Both were wearing the tattered gray and butternut uniform of the Confederate army. One had sergeant's chevrons, but the tunic was so filthy that they barely showed. He had a puffy scar, starting above his left eye, disfiguring the eye, then streaking down his cheek and jaw like a purple flash of lightning, twisting the left side of his mouth into a sneer. The other man was wearing a bushy black beard, but the most distinctive thing about him was his left ear. Only half of it was there, the earlobe having been shot off in the war. Both men were thin, and they had the look in their eyes and faces of men who had seen a lot of the war.

Warily, Martin nodded at them as he passed by them to go inside the building. The two Rebel soldiers returned the nod, but they never took their eyes off him. One of them spat a stream of tobacco juice in the dirt, but neither of them spoke.

The interior of the inn was a study of shadow and light. Some of the light came through the door and some through windows that were nearly opaque with dirt. Most of it, however, was in the form of gleaming dust motes that hung suspended in the still air, illuminated by the bars of sunbeams that stabbed through the cracks between the boards.

Martin found a table in the back corner of the room, near the stove. Since it was warm outside, the stove wasn't being used, but the smell of burnt wood clung to it like the low-lying, early morning fog on a grassy meadow.

The proprietor of the establishment came over to his table. Picking some sort of bug from his beard, he examined it for a moment, then flicked it away.

"What can I get for you?"

"What do you have to eat?"

"Beans, bacon, biscuits."

"All right, I'll have that. Do you have beer?"

"I've got whiskey."

"A glass of whiskey and some tobacco."

"Chewin' or smokin'?"

"Smoking."

"I've got a woman here iffen you'd like to spend a little time with her. It'll cost you six bits," the proprietor said. He nodded toward a woman who was sitting a few tables away. She smiled a toothless smile at him, and brushed an errant tendril of hair back from her forehead.

"No, thanks," Martin said. "I've got a woman of my own, and two kids, waitin' for me back home."

"Suit yourself," the proprietor said. "I'll get your vittles." He turned away from the table and walked back into what Martin assumed was a kitchen.

Even as he was giving his order to the proprietor, Martin saw the two Confederate soldiers come inside. They sat at a table near the door, but he noticed that both of them sat in such a way as to be facing him. Something about the way they were looking at him made him suspicious, so he eased his pistol out of his holster and held it under the table.

"Cap'n?" one of the men said. This was the one with sergeant's stripes. "You are a Yankee cap'n, ain't you?"

"The war's over, boys," Martin said. "I'm a civilian now, same as you two."

"Ain't quite the same," the sergeant said. "You still got your horse. The Yankees took our horses."

"I'm sorry to hear that."

"The name is Payson. Clyde Payson," the sergeant said. "This here is Garvey Laird. It's like I was tellin' Garvey, we got us a long way to go and the way things is now, 'bout the onliest way we got of gettin' there is by shank's mare."

"Well, Sergeant Payson, I feel for you, I truly do," Martin said. "I've got a long way to go myself, and I'd hate to have to make the whole trip without a horse."

"Yeah, well, here's the point," Payson continued. "Me'n Garvey here was thinkin' on maybe takin' your horse."

"What good would that do you?" Martin asked. "There are two of you, there's only one horse."

"We figure we could double up till we come up on another horse," Payson said.

"Oh, I don't think I would like that," Martin said. "And I know my horse wouldn't like it—being ridden double like that, I mean."

Garvey barked what might have been a laugh. "Well, now, that's real funny," he said. "Specially seein' as the horse ain't goin' have no say-so in the matter. And like you say, there's two of us and only one of you."

Payson and Garvey stood up from their table and made a point of turning to face Martin.

Martin moved the pistol out from under the table and pointed it at them.

The two soldiers, surprised to see that Martin was holding a gun on them, stopped in their tracks.

"Hold on, mister, we didn't mean nothin' like that," Payson said. "We was just goin' to palaver a bit, that's all."

"I'd feel a mite more comfortable if you boys weren't wearin' guns while we were palaverin'," Martin said. "How about comin' over here and droppin' 'em down in the stove?"

"Now why would we want to do a fool thing like that?" Garvey asked.

"Because I'll kill you if you don't," Martin said easily. He punctuated his comment by pulling back the hammer on his pistol. It made a deadly-sounding click as the sear engaged the cylinder. "I killed my share of men wearing that uniform. I wouldn't lose any sleep over killin' two more."

The two Confederate soldiers stared at him for a long moment, but did nothing.

"Use your thumb and finger to pull your guns out, then carry them over here and drop them in the stove," Martin said.

The two did as Martin ordered.

"Now what?" Payson asked.

"How long has it been since you two boys had anything to eat?" Martin asked.

"We had some hardtack yesterday," Garvey said.

"Nothing since?"

Both shook their heads.

"Sit down over there," Martin said, waving his pistol toward one of the tables.

The two complied.

"Innkeeper," Martin called.

"Yes, sir?" the innkeeper replied. It wasn't until then that Martin noticed the innkeeper was standing just inside the door from the kitchen, holding a plate of beans, bacon, and biscuits. He had watched the entire drama unfold.

"How about feeding these two boys?" Martin said. "On me."

"Cap'n, you'd do that for us after we was goin' to steal your horse?" Payson asked.

"Yeah, why not?" Martin answered. "And it isn't captain, it's mister now," Martin said. "Name's Cavanaugh. Like I said, the war's over. No need for us to be killin' each other anymore."

Fellsburg, Kansas

Matt Cavanaugh knocked on the door of the office of the R.D. Clayton Livery Stable.

"Come on in, Matt."

Although only nine years old, Matt was a big boy for his age and had proven to be a good worker for the owner of the livery.

"I'm all finished, Mr. Clayton," Matt said.

"Every stall is mucked out?" Clayton asked.

"Yes, sir, every one," Matt said.

Clayton was in his late sixties, a bald-headed, fat man with chin whiskers.

"Don't think I'm not going to inspect the stalls," Clayton said. "I'm paying you fifty cents a week to keep 'em clean. I don't intend to throw away good money on a bad job."

"You can check, Mr. Clayton," Matt said. "I cleaned them all."

"You wait here till I get back," Clayton said.

"Yes, sir," Matt said.

Matt picked up the newspaper and began reading it as he waited.

FREE LAND IN THE WEST

> Reports have reached this city of much free land in the West. With the rebellion now put to rest, the government is anxious to see enterprising citizens occupy land in the more western extremes of the nation, thus expanding the reach of civilization and enterprise.

"Here, boy," Clayton said, returning to the office. "If you want to read the paper, you will have to pay for it the same as I did."

"I'm sorry," Matt said. "I meant no harm."

Clayton ran his hand through his hair, then sighed. "Go ahead, take it," he said. "I have finished with it." He stuck his hand in his pocket and pulled out a coin. "Here is your half-dollar. You did good work."

"Thank you," Matt replied, taking the coin.

Matt's mother, Mary, and his fourteen-year-old sister, Cassie, were hanging clothes on a line. They took in washing while Matt worked at the stables to make enough money to buy food. They were living in an old cabin that was within sight of a burned-out house and barn. The house and barn were part of what had once been a very fine ranch. It had been destroyed by Bushwhackers two years earlier.

"Here's my week's pay, Ma," Matt said, handing the half-dollar to his mother.

"Oh, Matthew," Mary said, putting her arms around her young son and pulling him to her. "You are such a help. I am so proud of you. You work so hard for the money that I just wish you could keep it for yourself."

"Someone's coming up the road, Mama," Cassie said.

"A soldier?" Mary asked.

"It looks like a soldier," Cassie replied.

"No doubt someone going home," Mary said. "We'll have to set an extra plate for supper."

"Mama, why do we have to feed all the strays?" Cassie asked.

"Child, your pa is on the road somewhere, coming home to us," Mary replied. "Wouldn't you like for someone to be feeding him, if he's hungry, or giving him a place to get out of the rain?"

"Yes, ma'am, I reckon you're right," Cassie said.

"You go set the extra plate, I'll invite him," Mary said. "Maybe he knows something about . . ." Mary stopped in mid-sentence and stared long and hard at the approaching rider. "It's him," she said in a small, quiet voice.

"Mama?"

"Praise be to God, it's him!" Mary said, shouting loudly this time. "Children, it's your father, come safely home to us!"

Spreading her arms wide, Mary started running toward the rider. The rider spurred his mount into a gallop, then leaped down from his horse just as Mary reached him. They embraced in the middle of the road.

"Is that Pa?" Matt asked.

"Of course it is," Cassie said. "Don't you remember him?"

"Yeah," Matt said, "I remember him."

Though Matt said the words, he wasn't sure he remembered his father well enough to recognize him. Matt had been five years old when Martin Cavanaugh left home as a lieutenant in the Ninth Cavalry Regiment of Kansas. His memory was hazy, and consisted mostly of seeing a tall man, in uniform, riding away on the horse Buster.

"No, I didn't bring Buster back," Matt's father said over supper that night. "Buster was killed at a place called Pleasant Hill."

"Poor Buster," Mary said. "He was such a good horse."

"Yes, he was," Martin agreed. He got up from the table to pour himself another cup of coffee. Then he stood at the window for a long moment, looking toward the burned-out house and barn.

"When did that happen?" he asked, nodding toward the ruins.

"Three years ago," Mary said. "Bushwhackers came by, burned us out, and took what livestock we had left."

"I'm sorry," Martin said. "Here I go off to fight the war, thinking I'm protecting you, and the war comes here to you."

"It doesn't matter," Mary said. She walked over to put her arms around him. "You are home now. Everything will be fine."

"Mama, what about the bank?" Cassie asked.

"The bank? What about the bank?" Martin asked.

"It's nothing. We can discuss it later."

Martin shook his head. "It won't go away by putting it off, will it?"

Mary sighed. "No, I don't suppose it will," she said.

"What about the bank?"

"I—I'm sorry, Martin. I had no choice, I had to mortgage the place."

"And now the bank wants to foreclose?"

Mary wiped a tear away as she nodded.

"I'm so sorry," she repeated. "I know how important this place was to you."

"Nonsense," Martin said. "This is just a place. I've seen hundreds of places in the last five years. You and the children are all that's important to me now."

"Mama took in laundry and I helped," Cassie said proudly. "And Matt works down at Clayton's Livery."

"I muck out the stalls," Matt said.

"You've taken in your last laundry and you've mucked out your last stall," Martin said.

"But what are we going to do? The bank wants the money and we don't have enough, do we? Did you bring any money home with you?"

"How much do we owe the bank?"

"Five hundred dollars."

Martin shook his head. "I don't have that much. But I have enough for us to start over somewhere else."

"Start over where?" Mary asked.

"Out West!" Matt said excitedly.

"Out West?" Mary chuckled. "Matthew, wherever did you get such an idea?"

"I read about it in the paper in Mr. Clayton's office," Matt said. "There's free land out West for people who want it."

"Free land. I've never heard of such a thing," Mary said.

Martin held up his hand. "No," he said, "I've heard that. I wasn't sure whether or not it was true, but I have heard it." He looked over at Matt. "You say you read this in the paper?"

"Yes, sir, I read it today," he said.

"Free land in the West, huh?"

"Martin, what are you talking about? Surely you don't intend to just leave here, do you?"

"What is there here for us, Mary?" Martin asked. "My parents are dead, your parents are dead. Neither one of us have a brother or sister. What's keeping us here?"

"Well, nothing, I guess," Mary replied. "But how are we going to get there?"

"You let me worry about that," Martin said. "First thing I'm going to do tomorrow is find out how a person gets hold of some of this free land. Then, if I see it's somethin' we can do, I'll figure out a way to get us there."

"All right," Mary said. "Whatever you decide is fine with me."

"It's real good to see you back, Martin," C.D. Folsom said the next morning when Martin rode into town to see him. Folsom was president of the Fellsburg Bank. "Yes, sir, it's good to see all our men back home from that war."

"Not everyone made it back," Martin said.

"No, sir, they didn't and that's a fact," Folsom said. "How many did we lose?"

"Three officers, one hundred ninety-two enlisted men," Martin said.

Folsom shook his head. "Well, now, that is a shame," he said. "That is truly a shame." Folsom cleared his throat. "But I'm sure you came to discuss business, right?"

"I did," Martin said.

"Your note is for $594.60," Folsom said. "I'm sure you will want to pay that off so you can get back to running your ranch."

"Five hundred ninety-four?" Martin said, surprised by the figure.

"And sixty cents," Folsom added.

"I thought the note was for five hundred dollars."

"It was originally. But with compound interest for three years, it comes to $594.60. You do have the money, don't you?"

Martin shook his head. "No," he said. "No, I don't."

Folsom blew air through pursed lips and tapped his fingers on his desk for a moment. "I see," he said. "Uh, Mr. Cavanaugh . . ."

Martin couldn't help but notice that the friendly "Martin" had changed to the more businesslike "Mr. Cavanaugh."

"I hope you weren't counting on the bank extending your note any longer. We extended it once for your wife last year. Of course, I suppose if you could pay just the interest . . ."

"I don't have enough money to pay the interest either," Martin said.

"Then what exactly do you propose?"

"I would sell my ranch to the bank," Martin said. "You can give me the difference between what the ranch is worth and what I owe."

"You have to be joking."

"No, I'm very serious."

"Mr. Cavanaugh, you owe almost six hundred dollars. If the buildings had not been burned out during the war, it might be worth a thousand dollars. But with the buildings gone, it is barely worth what you owe."

"But it is worth what I owe?" Martin asked.

"Barely."

Martin sighed. "If I signed the ranch over to the bank, would it clear the books for me?"

"We are a bank, Mr. Cavanaugh, not a realtor."

"And yet, when you loan money on property, don't you always run that risk?" Martin asked.

Folsom nodded. "We do."

"Then I ask you again. If I sign the ranch over to you, will it clear the books?"

"I hate to see you do that," Folsom said.

"I don't see as I have any choice," Martin said. "Nor you either, for that matter. Because I'm either going to walk away from here after making a deal with you, or I'm simply going to walk away. In either case, you are going to wind up owning the ranch, but in the latter case, you are going to be out the legal expenses of foreclosure."

"I don't like being put over a barrel like this, Cavanaugh," Folsom said. Now, even the "Mr." had been dropped.

"Believe me, Mr. Folsom, I don't like this any more than you do. But I know that my ranch, even without the house and barn, is worth almost a thousand dollars. I figure that, in the long run, you are making out on the deal."

"All right," Folsom finally said after a long moment of contemplation. "I'll have Miss Steward draw up the papers for you to sign."

"Thank you," Martin said.

"Where are you going now?" Folsom asked.

Martin smiled.

"Out West," he said.

Chapter Two

With Smoke Jensen

As Matt Cavanaugh and his family prepared to start their trek West, another young man, some eight years older than Matt, was standing in front of a trading post, watching his own father ride away. When he and his father had come West a year earlier, they'd met up with an old mountain man known only as Preacher.

Preacher had befriended the men, taking a special interest in young Kirby Jensen, providing him with an education in survival that was the equal in intensity and thoroughness to a doctorate in any chartered university.

Kirby had already proven his worth in a short, but savage Indian battle and, though he was only seventeen years old, he could hold his own with anyone. Preacher had given him the nickname Smoke, and already, Smoke thought of himself in that way.

"Where's Pa goin', Preacher?" Smoke asked the old mountain man.

Preacher squirted out a stream of tobacco juice, then swiped the back of his hand across his mouth before he answered.

"Your pa ever tell you about a man by the name of Casey? Ted Casey?"

"I've heard the name," Smoke said. "And from the way he said it, I figured there was bad blood between them. But he never told me anything specific."

"I reckon that's because he still sees you as a boy, and not a man," Preacher said. "Maybe a pa always looks at his son that way."

"Pa's goin' to look Casey up?"

Preacher nodded. "He's got some business to take care of with him," the old man answered.

"Killing business?"

Preacher nodded. "I reckon so. Problem is, Casey ain't likely to be alone."

Smoke watched as his father stopped, turned his horse around, and waved. Smoke returned the wave; then his pa was gone, dipping out of sight over the rise of a small hill.

Smoke's pa had taken a few gold coins with him, but he'd left the bulk of his money with his son. Smoke felt the weight of the money in his pouch, then cleared his throat before he spoke. He had to, because he knew that he would have a catch in his throat if he hadn't, and he didn't want to sound like a baby to Preacher.

"He won't be coming back, will he, Preacher?"

"Like as not, he won't," Preacher said. "If you want to cry, Smoke, why, there ain't no shame in it. You could step around behind the trading post and have yourself a good cry all alone."

"I haven't cried since my ma died," Smoke said. "Don't reckon I'll be doin' any cryin' now."

Smoke made a few purchases with the money his father had left him and now, with a new pistol, knife, and Henry rifle in his saddle sheath, he rode with Preacher through the thick timber and up into the high country. It was their way to ride without talking, so Smoke saved all his questions for nighttime, when they were camped by a small fire that popped and snapped and sent sparks up as it cooked the bacon and warmed the coffee.

"How old were you when you come out here, Preacher?"

"Fourteen or so," Preacher said. "I run away from home at twelve, fought in the Battle of New Orleans, cordelled upriver to St. Louis, then found my way out here. Been here ever since."

"You've never been back East?"

"Once, I went to Philadelphia to kill a man that needed killin'," Preacher said matter-of-factly. "But for the most part, I been out here all along."

"You never got married?"

"Injun married," Preacher said.

"You got 'ny kids?"

"You ask a lot of questions."

"How'm I goin' to learn if I don't ask questions?" Smoke replied.

"You'll learn what I want you to learn," Preacher said. "Get some sleep now. We got us a lot of ridin' to do yet."

With Matt Cavanaugh

Matt wondered if this was what it was like to be at sea. For the last two weeks, they had been following a set of wagon tracks that stretched front and back from horizon to horizon, broken here and there by deeply cut gullies and rock outcroppings. The wagon tracks were from the days of the great wagon trains, two decades earlier. Now their wagon was all alone, its movement providing the only animation on the vast, open plain.

Matt and his father were walking alongside the wagon,

which was being driven by Matt's mother. Cassie had been walking as well, but a few minutes earlier had climbed up onto the seat to ride beside Mary.

"Pa, what was it like in the war?" Matt asked.

"It was like hell," Martin answered.

"Really? You mean like it says in the Bible, with the Devil and a burning pit of fire?"

"You might say that," Martin said. "There was fire, and there certainly was a Devil, though just who he was depends on the tellin', I reckon."

"Martin," Mary said, calling down from the wagon seat. "Over there."

Martin moved up to the front of the wagon so he could look to the other side, in the direction pointed out by Mary. He saw six riders coming toward them.

"Indians, do you think?"

"No, I don't think so," Martin said. "Not from the way they're riding."

The riders, still about a half mile away, turned toward the wagon, approaching it at a leisurely gait.

"What do you think they want?" Mary asked.

"I don't know," Martin answered.

"Should I stop?" Mary asked.

"I see no need to stop," Martin said. "Just keep on going. I reckon we'll find out what they want when they get here."

The wagon continued to roll across the plains, the wheels creaking, the pots and pans banging back and forth, the tree chains clinking, the horse hooves rising and falling. All the while, Martin kept an eye on the riders who were coming closer and closer.

"Matt," Martin said. "Move the rifle over to where I can get to it."

"Martin, no," Mary said. "You are just one man. You know

you can't take them all on. And if they see you with a rifle, it might provoke them."

Martin ran his hand over his cheek, then nodded. "You may be right," he said.

The riders, all of whom were wearing long, tan dusters, came up to the wagon. Martin recognized two of them. One was the man with the puffy scar that disfigured his left eye, then streaked down his cheek and jaw like a purple flash of lightning, twisting the left side of his mouth into a sneer. One of the others was the man with half an ear.

"Payson, isn't it?" Martin said as the riders stopped. "Sergeant Payson?"

"You've got a good memory, Cap'n Cavanaugh," Payson said, stretching his mouth into what might have been a smile.

"What are you boys doing out here?" Martin asked.

"Just sort of ridin' around, lookin' at the countryside," Payson replied. He nodded toward the wagon. "Movin', are you?"

"Yeah," Martin said. "Wasn't much left for me when I got home, I'm afraid."

"So, you're startin' over, are you?"

"You might say that."

"You got 'ny money?" Payson asked.

"I beg your pardon?"

"Money," Payson repeated. "You don't really think you're goin' to be able to get a fresh start if you don't have no money, do you?"

Martin didn't like the way the conversation was going. "We don't have any money," he said. "I spent everything I had on the wagon and things we'd need to make a new start."

Payson turned to the others. "What do you think about this?" he said. "Here's a man who was smart enough to be a captain in the Yankee army, but is so dumb that he comes out here with no money."

"Well, hell, Payson, how smart do you have to be to be a cap'n in the Yankee army?" one of the others said, and all laughed.

"You!" Mary said to Payson. "You were one of them. And so were you." She pointed to the bushy-bearded man.

"We was one of who?" Payson asked.

"You were one of the ones who burned our house and barn."

"Could be," Payson agreed with a chuckle. "Garvey and me rode with Bloody Bill Anderson and we burned us up a lot of Yankee houses and barns. But that was war. You see that, don't you, Cap'n?"

"Yes," Martin agreed. "The war's over now, and I figure a lot of us have done things we'd just as soon not remember."

"You don't have any money, huh?"

"No, I don't. And I'd feel a lot better if you folks would just ride on and leave us be."

"What if we don't want to ride on?" Payson asked.

"Then I'd be obliged to make you move on."

"How you goin' to do that? There's only one of you and there are six of us."

"You seem to be the one in charge," Martin said. "I'll kill you."

Payson threw his duster to one side and raised a double-barrel shotgun. Martin snaked his pistol from his holster in a lightning-fast draw. Before Payson could shoot, Martin pulled the trigger. But the hammer made a distinct clicking noise as it misfired.

Payson pulled the trigger on his shotgun and the blast, at nearly point-blank range, opened up Martin's chest, cutting his heart to shreds. He was dead before he hit the ground.

"Martin!" Mary screamed.

"Get the two women down here!" Payson ordered. "If they ain't got no money, we may as well have us some fun."

"Matt, run!" Mary shouted.

Earlier, Matt had moved his father's rifle closer to the edge of the wagon. Now, he grabbed the rifle and darted into the rocks alongside the wagon trail.

"What about the boy?" one of the men shouted.

"You can have 'im if that's your taste," Payson said. "But for me, I'm goin' to have me one of these women."

The others laughed at Payson's comment. Then they grabbed Mary and Cassie and jerked them down from the wagon seat. Mother and daughter fought hard, biting and scratching.

"Damn you!" Payson said, jerking back from Mary. "Be still!"

Mary and Cassie continued to struggle, putting up such a fight that Payson and the bushy-bearded man, who had taken first dibs, couldn't get the job done.

"To hell with it!" Payson said. He took a knife from his belt, then slashed it across Mary's throat. Mary began gurgling as blood spilled onto the dirt.

"Mama!" Cassie shouted.

"Cut the bitch, Garvey!" Payson said, and the bushy-bearded man silenced Cassie.

Payson stood up then, and looked down at the bodies of Mary and Cassie.

"Damn," he said. "Why'd they make us do that? Hell, I don't want 'em now."

"I'll do it," one of the other men said.

"What are you talkin' about, Cooper? They're both dead," Payson said.

"What the hell difference does that make?" Cooper asked. "Hell, all I wanted was a poke. Wasn't aimin' to make her fall in love with me."

The others laughed nervously.

"Anyone else goin' to join in the fun?" Cooper asked as he began unbuttoning his pants.

* * *

By the time Matt found a place in the rocks that would let him see what was going on, his mother and sister were already dead. Matt was less than twenty-five yards away from the six men who were standing around his mother and sister. He aimed the rifle at Cooper's head, and pulled the trigger.

The sudden gunshot startled everyone.

"What the hell?" Payson shouted, spinning around. Behind him, Cooper was pitching back with blood and brain matter oozing from the top of his head.

The moment Matt shot, he pulled back from the rock where he had been, and slipped into a very narrow fissure between two large rocks. As a result, Payson didn't see Matt, but he did see a wisp of gun smoke hanging in the air from where Matt had fired.

"It's the kid!" Garvey shouted. "Somehow he's got hold of a rifle."

"Get him!" Payson ordered.

"He went in between them rocks," Garvey said.

"Lucas, you the smallest one of us, see if you can get in there and pull him out," Payson ordered.

Nodding, Lucas ran over to the two rocks, then started squeezing through the narrow opening between them.

"Can you get through?" Payson called.

"Yeah, it's tight but I can do it," Lucas called back as he struggled to work through.

From his position behind another rock, about ten yards beyond the fissure, Matt watched Lucas working hard to squeeze through. He was in a very contorted position when Matt noticed that, while both arms were through, his waist, and consequently his gun, was not.

Matt stood up then and stared pointedly at Lucas.

"Ha!" Lucas called. "Payson, Garvey, come on. We've got his ass now."

"No," Matt said as he raised the rifle to his shoulder. "I've got yours."

"What?" Lucas shouted. In an instant, his sense of triumph turned to terror. "No, kid, no!" he shouted.

Matt pulled the trigger and felt the rifle kick back against his shoulder, watching as a black hole appeared in Lucas's forehead.

Matt had now killed two men in as many minutes.

"What are we going to do, Payson? Just stay around here until the little brat shoots us all, one at a time?" Garvey asked.

"Corey, Taggart, you find anything in the wagon?"

"No money, Payson," one of the men said. "Just some bacon, beans, coffee, flour, and sugar."

"Take the bacon and coffee and let's get out of here," Payson said. "And take the horses."

"What about the brat?"

"Leave him," Payson said. "He's out here in the middle of nowhere, all by himself. If Injuns or wolves don't get him, he'll likely starve to death, or . . ." Payson took an ax from the side of the wagon and smashed the water barrel. The water that Matt and his family had been so preciously hoarding spilled to the ground in one quick splash. "Die of thirst," Payson concluded.

"What about Lucas and Cooper?" Taggart asked.

"They're dead."

"I know they're dead. What are we goin' to do about 'em?"

"Leave 'em."

"We can't just leave 'em here."

"Why not?" Payson replied. "It ain't goin' to bother 'em none."

Garvey laughed.

"Come on, let's go."

"What about the wagon?"

"Burn it."

Matt could no longer hear them. He wasn't sure if they had actually left, or if they had just pretended to leave, so he stayed where he was, listening to the sound of burning wood, smelling it, and watching the smoke roil into the sky.

He spent the rest of the day there, then the whole night, then most of the next day. Finally, he decided to take a look, so he came out from the crevice, then climbed up on one of the rocks and looked down at the scene.

There was nothing left of the wagon except blackened residue and the iron bands around what had been the wheels, and the chain of the tree. There were five bodies, his mother, father, and sister, as well as the two he had killed. Four were on the ground; one was still wedged in the crevice between the rocks.

Matt started to climb down when he saw another wagon approaching. This wasn't the kind of wagon he and his family had been traveling in; this wagon was somewhat smaller and squared off with wooden sides. It was making a terrible racket as it rolled across the plains, and as it got closer, he could read the big red sign on the side.

MOE GOODMAN

Pots– Pans– Knives & Notions

Matt slipped back behind the rock and waited until the wagon approached. He watched as it stopped and the driver stared, in shock, at the carnage.

"Oh, my," he said, shaking his head. "Oh, my, what has happened here?"

The driver set the brake, then climbed down from the wagon and walked over to look at the bodies. He examined Matt's father, then his mother and sister for a long time. Then he walked over to look at Cooper, then took a cursory glance toward Lucas, who was still wedged in the crevice.

Shaking his head sadly, the driver walked back to his wagon, then untied a shovel that hung on the side. He started digging.

Matt continued to watch for several more minutes. Then, deciding that anyone who would take the time to dig a grave for someone he didn't even know must be a good man, he climbed down from the rock. He walked up behind the man, who, because of his digging, didn't notice Matt's approach.

"That's my ma and pa," he said. "And my sister."

Startled by Matt's unexpected appearance, the man jumped and grabbed his chest.

"Sorry," Matt said. "Didn't mean to scare you."

"Well, you did, boy, you like to give me a fit," the man said. His expression softened. "Your ma, pa, and sister, eh?"

"Yes, sir."

"And who might these two be?"

"There the ones I killed," Matt said.

The man looked shocked. "You killed?"

"Yes, sir. I killed 'em."

"How old are you, boy?"

"I'm nine."

"What's your name?"

"Matt Cavanaugh."

"I'm Moe Goodman," the man said.

"Thanks for buryin' my folks."

"Seems like the only decent thing to do."

"If you've got another shovel, I'll help dig."

"It so happens I do," Moe said, walking back over to his wagon. He opened the back door, reached inside, and pulled one out. "Brand-new," he said, "but I reckon using it one time won't keep me from sellin' it."

Matt took the shovel and, for the next several minutes, the only sound was the sound of the spades turning dirt.

"I'll say this for you, Matt," Moe said, finally breaking the silence.

"What's that?"

"You've got yourself one hell of a start in life."

Chapter Three

With Smoke Jensen

Smoke and his mentor, Preacher, ran across another old mountain man named Grizzly. They shared a meal of venison, potatoes mixed with wild onions, and gravy sopped up by a piece of pan bread Smoke had made for them.

The three ate in relative silence. Then Grizzly nodded toward Smoke, but addressed his remark to Preacher.

"All right to talk in front of the boy?"

"Don't ask me," Preacher said. "He's a man, full growed, ask him."

"Boy, uh, Smoke," Grizzly said. "This here is goin' to concern you, and I reckon it ain't goin' to be pleasant."

Smoke steeled himself for the worst. "I'm listenin'," he said.

"Man rode in here about two months ago. He was all shot up. Strange man he was, dug his own grave afore he died. It was like as if he just hung on long enough not to put anyone else out."

"He give you a name?" Smoke asked.

"Yeah. Said his name was Emmett. Emmett Jensen."

Smoke nodded. "That'd be my pa," he said.

"I reckoned it would be," Grizzly said. "He told me he had

a boy who would be travelin' with Preacher. And when I seen the two of you, well, I know'd who it was without askin'."

"Where's he buried?" Preacher asked. "Me'n Smoke here might like to visit the grave and pay our respects."

"Like I say, he chose his own spot," Grizzly said. "He's on a little plain at the base of the high peak, east of the canyon. You know where it is?"

"Yeah," Preacher said. "I know where it is."

Grizzly reached into a little bag and pulled out a heavy sack. He tossed the sack over to Smoke.

"This here belongs to you. Right smart amount of gold in there."

"You could've taken it," Smoke said. "You could've taken it and I would've never known anything about it."

"I reckon I could have, but that wouldn't have been the right thing to do now, would it?" Grizzly asked.

Smoke shook his head. "No, sir, it wouldn't have been."

"He left you a letter too," Grizzly said. "Figure you might want it." Grizzly handed Smoke another package, this one flat and wrapped in rawhide to protect it from the elements.

"Thanks."

Grizzly got up from the fire then, wiped off the seat of his pants, then walked over and mounted his pony. Taking the lead to his packhorses, he rode off without looking back.

When Preacher and Smoke awoke the next morning, Smoke started saddling his horse.

Preacher watched Smoke for a few minutes; then he filled his pipe and lit it from a small burning twig he took from the campfire. He took several puffs, not speaking until the pipe was well lit.

"Looks like you're leavin'," Preacher said.

"Seems right," Smoke replied.

"I wish you all the best."

Smoke mounted his horse before he spoke again. Then he looked down at the old man who had been such an important part of his life for nearly two years now.

"Preacher, you've taught me how to find my way around, how to shoot, what plants I can eat and what I should stay away from," Smoke said. "Fact is, I reckon I wouldn't be alive if it weren't for you."

"You was easy to teach," Preacher said. He pointed to the pistol at Smoke's side. "But one thing I didn't teach, 'cause you just got a God-given natural talent for it. And that's pullin' your gun."

Unconsciously, Smoke put his hand on the handle of his Colt .44.

"I ain't never seen no one who could pull a gun as fast as you, Smoke, or shoot it as well. That's goin' to come in real handy to you, but it's also goin' to be a burden."

"A burden?"

"Aye, boy, a burden," Preacher said. "There will be those who will hear about you, and they'll want to test you. That's where the danger is goin' to lie, 'cause you won't be expectin' it. It won't be anybody you've ever run into before. Like as not, you won't even have words with 'em. They'll know who you are, but you won't know who they are."

"I've thought about that," Smoke said. "I know what you mean."

Preacher nodded. "Uh-huh. I figured you was smart enough to understand it. But I wanted to warn you about it anyway."

Smoke leaned over and patted his horse on the neck. "Preacher, I think the time has come for me to be goin' off on my own now."

"You'll be lookin' for Casey, will you?"

"I reckon so," Smoke replied with a nod.

Preacher nodded. "What's got to be done has to be done,"

he said. "Don't be a stranger, you hear? Drop in to see an old man from time to time."

"I'll do that," Smoke said, slapping his legs against the side of his horse.

Two days later, Smoke found his pa's grave. Dismounting, he looked around until he located a rock that was just right; then, using a small hammer and a miner's spike, he chiseled his father's name and the year of his birth, 1815, as well as the year of his death, 1866, then put the rock at the head of the grave. He would have liked to put some sort of message on the head-stone, but it was hard enough just to get the name and dates on.

That done, Smoke hung a small coffeepot over the camp-fire, then found a comfortable place to read the letter his father had left him.

> *Son,*
>
> *I found the man who killed your brother, Luke, and stolt the gold that belonged to the Gray. But he had more with him than I thought he would. I killed two of 'em, but they got led in me and I had to hitail it out. I come here to this place, but I'm not goin to make it. Son, you don't have no call to try and settle accounts for me'n your brother, so don't get it in your mind you do. Make yourself a good life.*
>
> *I'm getting tard and seein is hard. Lite fadin. I love you Kirby-Smoke.*
>
> *—Pa.*

With Matt Cavanaugh

His name was Landers, "Brother Charles G. Landers, a simple man of Gawd," was the way he had introduced him-self to Moe Goodman.

Goodman had explained how his life as a peddler wouldn't allow him to keep the boy, and he asked Landers if he could find a home for Matt.

"Indeed I can," Landers said. "There are many among my scattered flock who would take great joy in receiving into their bosom a wonderful young man like this."

From the moment he laid eyes on Landers, there was something about him that didn't set well with Matt. He wanted to ask Moe not to give him to the itinerant preacher, wanted to beg to be allowed to stay.

But he said nothing.

Landers was unlike any preacher Matt had ever seen. On the four days they had been on the trail, Landers had cursed, gotten drunk, and once paid an Indian woman to be with her. Matt didn't know what family Landers was going to leave him with, but anything had to be an improvement over the current situation.

On the fifth day, they came into a town, identified by a sign just outside the town as Soda Creek.

Soda Creek had one main street, fronted on both sides by ripsawed, weather-beaten, false-fronted buildings. From what Matt could tell from his position on the horse behind Landers, it consisted mostly of saloons. One building, which didn't have a sign to identify it, had several women sitting out on an upstairs porch. As Landers rode by, a couple of the women stepped up to the railing and looked down.

Matt glanced toward them, then cut his eyes away in quick embarrassment. It looked almost as if the women had come outside in their underwear. The two who leaned over the rail were showing the tops of their breasts.

"Hey, Preacher Man, where'd you come by that little boy?" one of the women asked.

Landers stared straight ahead.

"Why don't you leave him with us?" one of the other women called. "It'd be nice to have a young boy around."

"Yes, we'll raise him right. Why, by the time he gets old enough, he'll know how to treat a woman real good."

The other women laughed, though Matt wasn't sure what was so funny.

"Brother Landers, who are those women?" Matt asked.

"Boy, don't you pay them no never-mind," Landers said. "They're nothin' but harlots, the lot of 'em."

"What's a harlot?"

"It's a woman that a man pays to be with," Landers explained.

"Like the Indian woman you were with the other night?"

"Shut up about that, boy," Landers hissed. "Don't you say nothin' to nobody 'bout that. What I was doin' was savin' that poor heathen's eternal soul. Most folks wouldn't understand that, 'cause most folks got dirty minds."

"Yes, sir," Matt said. "Where's the family that's goin' to take me?"

"There ain't no family goin' to take you."

"But you said . . ."

"I know what I said, but it don't work like that," Landers said. "First thing I got to do is get you into the orphanage. They can't nobody take you in 'lessen the law says it's all right, and the law's got to go through the orphanage."

"Oh," Matt said. He had not considered an orphanage, though as he was now an orphan, he supposed that it made sense. "Where is the orphanage?" Matt asked.

"Boy, you ask too many questions," Landers replied. "Thing's will go a lot better if you just keep your mouth shut and do as you're told."

"Yes, sir," Matt said contritely.

* * *

Emanuel Mumford had been elected as captain of the First Idaho Cavalry during the Civil War. The First Idaho was never activated, but Mumford continued to call himself Captain Mumford, and insisted that all who dealt with him refer to him in that way.

Captain Mumford was director of the Soda Creek Home for Wayward Boys and Girls. There had been some who suggested that the term "Wayward" implied that the children were behavioral problems, when most were merely orphans.

However, as Mumford pointed out, several of his residents were children of prostitutes who had died either of disease, or of alcoholism, or even giving birth. "And those children, being issue of wayward women, are by inheritance wayward," he insisted.

When Landers came in to see him, Mumford was going over his books. He had three ways of supporting the Home. One was a grant from the territorial government in Boise. A second was from generous donations made by the three churches in town. And the third, and most lucrative, was from wages earned by the children Captain Mumford farmed out to the various businesses and individuals in and around the town of Soda Creek.

"Captain Mumford, I wonder if I may have a word with you, sir," Landers asked.

Mumford shook his head. "We have been through all this before, Landers," he said. "I am not going to allow you to conduct a church service in the Home. Why, it would be so disruptive that we would wind up losing at least half a day's earnings, maybe more."

Landers held up his hand and shook his own head. "No, it's nothing like that," he said. "I understand your position and would never try and compromise it."

"Well, I'm glad you see it that way, Landers. Now, what can I do for you?"

"It's more in order of what I can do for you," Landers replied.

Mumford's face brightened. "You have a donation for the Home? How marvelous of you."

"No, no, nothing like that," Landers corrected quickly.

"Oh," Mumford said. He was obviously disappointed.

"What I do have for you is another guest."

"Another mouth to feed? No, impossible. We are over-crowded as it is."

"But this is a fine, strong young boy," Landers pointed out. "I'm sure that you will be able to find a position for him somewhere that will prove to be quite lucrative for you."

Mumford stroked his chin. "You say he's a strong boy?"

"Yes."

"How old is he?"

"I think he is about twelve," Landers lied. He knew that Matt was not yet ten.

"Well, perhaps I could find a place for him," Mumford said. "A young man like that can always bring in enough money to support himself."

"Good, I thought you might see it that way," Landers said. "You can have him for twenty-five dollars."

"What?" Mumford gasped. "Are you out of your mind?"

"Not a bit of it," Landers replied. "If you aren't interested in buying the boy, I can always sell him to some farmer or rancher who lives nearby."

"You aren't going to find anyone who will give you twenty-five dollars for him."

"Then I'll sell him for what I can get."

"I'll give you five dollars."

"Twenty."

They eventually settled on twelve and a half dollars, and after Landers counted and pocketed the money, he went back outside to where Matt was leaning against the hitching post, watching the activity of the town.

"I've got it all set up for you," Landers said. "It's costing me twelve and a half dollars, but I'll have the personal satisfaction of knowing you will be safe."

"Thank you, Brother Landers," Matt said.

"I'm only doing my Christian duty, boy," Landers replied. "You learn from that, so you can grow up to be a decent, God-fearin' man."

"Yes, sir," Matt said.

"You go on in now," Landers said as he swung back into the saddle.

Johnny reached for his rifle, but Landers put his hand out to stop him.

"You won't be needin' a gun in a place like this," Landers said.

"But it was my pa's rifle," Matt said.

Landers shook his head. "Let's just say it's you payin' me back for the twelve and a half dollars I just spent on you."

"But . . ."

"You goin' to argue with me, boy?" Landers asked in a sharp voice. "S'posin' I give you your rifle back, what good will that do? They'll take it away from you soon as you go inside. And like as not, it'll wind up gettin' sold and you won't get one penny for it. Leastwise, this way you know it's goin' to someone that was out some considerable money to get you situated."

Matt nodded. "Yes, sir, I guess you're right," he said. "All right, you can keep Pa's rifle."

"I'm glad you come to your senses. Go on in. The man you want to see is Captain Mumford."

Matt's eyes brightened somewhat. "My pa was a captain," he said. "Maybe Captain Mumford knew him."

"Maybe," Landers said. He slapped his legs against the side of his horse, clicked at it, and rode away.

Matt looked at the front door of the home. He remembered back on the farm in Kansas, how he would sometimes go swimming in the swimming hole. In the late spring the water would still be really cold, and he would have to take a deep breath and get up his courage before jumping in.

For some strange reason, he felt like that now, so taking a deep breath and squaring his shoulders, he walked up the brick walk, then opened the door and went inside.

"Boy, have you no manners?" the man who was inside asked gruffly.

"Sir?"

"You don't walk into someone's home without knocking on the door," he said.

The man was thin and bald except for the side of his head. And that hair came down in bushy sideburns, though they did not join to make a beard.

"I thought this was the orphanage," Matt said. "Maybe I'm in the wrong place. I'm sorry." He turned and started to leave.

"Did you come with Landers?" the man asked.

"Yes, sir."

"Then I already paid for you. You are in the right place."

"You paid for me?"

"Twelve and a half good dollars," the man said. "You'll be workin' that off."

"But he took my rifle."

"Who took your rifle?"

"Brother Landers. He said he paid you so I could stay here, and he took my rifle to pay him back."

The man chuckled. "Let that be a lesson to you," he said. "Don't trust somebody just because they tell you they are a preacher."

"Isn't he a preacher?"

"He is sometimes, I reckon. What's your name?"

"Matthew Cava . . ."

The man held up his hand. "Your ma and pa alive?"

"No, sir."

"Then you don't have a last name."

"But my last name is . . ."

"You don't have a last name," the man said again. "Do you understand that?"

"Yes, sir."

"Yes, Captain Mumford."

"What?"

"When you talk to me, you will always address me as Captain Mumford."

"Yes, Captain Mumford," Matt said.

"You're awfully small for twelve years old."

"I'm not twelve," Matt said.

Mumford slapped Matt in the face, not hard enough to knock him down, or even bring blood, but hard enough that it stung.

"What did you say?"

"I said I'm not twelve," Matt repeated.

Mumford slapped him again. "You don't learn very well," he said. "Now, I'm going to ask you again. What did you say?"

"I said I'm not twelve—Captain Mumford," Matt said, getting the last part out just before Mumford slapped him again.

Mumford smiled. "Well, maybe you aren't so dumb after all. Not twelve, huh? How old are you?"

"I'm nine, Captain Mumford."

"Nine, huh? Well, you are a big enough boy for nine. I'm sure I can find something for you to do. Connors!" he called loudly.

An older boy came into the office from the back of the house.

"Yes, Captain Mumford?"

"Here is a new boy," Mumford said. "His name is Matthew. Take him into the back and"—Mumford paused for a moment, then smiled, though Matt found the smile frightening, rather than comforting—"break him in."

"Yes, Captain Mumford," Connors said, his own smile as malevolent as that of Mumford.

Connors led Matt through a door and down a hall. Matt saw a room with a lot of bunk beds, and he started toward it.

"Nah, that's for the girls," Connors said. "Boys is this way."

"There are girls in this place?" Matt asked.

"Yeah," Connors said. "But don't get no ideas about any of them. All the girls belong to me'n Simon."

"What do you mean they belong to you and Simon?"

Connors looked at Matt and laughed. "Never mind," he said. "You're too young to know."

Chapter Four

The room was long and relatively narrow. The floor was made of wide, unfinished boards and the walls were nothing more than studs and outside planking. There was only one window in the entire room.

The beds that ran in rows down either side of the room were crowded so close together that there was barely room to get between them. Most of the beds looked to be very spartan; small, even for children, with blankets with holes and lumpy cotton mattresses. There were no sheets.

"You'll sleep here," Connors said, pointing to one of the beds. Stuffing was coming from the mattress, and roaches were running across the filthy blanket.

"Where do you put your clothes?" Matt asked.

"You got 'nything other than what you are wearin'?" Connors asked.

"No."

Connors chuckled. "Then don't worry about it."

Glancing toward the far end of the room, under the window, Matt saw two beds that were set aside from the others. These beds were larger, had sheets, pillows, and blankets. There was also a rack and shelf on the wall beside each bed and a trunk between the beds. Several changes of clothes hung from the racks, and boxes were stacked on the shelves.

The open window provided some relief from the sweltering heat outside, though none of that relief reached the rest of the room. There was a stove there too, and though the stove was now cold, it didn't take much thought for Matt to realize that what little warmth it would produce in the wintertime would be confined to the area immediately around it.

"Who sleeps there?" Matt asked, pointing to the two beds.

"The bed on the left is mine," Connors said. He pointed at Matt. "And don't ever let me see you down there. The other bed belongs to my friend, Simon."

"How come you two get the good beds?"

Connors laughed. "You'll find out soon enough," he said. Matt heard voices from outside.

"The others is comin' back for supper," Connors said. "To show you what a good guy I am, I'm goin' to let you eat with us tonight, even though you ain't done no work yet to earn it."

"You are going to let me eat? I thought Captain Mumford was in charge."

"He is in charge," Connors said. "But you'll mostly be dealin' with me'n Simon." Connors smiled proudly, and hooked his thumbs under his armpits. "Cap'n Mumford says that me'n Simon is his sergeants."

"Am I supposed to call you Sergeant?"

Connors laughed. "You don't even talk to me, boy, unless I talk to you first," Connors said. "I'm just talkin' to you now 'cause you're new and you need to know the rules. Come on, I'll show you where we eat."

The dining room was about the same size as the dormitory. It had two long tables, flanked on either side of the table by a wooden bench. One of the tables appeared to be for the girls, the other for boys. At the back of the room there was one smaller table. Matt didn't have to ask who that table belonged to.

"From here on, you are on your own," Connors said as he walked away.

Matt saw a line of boys and girls and, figuring they were waiting to be fed, he joined them. At nine years old, he decided he was one of the youngest—if not the youngest—but he wasn't the smallest.

Matt had been around other children before, at school and in church, but he had never seen such dispirited expressions as he saw here. Not one person was smiling, there was no animated conversation, and in fact there was very little interaction of any kind. They just stood there in silence until a couple of women came out, carrying a large pot and a plate of bread. The woman carrying the pot was very fat. The one carrying the tray of bread was very skinny.

"Bow your heads!" the fat woman shouted.

Matt bowed his head, but he looked up with his eyes to see what the others were doing.

"Lord, for the blessing of this food, we thank you!" the fat woman shouted.

Once the blessing was given, the atmosphere changed. The boys and girls who were standing in line became much more animated, engaging each other in conversation. The boy just in front of Matt turned to him.

"You just get here today?" he asked.

"Yes."

"My name is Eddie, what's yours?"

"Matt Cavanaugh."

"Shh!" Eddie said, putting his finger across his lips. "Don't let nobody hear you say that."

"Say what?"

"Your last name," Eddie said. "We don't have last names in here. Don't none of us have last names."

"That's right. Captain Mumford told me that."

"It could get you a beatin'," Eddie cautioned.

"I wonder what's for supper," Matt said.

Eddie laughed. "Can sure tell you are new," he said.

"Why is that?"

"'Cause what is for supper is what we have for supper ever' night. Pease porridge. Pease porridge and bread. There's s'posed to be some bacon in the pease porridge, but ain't nobody ever seen none."

"You have that every night?" Matt asked.

"Oatmeal for breakfast ever' mornin' and pease porridge for supper ever' night."

"What about them?" Matt asked, pointing to the table at the back of the room. There he saw Connors and another boy as big as he was. They were eating fried chicken and mashed potatoes, talking and laughing with each other.

"That's Connors and Simon," Eddie said. "They don't count. They're Captain Mumford's toadies," Eddie said.

"Toadies?"

"Yeah, they get the best food, the best clothes, the best everything. Wait until you see where they sleep," Eddie said.

"I did see it. Why do they get such good treatment?"

The boy that was standing just in front of Eddie laughed. "For one thing, they are the oldest. They're both thirteen. And for another, they are tattletales. They tell Captain Mumford everything we do."

"Oh."

"I'm Timmy," the second boy said.

"Matt Cava—uh, Matt," Matt said, remembering to correct himself.

"I'll bet they don't have any friends," Matt said.

"They don't need friends. They've got everything else," Timmy said.

Matt took his bowl of pease porridge and a hunk of bread

to the table where he sat with Eddie and Timmy. Eddie introduced him to some of the others, though, for the moment, the names sort of passed him by. He knew that if he stayed here long enough he would eventually learn everyone's name, so he didn't ask anyone to repeat it.

Matt looked down at his pease porridge with obvious distaste. "This is what we have for supper every night?" he asked.

"Every night."

"What do we have for dinner?"

"We don't eat dinner here," Eddie said. "But most of us get lunch from the place where we're workin'. And that's generally the best. Where will you be workin'?"

"I don't know."

"You ever worked anywhere before?"

"I've mucked stable stalls," Matt said.

"Yeah, well, you don't want to have to do that if you can help it. Best thing is to get a job with a café or a saloon. You'll be sweepin' out and washin' dishes, but you get to eat good there."

"How do I get a job there?"

"I'll talk to Mr. McDougal down at the saloon and see if he'll ask for you," Eddie said.

The bread was good and Matt was hungry, not having eaten since the day before when Landers had shared some jerky with him. But not even hunger could make him eat the pease porridge. He took one bite, then pushed the uneaten gruel away.

"If you aren't going to eat that, can I have it?" Timmy asked.

"How can you eat it?" Matt asked.

"After you been here a while, it'll taste just like apple pie to you," Timmy said.

The others at the table laughed. "When have you ever had apple pie?"

"Well, I know it's good because I've heard said it was good," Timmy said.

Matt thought of the last apple pie his mother had made. She had used dried apples and made the pie on the trail for them, just about two days before Payson and the others had attacked them.

Matt's eyes filled, and tears began streaming down his cheeks, but he didn't sob out loud.

Timmy looked at Matt.

"You thinkin' about apple pie your mama made?" he asked.

Matt nodded, but didn't speak.

"I'm sorry I brung up the memory," he said. "Me, I ain't got no memories like that. They say my mama was a whore, but I got no way of knowin' that. I don't even remember her."

Matt slid his bowl of porridge across.

"No," Timmy said, pushing it back. "Even if you don't like it, you better eat it."

"Like you say, there will come a time when I can eat it," Matt said. "But I can't eat it now, so you may as well take it."

"Thanks, Matt. So now you got two friends in here. Me'n Eddie. That's good. Boys that come in here and don't make friends, they are the ones who have it the hardest."

Matt looked back at Connors and Simon, salivating as he saw them eating the fried chicken with such relish.

Chapter Five

With Smoke Jensen

The name of the little town was Prosperity, and it sat on the banks of the Cuchara River. Prosperity was a ranching and farming community with a sign posted just outside the town limits with the proud boast:

Come Watch Us Grow

Progress and <u>PROSPERITY</u> in Colorado

The city marshal, having seen Smoke approaching from some distance away, met him just outside of town.

"Welcome to Prosperity, stranger," the marshal said. "The name is Crowell, Marshal Crowell." He put his hand to his badge, even though Smoke had already seen it.

"Marshal," Smoke said, touching the brim of his hat.

"I didn't catch your name," Marshal Crowell said.

"Folks call me Smoke."

"Smoke?" The marshal chuckled, more in dismissal than in humor. "That's it? Smoke? Smoke what?"

"I've been spending some time in the mountains," Smoke said. "One name is all anybody needs up there."

"Well, Smoke, if you're just makin' a friendly visit to my town, then you're welcome," Crowell said. "But if you're comin' here for any other reason, well, I'm goin' to have to ask you to just keep ridin'."

"I'm looking for a man named Casey," Smoke said. "Ted Casey."

"What do you want with him?"

"That's my business."

"I'm the law here'bouts," Crowell said. "I reckon that makes it my business."

"Is that a fact?"

"You know what, mister, I don't much like your attitude," Crowell said. "Why don't I just . . . ?"

That was as far as Crowell got. He was reaching for his gun, but stopped in mid-draw and mid-sentence when he saw the pistol in Smoke's hand.

"What the hell?" Crowell gasped. "I didn't even see you draw!"

"Like I said, where is Casey?" Smoke asked. He neither raised his voice, nor made it more menacing. Ironically, that made his question all the more frightening.

Crowell hesitated for a few seconds. "His ranch is southeast of here, on the flats. You'll cross a little creek before you see the house. I ought to warn you, though, he's got several men workin' for him, and they're all good with a gun. Maybe not as fast as you, but there's only one of you."

"You got an undertaker in this town?" Smoke asked.

"Of course we do. Why would you ask?"

"I'm about to give him some business," Smoke said.

Ten miles out of town, Smoke encountered two rough-looking riders.

"You're on private land," one of the men said. "Turn your horse around and git."

"You're not being very hospitable," Smoke said.

"Don't intend to be. Strangers ain't welcome here."

"I'm looking for Ted Casey."

"You deef or somethin'? I told you to git."

"I'm looking for Ted Casey," Smoke repeated.

"What do you want with Casey?"

"Just to renew an old friendship from the war," Smoke said.

"From the war?" one of the men said with a laugh. "Boy, you're still wet behind the ears. You ain't old enough to have been in the war."

"I'm sorry, I wasn't very clear. I'm actually looking him up for my pa."

"What was your pa's name?"

"Jensen," Smoke said. "Emmett Jensen."

"Jensen?"

"Yeah. You remember him, don't you?" Smoke said. His words were calm and cold.

"Kill 'im!" one of the riders shouted, and both grabbed for their guns.

They were too slow. Smoke had his pistol in his hand and he fired twice, the shots coming so close together that there was no separation between them.

The two riders were dumped from their saddles, one dead, the other dying. The dying rider pulled himself up on one elbow. Blood poured through his chest wound, pink and frothy, indicating that the ball had passed through a lung.

"Figured when we killed your pa that would be the end of it," he said. He forced a laugh, and blood spattered from his lips. "You're good, a hell of a lot better'n your brother. Casey shot him low and in the back. It took him a long time to die too. I enjoyed watchin' him. He was a coward, squealed like a pig and cried like a little girl."

Smoke made no reply.

"So was your pa a coward."

Smoke was quiet.

"What's the matter with you?" the rider asked. "You just goin' to let me talk about your folks like that? You're yellow."

Smoke turned his horse and rode around the two men, following the road in the same direction from which the two riders had come.

"Shoot me!" the rider shouted. "You yellow-bellied coward, don't leave me here to die like this! Shoot me!"

Smoke continued to ride away. Thirty seconds later he heard a gunshot, the sound muffled by the fact that the shooter had put the barrel in his own mouth.

Smoke didn't bother to look around.

Stopping in a copse of trees a short distance from the ranch house, Smoke studied it for a moment or two. The house was built of logs with a sod roof. If it came to it, it would burn easily.

"Casey!" Smoke called. "Casey, come out!"

"Who's callin'?" a voice shouted from within the house.

"Jensen."

"Jensen? I thought we killed you."

"That was my pa. And my brother," Smoke said.

"What do you want?"

"I'm here to settle up."

There was a rifle shot from the house, and though it missed, the bullet came close enough for Smoke to hear it whine.

Smoke took his horse into a ravine that circled the house. Fifty yards behind the house, he dismounted, snaked his rifle from the saddle sheath, then lay against the bank of the arroyo. Inside, he saw an arm on the windowsill. He shattered the arm with one shot from his new Henry. A moment later, he saw someone's outline through one of the other windows and he shot him, hearing a scream of pain.

"You boys in there," Smoke called. "You want to die for Casey, do you? I've already killed two of you back on the road."

"Your daddy ride with Mosby?" someone called from inside.

"That's right."

"You had a brother named Luke?"

"I did."

"Yeah, well, he was shot in the back and the gold he was guardin' was stole. Casey done it, not me! You got no call to come after me."

Smoke fired several more rounds into the house.

"Jensen! The name is Barry! I come from Nevada. Din't have nothin' to do with no war, never been East. They's another fella in here just like me. We herd cattle for wages, we ain't got no stake in this fight."

"Come on out and ride away then," Smoke called. "I won't shoot you."

The cabin door opened and two men came out with their hands up.

"We're just goin' to get our horses," one of them shouted.

"Go ahead."

The two men were moving toward the barn when a couple of shots rang out. Both were shot in the back by someone from within the house.

"What'd you do that for, Casey?" Smoke shouted. "They weren't part of this."

"When I pay men to work for me, I expect loyalty," Casey called back.

Smoke didn't answer. He was quiet for several moments, trying to decide what he should do.

"Jensen? Jensen, you still out there?" Casey called.

Casey's voice was getting nervous.

"Jensen? Come on down. Come out in the open so I can see you and we can talk."

Smoke still didn't answer.

"Jensen, you there?"

"I think he's gone," another voice said.

"That's what he wants us to think, you fool," Casey's voice replied.

Smoke followed the arroyo on around to the bunkhouse. In a pile behind the bunkhouse he found a bunch of rags, and in the bunkhouse, a jar of coal oil. He stuck the rags down into the mouth of the coal-oil jar, lit it, then threw it at the ranch house. The jar broke and the fire erupted almost immediately. As the logs burned, they began filling the house with smoke and fumes.

From inside the house, Smoke heard coughing. Then one man broke from the cabin and started running. Smoke cut him down with his rifle. A second began running and Smoke pulled the trigger on the rifle, only to hear the hammer fall on an empty chamber. He pulled his pistol and shot the man once, watching him double over with a slug in his gut.

Casey waited until the last minute before he stumbled out into the yard, his eyes blinded from the smoke and fumes. He fired wildly as he stumbled around, finally pulling the trigger repeatedly on an empty gun.

Smoke walked calmly up to him, even as Casey was trying to reload, and knocked him out.

Just outside the little town of Prosperity, Smoke dumped a bound and gagged Casey onto the ground. Curious about what was going on, several townspeople came forth to watch as Smoke took a rope from the saddle of Casey's horse and began making a noose.

"What do you think you are going to do here?" Marshal Crowell asked.

"Obvious, isn't it?" Smoke replied. "I'm going to hang the son of a bitch who killed my brother and my pa."

"I am an officer of the law. What if I ordered you to stop?" Crowell asked.

"Then I'd just kill you and hang him," Smoke answered.

"But you can't do this," Crowell insisted. "He hasn't been found guilty."

"Yeah, he has. He's already admitted it to me," Smoke said. "I also watched him kill two of his own men. He shot them in the back."

"That doesn't make what you are doing right," Crowell said.

"It's right in my book," Smoke said. He put the noose around Casey's neck, then threw the other end of the rope over a tree limb. "Get up on your horse," he ordered.

"You go to hell," Casey said, spitting at him.

"Have it your way," Smoke said. He tied the end of the rope to the saddle horn, and started to slap the horse on the rump.

"No, wait!" Casey shouted. "Not that way." Casey's hands were tied in front of him, but he put them on the pommel, then swung himself into the saddle.

"You got anything to say before I send you to hell?" Smoke asked.

"Yeah. I already sent your brother and your pa there, and when I get there I'm going to kick them both in the ass. Now, do your damn'dest, you son of a bitch."

Smoke slapped Casey's horse on the rump. With a protesting whinny, it leaped forward and Casey, dying quickly from a broken neck, swung back and forth, the only sound being the creaking of the rope and the cawing of a distant crow.

"I'll be notifying the governor about this," Crowell said.

"You do what you think you need to do," Smoke said. Without looking back, Smoke walked over to his horse, swung into the saddle, and rode away.

"Son of a bitch," someone said, almost reverently. "That's the damn'dest thing I done ever seen."

Chapter Six

With Matt Cavanaugh, three years later

True to his promise, Eddie managed to get Matt a job at McDougal's Saloon. There, Matt emptied and shined the spittoons, swept and mopped the floors, washed dishes, chopped wood in the wintertime, and swatted flies in the summertime.

During the school year, they came to work at the saloon for two hours before school opened, then worked from three o'clock until eleven every night. Despite the long hours, the owner of the saloon, Drew McDougal, did treat them fairly, and he did provide them with lunch every day.

For their labors, Matt and Eddie were paid a dollar and a half per week, but the money went to the Home, not to them.

"This money is needed to pay the expenses," Captain Mumford informed them.

As time went by, Matt learned that every penny any of the home residents earned went directly to Captain Mumford. And while he claimed to spend it all on upkeep, there was no one to look over his books but him. Whatever he spent it on, Matt was certain it wasn't spent on food or clothes. He got new clothes only when he outgrew what he was wearing, or when he wore them out.

In Matt's case, it was generally a matter of outgrowing them because he had grown considerably in the three years he had been there. Although there were several kids who were older than his twelve years, only two, Connors and Simon, both of whom were sixteen, were bigger than he. And in their case, they were only marginally bigger.

In the early days of Matt's stay in the Home, Connors and Simon had sometimes taken it upon themselves to punish him for real, or imagined, infractions. But there came a time when Connors told Matt to bend over and grab his ankles so he could swat him.

"Hit me with that paddle one more time and I'll cram it down your throat," Matt responded menacingly.

Startled by Matt's challenge, Connors walked away without administering punishment, and now neither Connors nor Simon was courageous enough to take him on by himself.

Matt's size, courage, and demeanor had made him a popular leader among the others in the Home, and even those who were older than Matt looked up to him.

That is why when Matt told them all to follow his lead and not eat supper one night, no one questioned him as to why they should do such a thing. When they went through the line for supper, they accepted their bowls of pease porridge, then went to their tables. As they looked toward Matt, he reminded them by sign and signal that they were not to eat their porridge.

In the meantime, they watched as Connors and Simon walked confidently back to their table. Unlike the other residents of the home, neither Connors nor Simon had to go through the line. Instead, they were served at their seats.

One of the kitchen workers brought two bowls out to them and set them on the table in front of Connors and Simon.

"Here, hold on!" Simon called out as the woman started back toward the kitchen. "What is this?"

"It's your supper," the woman answered.

"The hell it is. We're having ham tonight."

The kitchen worker shook her head. "No ham," she said.

"What's going on here? What happened to our ham?"

"I haven't seen any ham," the woman answered.

Though none of the other residents laughed out loud, they all repressed giggles and smiles while they watched the frustration of the two oldest of their number as they tried to eat the pease porridge.

"What is this?" Connors shouted in anger. "Nobody can eat this shit!"

Again, there were repressed giggles from the other residents. Then, at a nod from Matt, everyone got up from the table and took their untouched bowls of porridge to the garbage can. There, they dumped the porridge, turned the bowls in, then filed out of the dining room.

"Connors, did you see that?" Simon asked.

"Did I see what?"

"None of them ate."

"Yeah, well, who can blame them?" he replied, looking at his meal with disgust.

"No, you don't understand," Simon said. "None of them ate so much as one bite. They always eat."

"Yeah," Connors said. "Yeah, you're right. I wonder why not. Why don't you follow them, Simon, and see if you can figure out what's going on."

"Yeah," Simon said. "I will."

Simon slipped out of the dining room, then hanging back a little, watched as the others went into the chapel. Curious, he moved up to the door of the chapel, then looked inside. Everyone was sitting quietly in the pews, with their heads bowed and their eyes closed.

"Simon," Matt called, seeing Simon standing at the door. "It's so good to see you here. Come on in."

"What?" Simon asked.

"Why don't you go get Connors and bring him with you? We would love to have you two join us."

"What are you doing?"

"Why, we're having a prayer service, of course," Matt said.

"What do you mean you're having a prayer service? How can you have a prayer service if there ain't no preacher here?"

"You don't need a preacher to have a prayer service," Matt said. "All you need to do is pray. Won't you join us?" He reached out as if to grab Simon and pull him on into the chapel.

Simon held out his hands as if warding Matt off. He shook his head.

"No," he said. "I ain't doin' no prayin'."

"What about Connors? Won't you ask him to join us?"

"You're crazy," Simon said. "There ain't neither one of us goin' to be comin' in here and sayin' a bunch of prayers."

"Then we will pray for you," Matt said.

"You're crazy, I tell you. Every last one of you."

"Oh, Simon?" Matt called as Simon started to leave.

"What?" Simon responded in a belligerent bark.

"Enjoy your pease porridge."

The others laughed out loud.

"You're crazy," Simon repeated.

Matt waited for a moment, then looked over at Eddie. "Make sure he's gone."

Eddie went to the door, looked through it, then turned back. "He's gone," he said.

"Let's eat," Matt said, and with that, everyone crowded up to the altar where, from beneath the pulpit, Matt pulled out a large cooked ham.

"Oh, this looks so delicious," Tamara said. Tamara was two years older than Matt. In the early days, when Matt first came to the home, it had been Tamara who recognized the grief he was suffering, and who had tried, as well as she knew how, to comfort him. "Where did you get it?"

"The ladies of the Episcopal church cooked it especially for us," Matt said. "I just happened to be outside Captain Mumford's office when they brought it. Captain Mumford thanked them for it, then told Connors that he and Simon could both have a little of it before he took it home."

"Took it home? He was going to take it home?" someone asked.

Matt nodded. "Yeah. You think pease porridge is all we ever get? Churches and the like been bringing us food ever since I got here, only we don't ever see any of it," Matt said.

"That ain't right," one of the boys said. He had only been there about six months.

"I agree, Billy, it isn't right, so that's why I decided to do something about it," Matt said.

"Get this ham?"

"Yeah, get this ham. I waited until Captain Mumford stepped out of the office, then I took it and brought it here."

"I wouldn't have had the nerve to do that," one of the others said.

"Sure you would have," Matt said. "All you would have had to do was smell it when you were hungry."

"When is anyone not hungry in here?" one of the other girls asked, and they all laughed.

Timmy carved the ham and several came back for seconds, until everyone had eaten their fill. Now, the only thing remaining was the large ham bone.

"What are you going to do with the ham bone?" Eddie asked.

"My mama always made beans with it," Matt said. "Beans and cornbread."

"Oh, beans and cornbread. If I weren't so full right now,

that would make me really hungry," Timmy said, and again, everyone laughed.

"Seriously, what are you going to do with it? If you just throw it away and Captain Mumford discovers it, we're all going to get in trouble," Eddie said.

"Yeah," Matt said with a big smile. "If Captain Mumford discovers it, he really will be mad, won't he? I mean, really mad. There's no tellin' what he might do." Matt chuckled.

"I'll say," Eddie started. "He would . . ." Eddie paused in mid-sentence. "Wait a minute! You are up to something, aren't you? What are you going to do?"

"You'll see," Matt said.

"Matt, do be careful," Tamara said.

"I will be," Matt promised.

The next evening, just before supper, Captain Mumford came into the dining room.

"I want all of you to line up!" he shouted. "Boys on the right, girls on the left."

Everyone began to do as he ordered, though nobody had any idea what is was all about. They began talking among themselves, asking questions and speculating as to what this was about.

"Shut up!" Mumford shouted. "All of you, just shut up!"

"Cap'n Mumford, you want me'n Simon to go take care of some of the loudmouths?" Connors asked.

"I do not, sir!" Mumford said in a cold and calculating voice. "I want you two to stand over there with the boys."

"You—you are asking us to stand over there with them?" Connors asked, surprised by the request.

"I'm not asking you anything," Mumford said. If anything, his voice was even colder now than it had been earlier. "I am telling you."

Simon and Connors exchanged worried and confused glances, then walked over to stand against the wall with the others.

Mumford was holding a gunnysack.

"Any time you get several people living together as we do here, the one thing that you must be able to count on is trust," Mumford said. "You must be able to depend upon one another to be loyal, and honest. The worst thing that can happen in a society such as ours is that one might steal from another."

Mumford stuck his hand down into the gunnysack, then pulled out the remnants of the ham the residents had eaten the night before.

"This ham was to have been a gift to you." He took in the residents with a wave of his hand. "To all of you," he continued. "It was provided to us by the ladies of St. Paul's Episcopal Church. I had it on my desk, ready to take back to the kitchen for your supper. I stepped out but for a moment, and when I came back, it was gone."

No one made a sound.

"Stolen!" he shouted loudly.

He looked over at Simon and Connors. "Then, this morning, I found this ham bone in the trunk shared by these two."

"What?" Connors shouted. "Look here, we didn't have nothin' to do with stealin' that ham!"

"I will not tolerate stealing, sir, and I will not tolerate lying," Mumford said coldly.

"But we didn't . . ." Simon said.

"Hush, sir! Hush your foul mouth," Mumford said. "You are both sixteen years old. I have kept you on here out of the goodness of my heart. But I am not required to keep anyone beyond the age of sixteen. So, I am ordering both of you out of here tonight."

"What do you mean out of here? Where are we supposed to go?"

"I don't care where you go," Mumford said. "As long as you aren't here. If I see either of you here ever again, I shall go to the sheriff's office and have you both charged with trespassing."

"I don't know who did this to us," Connors shouted to the boys and girls who were lined up on either side of the dining hall. "But when I find out, I will get you. I will get you for this, I promise!"

"Get out," Mumford said.

Connors and Simon both left, followed by the cheers, jeers, and catcalls of the ones they were leaving behind.

The next day, Mumford asked Matt to come to his office.

"Yes, Captain Mumford?" Matt said.

"I've been watching you, Matt," Mumford said. "And I like the way you handle yourself."

Matt didn't answer, because he had no idea where the discussion was going.

"Connors and Simon served their purpose well, as long as they were here," Mumford continued. "But they outlived their purpose, and it was time for them to go."

"I think everyone was happy to see them go," Matt said.

"Maybe so," Mumford said. "Still, as I say, they did serve their purpose. Matt, when you are in charge of something like this, you need people to help you. Specifically, you need someone who is himself a resident, someone who knows what is going on, who knows what the others are talking about. Someone who can report back when they see misbehavior."

Matt said nothing.

"I'm sure you saw how much better Connors and Simon had it than the rest of you," Mumford said.

"Yes, we all saw that."

"It is a necessary part of the procedure," Mumford said. "I could not expect someone to work for me without some sort of compensation. In the case of Connors and Simon, I compensated them by allowing them to eat better, to have better accommodations. And of course, I will do the same thing for you."

"For me?"

"Yes. Winter is coming on, this will be your third winter. I'm sure you remember how cold and drafty the dormitory is. But if you move down to the end, where Connors and Simon were, you will find it much warmer and much more comfortable."

"Why would I move down there?"

"If you are working for me, then it is your due," Mumford said.

"You want me to do what Connors and Simon did? You want me to spy for you?"

"Yes."

Matt shook his head. "No," he said. "No, I won't do it."

The smile left Mumford's face. "You have no choice," he said. "You will do it because I am ordering you to do it."

Chapter Seven

"I can't do it," Matt told Tamara later that night. The two were sitting on the back porch of the home, listening to the frogs and the night-calling insects. "I won't do it."

"I thought you said he ordered you to do it," Tamara said.

Matt nodded. "He did order me to do it. But I'm not going to. I can't be like Simon and Connors. I can't turn on the others in here."

Tamara reached up to brush a fall of hair back from Matt's forehead.

"You wouldn't be like them," she said. "You couldn't be like them."

"There might be some who wouldn't understand," Matt said. "They would think I had turned against them."

"There might be some who would think that," Tamara agreed. "But I would know better. So would Eddie, and Timmy, and Billy."

Matt shook his head. "Maybe," he said. "But I'm not going to take that chance."

"What do you mean? What are you going to do?"

"I'm leaving this place."

"Leaving? But where will you go? How will you live?"

"I don't know, but anyplace is better than this."

"When are you going?"

"Tonight," Matt said. "When I know everyone is asleep."

Tamara didn't answer right away, and for a long moment the silence was invaded by the bleat and thrum of the frogs and insects. Finally, she reached over and put her hand on his.

"Matt, take me with you," she said.

"Tamara, I can't," Matt answered. "Like you said, I have no idea where I'm going or what I am going to do. Winter is coming on. I could freeze to death up in the mountains, if I don't starve first."

"I don't care," Tamara said. "I'm willing to take that chance if you are."

"Tamara, I . . ." Matt started.

"Matt, please. I'm fourteen years old now. Next year I'll . . ." She paused in mid-sentence.

"You'll what?"

"Matt, don't you know what Captain Mumford makes the older girls do to earn money?"

"I thought all the older girls worked at Emma Smith's Boarding House."

"And you have no idea what goes on there?"

"Don't you just clean and cook and make up the beds and such?"

"Beds, yes," Tamara said. "Only we don't just make them up."

Suddenly Matt realized what Tamara was talking about.

"Are you saying that Captain Mumford makes you be with men?" he asked.

Tamara nodded, and her eyes brimmed over with tears. One began sliding down her cheek, and she reached up to brush it away with the tip of her finger.

"I didn't know that," Matt said. "I've been here for three years, and I didn't know that."

"Captain Mumford says he will horsewhip any girl who tells," Tamara said. "Besides, it's not something anyone would want to tell anyway."

"Are you . . . ?" Matt began.

"Not yet," Tamara said. "He doesn't make anyone start until they are fifteen."

"I'll take you with me," Matt promised.

"Oh, thank you! Thank you!" Tamara said, spontaneously embracing him and kissing him on the cheek.

"Be ready to go tonight."

"What time?"

"I don't know, after midnight sometime, when everyone else is asleep," Matt said. "You be standing in the door of the girls' room, looking for me. I'm not coming in there."

"I'll be there," Tamara said.

Matt wasn't sure exactly what time it was when he left. He knew it was late at night because everyone was asleep and he could hear the snores and rhythmic breathing of the others. It was getting colder outside, and he had no overcoat, so he decided to take the blanket off his bed.

He walked down to the hall and stood just outside the girls' dormitory. When Tamara didn't come out, he decided to leave without her, but suddenly she was there.

"When I saw you with the blanket, I thought that might be a pretty good idea," she whispered. "So I went back to get mine."

"All right, let's go, but keep quiet," Matt said.

Leaving the dormitory, Matt and Tamara tiptoed through the darkened building, passing through the dining room, then making their way into the kitchen. There, they found several chunks of stale bread, which they stuck down into their pockets. Then, wrapping themselves in the blankets, they sneaked out through the back.

Once outside, they looked back toward the building that housed the Home for Wayward Boys and Girls. For a moment, Matt almost went back in. It wasn't much, but it was the only home he'd had for the last three years. For some of the residents, it was the only home they had ever known.

"Are you sure you want to go with me?" Matt asked. "I mean, when you think about it, the Home kept us warm in the winter, gave us a place to sleep, and provided meals."

"Such as they were," Tamara said.

"We are giving up a safe haven for the unknown," Matt said.

"Who are you trying to talk out of going? Me or you?" Tamara asked.

"I don't know," Matt answered honestly. "Both of us, I guess." He shook his head. "But I can't stay. I cannot and I will not replace Connors and Simon."

The moon was full and bright, and it lit the path for them. A cool night breeze caused Matt to shiver, though in truth he didn't know if his trembling was entirely from the cold, or from nervousness over his uncertain future. He pulled the blanket around himself, then began walking.

The Home for Wayward Boys and Girls was three blocks from Muddy Creek, and while that had not been a conscious goal, Matt quickly found himself on the bank of the creek, looking down at the water. That's when he saw the boat.

"There," he said excitedly, pointing to the boat. "That's our way out of here!"

"We're going to steal a boat?" Tamara asked.

"Nah, we're not stealing it," Matt said. "We're just borrowing it. You keep a watch out while I untie it."

Scrambling down the creek bank, Matt started untying the boat. That was when he heard the dogs barking.

"Tamara!" he called up the embankment. "Tamara, what is it?"

"Someone's coming," Tamara called down.

"Come on, hurry!"

"No!" Tamara said. "You go ahead. I'll lead them away from the water."

"Tamara, no, come on!" Matt said. "Hurry, we have to go now!"

"You go on!" Tamara called.

Matt saw Tamara turn and run away from the top of the bank.

"Help!" Tamara called. "Help me!"

"What are you doing out here, girl?" a man's voice asked.

"I don't know," Tamara answered. "I think I must have been walking in my sleep, I just woke up out here. I'm lost and frightened. Please, help me get back to the Home."

As Tamara distracted whoever had been alerted by the dogs, Matt stepped into the boat and pushed himself off. Picking up the paddle, he helped the swift-flowing water propel him downstream.

It was five or six miles before the creek was no longer wide enough or deep enough to support the boat. There, Matt abandoned it, and started walking. He stayed close to the creek because it was a source of water and because he had an idea that it might eventually lead him somewhere.

He ate the last of his bread on the third day. On the fourth day he found some wild onions and ate them, though the taste was so bitter that he could barely keep them down.

He had nothing at all to eat on the fifth day, but on the sixth he managed to catch a frog. He remembered eating frog legs back in Kansas, but they were rolled in batter and deep-fried. He had no way of cooking these legs; he had no matches. But he did have a pocket knife and he cut off the legs, skinned them, and ate them raw.

An early snow moved in just before nightfall of the sixth day, and the single blanket Matt had brought with him did little to push away the cold. It was also tiring to try and hold the blanket around him while walking, and he considered cutting a hole in the middle, but decided against it because he thought it would be less warm at night that way.

As the snow continued to fall, it got more and more difficult to walk. At first, it was just slick, and he slipped and fell a couple of times, once barking his shin on a rock so hard that the pain stayed with him for quite a while.

As the snow got deeper, he quit worrying about it being slick, and concerned himself only with the work it took just to keep going. His breath started coming in heaving gasps, sending out clouds of vapor before him. Once he saw a wolf tracking him, and he wished that he had his father's rifle.

He found a limb that was stout and about as thick as three fingers. Using his knife, he trimmed the smaller branches off it, then managed to cut it to just the right size. He was able to use the limb as a cane to help him negotiate the deepening snowdrifts.

Just before dark, he sensed more than heard something behind him and, turning quickly, saw that the wolf, crouched low, had sneaked up right behind him. With a shout, and holding the club in both hands, he swung at the wolf and had the satisfaction of hearing a solid pop as he hit the wolf in the head. The wolf yelped once, then turned and ran away, trailing little bits of blood behind it as it ran.

Matt felt a sense of power and elation over that little encounter. He was sure that the wolf would give him no further trouble.

After the sun set, he found an overhanging rock ledge and got under it, then wrapped himself in the blanket. When night came, he looked up into the dark sky and watched as the huge, white flakes tumbled down. If it weren't for the fact that he was probably going to die in these mountains, he would think the snowfall was beautiful.

"Lord," he said, praying aloud. "I reckon I haven't been all that good at prayin', even though we had a chapel back at the Home. But I know that Mama used to pray to you all the time, and she seemed to take a lot of comfort in it, so if you don't mind hearin' from someone like me, I'm goin' to pray to you now.

"I want you to look out for Eddie and Timmy, and all the other kids back at the Home. Truth is, Lord, I probably shouldn't have left. Without me there to take care of them, there's no tellin' what Captain Mumford is goin' to put them through. And there's no tellin' who he's goin' to get to take the place of those two no-accounts, Connors and Simon.

"But that's spilt milk, Lord. The Home is back there, and I'm here, and I probably wouldn't live long enough to make it back there even if I tried. I'm probably goin' to die pretty soon now. Of course, I don't reckon I have to tell you the way things are right now. I'm out of food, it's gettin' colder, and the creek has quit so I'm out of water too. I know Mama is up in heaven with you, 'cause she was a very good woman. And Cassie is up there too. And though I didn't know Pa all that well, seein' as he was off to war for most of my life, well, I figure he's probably up there also, 'cause I don't think Mama would've married a bad man.

"But now it comes to me, Lord, and I have to confess that my chances don't look all that good. I killed those two men back at the wagon. Well, I don't have to tell you about it, you saw me do it. I can't rightly say that I shot either one of them to save my family because, as you know, my family was already dead. The only reason I shot 'em is because they needed killin'. And I have to be honest with you, Lord, I aim to hunt down Payson and Garvey and the others who were with them, and kill them as well. So if you let me live through this, then I'm going to take it that it's all right with you. And if it isn't all right with you, Lord, then I hope you just go ahead and take me tonight.

"Amen."

Finishing his prayer, Matt pulled the blanket more securely around him, pulled up his legs, then leaned back against the rock. Strangely, the cold seemed to be less intense and he felt his body warming. He also felt his eyes growing very heavy and he closed them, then drifted off to sleep.

Chapter Eight

With Smoke Jensen

The sudden snowfall had caught Smoke by surprise. It shouldn't have caught him by surprise. Preacher had taught him well how to gauge the change in weather.

"When the clouds is low in the west and there's these long, scraggily tails hangin' down from 'em, then like as not you'll be gettin' snow soon as they start movin' over the mountains."

Smoke needed to be on the other side of the mountain range, and he was afraid that the snow might be so heavy as to close the pass. So, though every ounce of him wanted to hole up somewhere long enough to ride the storm out, he pushed on through, fighting the cold, stinging snow in his face until he reached the top of the pass. He made it through, and had started looking for a place to spend the night when he saw the boy.

He almost didn't see him; there was a big drift of snow so that only the boy's head and shoulders were sticking out. He was under an overhanging ledge, and his head was back and his eyes were closed.

"Damn, who is that?" he asked aloud. "And what's he doing here?"

Smoke stared in shocked surprise at the young boy. Was he sleeping? Or was he dead?

The boy's face and lips were blue, and there were ice crystals in his eyebrows and hair. The blanket around him, which was his only protection against the cold, was frozen.

It didn't look good.

"Here, try some of this."

Matt opened his eyes and saw a man sitting on the bed beside him, holding a cup. He took the cup and raised it to his mouth, but jerked it away when it burned his lips.

The man who handed him the cup laughed. "Oh, maybe I should have told you it was hot."

Matt tried again, this time sipping it through extended lips. It was hot, and bracing, and good.

"What is it?" he asked.

"Broth, made from beaver," the man said.

"Don't know that I've ever tasted beaver before," Matt said calmly.

Smoke laughed.

"What's so funny?"

"I'll say this for you, boy, you do have sand," Smoke said. "You sure seem to be taking this in stride."

Matt took another swallow, then looked around. He was in a room, or more accurately, a one-room cabin. There was a fireplace on one side in which a fire was burning briskly, putting out enough heat to warm the entire room. The interior walls were made of mud-chinked logs. There was a table and several chairs, a couple of chests, and a wall rack that held three rifles and a shotgun. There were antlers on the wall, and bearskins on the floor. The very bed he was lying on had skins and well as blankets.

"Beaver broth is good," he said.

"I made some biscuits," the man said, handing one to Matt.

Matt took one of the biscuits and began eating it hungrily.

"Whoa, slow down, slow down, you'll make yourself sick," he said. "How long has it been since you ate?"

"I don't know," Matt said. "I don't even know how long I've been here."

"I brought you here night before last," the man said. "You've been asleep for the whole time. In fact, I wasn't sure I'd ever be able to wake you up. I was thinking I would have to bury you out back somewhere."

"Where is here?"

"I'll tell you where here is after you answer some of my questions. Who are you?"

"My name is Matt."

"Matt what?"

"Just Matt."

The man nodded. "All right, Just Matt, that's good enough for me," he said. "My name is Smoke Jensen."

"Smoke? You mean, like smoke from a fire?"

"Yes."

"I've never heard of such a name."

"I've never heard of someone who was just Matt."

"I'm sorry," Matt said. "I guess if your name is Smoke, then that's your name."

"My real name is Kirby. Kirby Jensen. But folks have called me Smoke from the time I was a kid, so it sort of belongs to me now."

"You were going to tell me where I am."

"You are in my cabin in the Gore Range."

"Gore Range? What is the Gore Range?"

"It is a mountain range in Colorado," Smoke explained.

"Oh."

"Are you lost, Matt?"

"No, I'm not lost. I knew I was in Colorado," Matt replied.

Smoke laughed again. "Well, as long as you knew you were in Colorado," he said.

Matt took another swallow of the broth.

"Tell you what, Matt. As soon as you've got your strength, I'll take you back."

"No!" Matt said sharply. "No, I won't go back!" He tried to get up and get out of bed, but he was too weak and he fell back onto the bed.

"Here, hold on, hold on there," Smoke said. "You're too weak to be doin' that."

"I'm not goin' back," Matt said.

"All right, if you don't want to go back, I won't make you," Smoke said. "But don't you think your ma and pa might be worrying about you?"

"My ma and pa are both dead," Matt said. "They've been dead for three years."

"I see," Smoke said. "So, where is it you don't want to go back to? Are you living with relatives or something?"

Matt shook his head and finished the broth. He handed the cup to Smoke. "Is there any more?" he asked.

"Yes, there's more," Smoke replied.

"And another biscuit, please?"

Smoke refilled the cup with broth, then handed it and another biscuit to Matt.

"It's an orphanage," Matt said, answering Smoke's earlier question. "Only it's called the Home for Wayward Boys and Girls. None of us are really wayward, though. The only thing is we're all just orphans."

"So, if it's just an orphanage, why did you run away?"

"You wouldn't understand," Matt said.

"Maybe I wouldn't," Smoke agreed. "But in the meantime, you can put your mind at ease. I'm not going to make you go back."

"I don't want to be a burden on you, so as soon as I get my strength back, I'll be going on," Matt offered. "Just tell me the way to the nearest town so I can find a job somewhere."

"The nearest town is a good fifty or more miles from here," he said. "And even if you knew where it was, you wouldn't be able to make it. Most of the high passes are filled with snow by now. You wouldn't be able to get through."

"Oh."

"So, I'm afraid you are going to have to just stay here with me."

"Stay here? Stay here for how long?"

"Four or five months anyway," Smoke replied. "Until the high passes are open."

"I'm sorry."

"What are you sorry about?" Smoke asked.

"I'm sorry I'm goin' to have to stay here and put you out."

"Well, don't worry about it. In the first place, I could use the company. It gets awfully lonely sometimes, spending a winter in a cabin like this all by yourself. And in the second place, you won't be puttin' me out because I aim to see to it that you earn your keep."

"Yes, sir," Matt said. "I'll do whatever you ask me to do, Mr. Jensen."

"Is that a promise?"

"Yes, sir!"

"Then I'm going to ask you not to call me Mr. Jensen. The name is Smoke. That's what I'll be wanting you to call me."

"All right—Smoke," Matt replied with a big grin.

"First thing we're going to have to do is build you a bed," Smoke said. "The bed you've been sleeping in for the last two days belongs to me, and I don't plan on sharing it."

"I've made my bed, but I don't think I've ever built one before," Matt said.

"Matt, during your stay with me you're going to be doing a lot of things you've never done before," Smoke promised.

Chapter Nine

"It doesn't make the best coffee," Smoke said as he poured the dark substance into the bottom of a coffeepot. "But if you roast dandelion root, then crush it up and boil it, well, the coffee is passable."

"The meat smells good," Matt said. He was talking about a cut of venison that was cooking in a roaster that was sitting on a rock at the back of the fireplace. Wild carrots and wild leeks surrounded the meat and were now bubbling in the meat juices.

"The meat, carrots, and cattail roots will make us a fine meal," Smoke said. "Afterward, we'll have dessert of wild blueberry pie and coffee."

"I had no idea there were so many things you could eat in the wild," Matt said. "I mean, if you think about it, I nearly starved to death out there and there were all sorts of thing to eat."

"Well, don't feel bad about it," Smoke said. "I wouldn't have known about it either if it hadn't been for Preacher."

"Preacher must be quite a fella," Matt said. "I'd like to meet him someday."

"You will," Smoke promised. "The thing about Preacher is, he likes his time alone."

"Why is that?"

"He's an old-time mountain man," Smoke explained. "One of the originals."

"You're a mountain man too."

"I am," Smoke agreed. "But I don't plan to spend my whole life in the mountains. Truth is, I like civilization too much. One of these days I intend to get myself a ranch and settle down."

"Not me," Matt said.

"You don't want to settle down?"

"No, sir. I want to just wander around from place to place."

"I guess you'll get to see a lot of the country that way," Smoke said.

Matt was quiet for a long moment before he spoke. "After I kill some people," he said.

Smoke didn't reply.

"I reckon you think that's wrong of me, don't you? Saying that I'm going to kill some people."

"Depends on who you are going to kill, and why you are going to kill them," Smoke said.

"I only know the names of two of them," Matt said. "One is Payson and the other is Garvey."

"Are those first names or last?"

"I don't know," Matt said.

"Well, would you know these people if you saw them?"

"Yes, I'd know them. Payson has a long, ugly, purple scar on his face and it's made his eye look funny," Matt said, using his finger to illustrate the scar. "Garvey only has half an ear."

"You said your ma and pa are dead. Did these fellas kill them?"

"Yes, and my big sister too," Matt said. "They were also going to—uh—I mean, with my mom and my sister they were going to—uh—don't know how to say it."

"Rape?"

Matt was quiet for a moment. His eyes brimmed with tears; then they began flowing down his cheeks. He held back his sobs as he brushed the tears away. Finally, he nodded.

"Yes. One of them was going to rape my mom and sister," Matt said. "My mom and sis were already dead, but he was going to do it anyway."

"You said he was going to," Smoke noted. "But he didn't?"

Matt shook his head. "No."

"What stopped him?"

"I—I did," Matt said. "When they shot Pa, I grabbed Pa's rifle and I ran. Like a coward, I ran."

Smoke shook his head. "That wasn't being cowardly, Matt. That was being smart."

"I managed to get behind some rocks and I climbed up so I could see. But by the time I got up there, it was too late. Ma and Cassie were already dead, and one of them was standing over my ma, unbuttoning his pants, getting ready to . . ." He paused for a moment before he continued. "To be honest with you, Smoke, I was nine years old then, so I didn't really know what he was planning to do. I thought maybe he was going to pee on them. So I shot him in the head."

"Good for you," Smoke said.

"After I shot that one, one of the others tried to come after me, but he got wedged in between a couple of rocks and couldn't get to me. So I killed him too."

"How do you feel about that?" Smoke asked.

"What do you mean?"

"Do you think what you did was wrong?"

"I don't know," Matt admitted. "I mean, I know it's wrong to kill people, but I also know that soldiers kill people. My pa was a soldier in the war. He killed people and I know he wasn't a bad man."

"That is something to think about, Matt," Smoke said. "If

good men can kill good men during a war, then there can't be anything wrong with a good man killing an evil man."

Matt smiled and nodded. "Yeah," he said. "Yeah, I hadn't thought of it that way before, but I think you are right."

"It smells like supper is ready," Smoke said.

"That's good. I'm starving."

Smoke laughed. "If anyone else told me they were starving, I would figure they didn't know what they were talking about. But seeing as how you actually were starving when I found you, then I guess you don't fall into that category."

Throughout the long winter, Smoke began teaching his young protégé things he needed to know to get by. In the teaching, he felt almost as if he was doing nature's bidding, passing along things he had learned from Preacher. And just as it wasn't a father-son relationship between Smoke and Preacher, neither was this a father-son relationship. But the fact that they didn't share a familial bond didn't mean the relationship wasn't just as strong, nor the continuity as valid as it would have been if they had.

"Just because we're livin' out here in the wilds, doesn't mean we don't have laws that we follow," Smoke said, recalling almost the same conversation he once had with Preacher. "Only out here, it isn't laws that you find written on paper or in books. And it isn't laws that have to have sheriffs enforcing, or judges settling."

"What kind of laws are they?"

"You might say they are the laws of decency and good sense," Smoke explained. "For example, don't go putting your hands on another man's wife, don't steal from him, don't cheat him, and don't call him a liar. Do that, and somebody is going to get killed."

"Somebody? Don't you mean the man that's doing the wrong?" Matt asked.

Smoke shook his head. "Not always. Sometimes the one who is wronged has no choice but to try and defend those laws. But if the one who wronged him is faster and better with a gun, then the wronged man dies."

"I see what you mean."

"I hope you do see what I mean, Matt, because I'm going to teach you how to use a gun, And by the time I get through with you, there will be few, if any, in the country who will be able to stand up to you. But with that comes the responsibility of knighthood."

Matt chuckled. "Knighthood?"

"You've heard about knights, haven't you?"

"Yeah, I've seen pictures. They are the guys who wore the iron suits, right?" Matt asked.

"Right. Those suits were called armor. The knights were appointed by the king, and he made sure that he only appointed the best men for the job. You see, the knights were so strong they could kill anyone they wanted to. But they didn't. They took an oath never to use their power to enrich themselves, but always just to help others."

"Are you a knight, Smoke?"

Smoke nodded. "Yeah," he said. "In a manner of speaking, you might say that I am a knight. I respect the rights of others, and I settle my own accounts without running to the sheriff."

"How do you settle accounts?" Matt asked.

"Say a cougar is sneaking up on my horse," Smoke suggested. "Do you think I should go to a sheriff or a judge to complain?"

"No, sir," Matt replied.

"What would you do?"

"I'd shoot the cougar."

Smoke nodded. "Uh-huh. It's the same with a man, Matt.

If a man calls you out, you don't go to the sheriff or a judge, you deal with him, straight and simple."

"Like Payson and Garvey?"

"Like Payson and Garvey," Smoke agreed.

As soon as the streams melted and the water began flowing again, Smoke asked Matt to come down to the creek with him.

"Are we going fishing?" Matt asked.

Smoke chuckled. "Something like that," he said. He handed Matt a pan.

"Hmm. I've never fished with a pan before," Matt said, looking at the pan.

"That's because you've never fished for gold before."

"Gold? You fish for gold?"

"I do," Smoke said.

The walk from the cabin to the creek was about half a mile. There, a wide bed of gravel wound its way through the valley, and in the middle of the bed of gravel was a creek, approximately thirty yards wide. The creek ran cool and clear, except where the whitewater broke over the rocks.

"It's very pretty here," Matt said.

"Yes, it is," Smoke agreed.

"Is this where we are going to fish for gold?"

"Yes, but it isn't called fishing, it's called panning," Smoke said. "Pay attention."

"All right."

"The first thing you have to do is look around for the best location to work. Find yourself a spot where the water is at least six inches deep and flowing just fast enough to keep the muddy water from getting into your pan. Also, it's nice if you can find a rock that will let you sit down."

Smoke continued his lesson, demonstrating as he talked.

"Fill the pan about three-quarters full of gravel, then hold it deep enough so it is just under water. Shake it back and forth and from side to side, but not so hard that you wash anything out of the pan. Keep doing this until everything heavy goes to the bottom of the pan and the lighter stuff comes to the top. Then turn the pan just enough to pour out the lighter rocks," he said, continuing to demonstrate.

"After that, you sort of swirl things around in the pan to look at what you have and . . . ha!" he said, reaching down into the pan. "Here is what we are looking for."

Smoke held a little rock in his hand, not much bigger than a pea.

"That's just a rock," Matt said.

Smoke turned it, and Matt saw a quick flash in the sun.

"Not just a rock," Smoke replied.

"It's gold!" Matt said.

Smoke nodded.

"If there's gold in this creek, why aren't more people up here doing this?"

"Right now only three people know about it," Smoke said. "Preacher, me, and you. I'd like to keep it that way."

"Wow!" Matt said. "This is fun!"

Smoke chuckled. "I'm glad you think so," he said. "Because this is what we are going to be doing all summer."

Chapter Ten

Cedar Creek

There wasn't much to the little town of Cedar Creek. It was hot, dry, and dusty, out in the middle of nowhere and baking under the blows of the hot September sun. An old yellow dog was asleep under the front porch of the general store, the shade shared by a black-and-white cat.

School had just started, and on the school grounds a group of Miss Miller's second-grade students were laughing and playing during their afternoon recess.

As the children played and the rest of the town went about its business, a drama was taking place inside the Bank of Cedar Creek. Seven men, wearing yellow dusters and brandishing guns, were holding the bank employees and customers at bay. The bank robbers were wearing as masks bandannas tied around their faces. But the leader of the group had a puffy scar, starting above his left eye, disfiguring the eye and streaking down his cheek like a purple flash of lightning, then disappearing under the bandanna.

Even as Payson and his men were robbing the bank, Jason Feeler was coming up the boardwalk, carrying an envelope.

The envelope contained twelve dollars and seventy-five cents, a deposit from the livery stable. Jason, who was seventeen, felt pleased that Mr. Heckemeyer considered him responsible enough to take the overnight receipts to the bank.

As Jason reached the front of the bank, he looked in through the window, then gasped. Mr. Fitzhugh, the bank president, was standing against the wall with his hands in the air. So were several others. Mr. Boykin was on his knees in front of the safe, twisting the dial, while a masked man was standing beside him, holding a gun against his head. There were six other robbers in the bank.

Fitzhugh saw Jason, and made a slight motion with his head. Jason understood, nodded, then left the front of the bank. As soon as he was clear of the bank, he started running. A moment later, he pushed open the door to the marshal's office.

"The bank's bein' robbed, Marshal Cobb!" Jason shouted breathlessly.

"What?"

"They's some men with guns robbin' the bank," Jason said. "They're in there now!"

Marshal Cobb pulled a rifle down from the gun rack and tossed it to Jason; then he pulled another one down for himself.

"Get down to the general store," the marshal ordered. "Tell anyone you find there to get ready. I'm goin' to get some help from the saloon."

Spurred on by the warning and moving quickly and quietly enough to avoid giving the bank robbers any sign of what they were doing, the men blocked off both escape routes out of town. They pushed wagons across the street to use as barricades; then with rifles, pistols, and shotguns, they took up their positions. Armed and ready, they stared back toward the bank, watching and waiting.

* * *

Inside the bank, unaware of the ambush being set for them outside, the scar-faced man was holding his gun on the bank teller, who was kneeling in front of the vault door, nervously twisting the combination dial.

"Mister, if you don't have that lock open in thirty seconds, I'm going to blow your brains all over the front of this safe," the scar-faced man said menacingly.

"I'm trying to open it," the trembling teller replied. "But I'm so scared that I keep makin' mistakes."

The scar-faced man cocked his pistol and pressed the barrel against the teller's temple. "Yeah? Well, don't make any more, 'cause the next mistake will be your last one."

The teller began again.

"Garvey, what's it look like outside?" the leader asked.

"Damn, Payson, you said my name," Garvey said.

"Yeah, and you just said mine," Payson replied.

Like Payson, Garvey had a very distinguishing feature. The lobe of his left ear had been shot off, leaving him only half an ear on that side. He moved over to the window and pulled the green curtain aside so he could look out into the street.

"Never mind, what does it look like?"

"It looks quiet," Garvey said.

There was a click as the vault door came unlocked.

"There, that's more like it," Payson said with a wide, evil grin. He pulled a sack from the pocket of his duster and handed it to the teller. "Now, fill it up."

The teller reached for the coin drawer.

"To hell with them coins! I want greenbacks!" Payson ordered, waving his pistol toward the drawer that was full of banded stacks of bills.

"Yes, sir," the teller replied, and with trembling hands he

began scooping up the bank-note packages and dropping them into the bag.

"Hurry it up, hurry it up," Payson demanded. "We ain't got all day."

"Marshal, look!" one of the townsmen said, pointing toward the school.

Through all their preparation, no one had thought to warn Miss Miller and her second-grade pupils. The games of recess continued without interruption.

"Somebody needs to get them kids out of there!" another said.

"All right, go down there and . . ." Marshal Cobb began, but before he could finish the sentence, the front door of the bank swung open and seven men dashed toward the horses that were tied at the hitching rail. "No, wait, it's too late now," the marshal said.

Marshal Cobb raised up from his position and called out to the seven robbers.

"You men hold it right there!" he shouted. "You ain't a'goin' nowhere!"

At almost the same time Cobb shouted, he fired. His bullet went through Garvey's hat, knocking it into the dirt.

"What the hell?" Garvey shouted. "Payson, look out! It's a trap!"

"Poke, Syl, Clem, Bart, Pete, get mounted!" Payson shouted to the others. "Let's get out of here! Let's go, let's go!"

The other outlaws also began shooting as they started for their own mounts.

From the front porch of Lambert's Café, a citizen with food stains still on the front of his shirt appeared with a shotgun. He let go a blast, but the range was too great. His pellets peppered the outlaws without penetrating their skin.

Another man fired a shotgun from a little closer range, and the front window of the bank came crashing down.

Once the robbers were mounted, they started down the street at a full gallop, while two dozen armed townsmen fired at them from every possible position.

"I'm hit, I'm hit!" one of the outlaws shouted.

"Sonofabitch! They got Pete!" Poke yelled. He reached over to try and steady Pete on his horse, but the outlaw fell. "Payson, Pete's down!"

"Leave 'im!" Payson shouted back.

Payson and his gang reached the end of the street, only to find the barricade that had been erected.

"Damn! They got us blocked off! What'll we do, Payson?" Syl shouted.

"This way!" Payson answered, and leading the way, he started back through the town, riding back in the opposite direction. They were galloping hard when they came up on the barricade that had been erected at the other end of town. They had to pull up short. The horses, now as panic-stricken as the men, twisted around in nervous circles and reared up, anxious to run, but not sure where to go. It was all the riders could do to control them.

"They got us blocked off at both ends!" Clem yelled.

"There!" Bart shouted, pointing toward the school yard. "We can go through there!"

Without answering, Payson veered off the street and headed straight for the school yard, where the kids, who were by now frightened by the exploding gunshots, had gathered around Miss Miller. The teacher was also rooted to the spot by her own terror.

"Hold your fire, men! Hold your fire! We might hit one of the kids!" Marshal Cobb shouted.

With the marshal's order, the fire of the townspeople stopped, giving Payson and his men a chance to get away.

When Payson reached the alley behind the school, he and the others turned and fired back though the playground at the townspeople. Then they galloped away, followed by the shouts of anger and frustration from the men of the town. Marshal Cobb led them through the school yard to the alley, where they formed a skirmish line of shooters, firing at the cloud of dust as the riders grew smaller and smaller in the distance.

"Cease fire, cease fire!" the marshal shouted. "We're just wastin' ammunition now. They're well out of range."

"Marshal, you ain't gonna just let them get away, are you?"

"Nothing I can do about it," the marshal said. "They're out of town now, I've got no jurisdiction."

Looking back, they saw one of the outlaws lying dead in the street.

"At least we got one of them," Marshal Cobb said.

"Yeah," one of the others said. "And they got two of us. Look over there."

"My God," Marshal Cobb gasped when, for the first time, he saw that Miss Miller and a little girl were lying on the ground, victims of the outlaws' last fusillade. The fallen figures were surrounded by the other children, who were looking down at their teacher and their friend in shocked silence.

"Somebody get a doctor, quick!" Marshal Cobb called.

"We won't be needin' a doctor, Marshal," one of the men who had walked over to check them said. "What we need is an undertaker. They're both dead."

By now the outlaws were in full gallop, running away from the town. They ran the horses for several minutes before Bart Ebersole called out.

"Payson! If we don't give these horses a blow, they're goin' to drop dead under us!"

"Yeah, all right," Payson answered. "Pull up."

The six outlaws stopped the gallop, then dismounted, walked their horses to let them regain their breath.

"Anyone else hit?" Payson asked. "Garvey, Poke, Syl, Clem, Bart?"

"Nah," Garvey said. "Except for Pete, we come through fine."

Payson laughed. "Damn, boys, that was good. Jesse James don't have a thing on us!"

Chapter Eleven

Matt was standing just outside Smoke's cabin, throwing a knife at a target he had carved on a tree. The hunting knife, a gift from Smoke, was perfectly balanced for throwing, and whenever he had time during the long summer days, Matt would practice.

"Matt," Smoke called from the door of the cabin. "Let's see how good you really are."

Smoke threw his knife, hitting the target dead center.

Smiling, Matt threw his own knife at the target, hitting so close to the one Smoke had thrown that the blades were actually touching.

"Whoa, you've gotten pretty good with that," Smoke said.

"Thanks," Matt said, walking out to the tree and pulling both knives free.

"You remember what I said about going into town when summer was over?" Smoke said.

"I remember."

"Well, summer is over. Why don't you go out to the corral and pick out your horse?"

"*My* horse?"

"Yeah, your horse. A man's got to have a horse."

"Which horse is mine?" Matt asked.

"Why don't you take the best one?" Smoke replied. "Except for that one," Smoke added, pointing to an Appaloosa over in one corner of the corral. "That one is mine."

"Which horse is the best?" Matt asked.

"Uh-uh," Smoke replied, shaking his head. "I'm willing to give you the best horse in my string, but as to which horse that is, well, you're just going to have to figure that out for yourself."

Matt walked out to the small corral that Smoke had built and, leaning on the split-rail fence, looked at the string of seven horses from which he could choose.

After looking them over very carefully, Matt smiled and nodded.

"You've made your choice?" Smoke asked.

"Yes."

"Which one?"

"I want that one," Matt said, pointing to a bay.

"Why not the chestnut?" Smoke asked. "He looks stronger."

"Look at the chestnut's front feet," Matt said. "They are splayed. The bay's feet are just right."

"What about the black one over there?"

"Uh-uh," Matt said. "His back legs are set too far back. I want the bay."

Smoke reached out and ran his hand through Matt's hair.

"You're learning, kid, you're learning," he said. "The bay is yours."

Matt's grin spread from ear to ear. "I've never had a horse before," he said. He jumped down from the rail fence and started toward the horse.

"That's all right, he's never had a rider before," Smoke said.

"What?" Matt asked, jerking around in surprise as he stared at Smoke. "Did you say that he's never been ridden?"

"He's as spirited as he was the day we brought him in."

"How'm I going to ride him if he has never been ridden?"

"Well, I reckon you are just going to have to break him," Smoke said, passing the words off as easily as if he had just suggested that Matt should wear a hat.

"Break him? I can't break a horse!"

"Sure you can. It'll be fun," Smoke suggested.

Smoke showed Matt how to saddle the horse, and gave him some pointers on riding it.

"Now, you don't want to break the horse's spirit," Smoke said. "What you want to do is make him your partner."

"How do I do that?"

"Walk him around for a bit so that he gets used to his saddle, and to you. Then get on."

"He won't throw me then?"

"Oh, he'll still throw you a few times," Smoke said with a little laugh. "But at least he'll know how serious you are."

To Matt's happy surprise, he wasn't thrown even once. The horse did buck a few times, coming down on stiff legs, then sunfishing and, finally, galloping at full speed around the corral. But after a few minutes he stopped fighting, and Matt leaned over to pat him gently on the neck.

"Good job, Matt," Smoke said, clapping his hands quietly. "You've got a real touch with horses. You didn't break him, you trained him, and that's real good. He's not mean, but he still has spirit."

"Smoke, can I name him?"

"Sure, he's your horse, you can name him anything you want."

Matt continued to pat the horse on the neck as he thought of a name.

"That's it," he said, smiling broadly. "I've come up with a name."

"What are you going to call him?"

"Spirit."

Smoke nodded. "Spirit. That's a good name. The Indians will like that name."

"I wonder how long it will take him to learn his name," Matt said.

"Not too long," Smoke replied. "What do you say we get started into town now?"

"How far is town?" Matt asked.

"About fifty miles north of here," Smoke said. "We'll spend tonight on the trail, and get there sometime tomorrow."

"Smoke, we're not going to the town of Soda Creek, are we?" Matt asked.

"Soda Creek? No. Why the concern? Is that where the orphanage was?"

"Yes, and I don't want to go back there. I don't even want to go to the town."

"Don't worry about it. Soda Creek is south, and we're going north," Smoke said. "Do you know how to find north?"

"I know the sun rises in the east," Matt said.

"What if it's nighttime, and you can't see the sun?"

"I know about the North Star."

"That's good. Do you know how to find the North Star?"

"The Big Dipper," Matt said. "All you do is line up the two stars on the cup of the dipper, and you can find the North Star. Pa showed me how to do that when we were on the trail."

"Good for your pa," Smoke said. "That's a good thing to know. But what if you are in trees or something so that, for some reason, you can't see the stars? Did you know that you can also find the north with the moon?"

Matt shook his head. "No," he said. "I didn't know you could do that."

"On a fairly full moon you can see a crescent of shadows. The finger in the crescent points to the north. When the moon is at a phase where you can see where the shadow starts, you can find north by making an imaginary line from the tip of the shadow to the north."

"That's good to know," Matt said.

Smoke chuckled. "If you can keep a few things like that in mind, you might be able to locate yourself just a little closer than by saying you're in Colorado."

Matt laughed, remembering that he had insisted to Smoke that he wasn't lost because he knew he was in Colorado.

The two men rode on through the afternoon; then Smoke held up his hand as a signal to stop.

"We'll camp here tonight," he said, pointing. "There's water, and it's always good to camp by water, as long as you know the dangers."

"What's dangerous about camping near water?" Matt asked.

"All critters need water," Smoke explained, "squirrels, rabbits, horses, men, dogs, and the like. But so do bears, and mountain lions, and wolves. And some of them are pretty possessive. If they see you around their water hole, they aren't going to like it. So you're going to have to stay alert the whole time you are by a water hole."

Matt remembered his encounter with the wolf when he was on the trail, running away from the Home. "I see," he said.

"Also, the water might be poison."

"Poison? How, why?"

"Don't always know why the water would be poison, but there is bad water out there and you'll run across it from time to time."

"How do you tell if it's poison? By taste?"

Smoke shook his head. "No, that's not good enough. Some bad water tastes pretty good, some good water tastes awfully bad. About the only way you can really tell is to take a look around it. If you see the bones of dead animals real close to a water hole, the chances are they died drinking the water. That's a good sign for you to just keep moving on."

"I'll try to remember that," Matt said.

"You'll try? I hope you remember everything I'm telling you," Smoke said. "Otherwise, I'm just out here batting my gums for nothing."

"I will remember," Matt promised.

Mule Crossing, Colorado

There was no town called Mule Crossing. It was a place about fifteen miles west of Meeker, where the White River could be forded. Here, a man named John Grant had built a saloon and general store.

The man who came into Grant's saloon stood at the door for just a minute, allowing his eyes to adjust to the darkness. He was about average size, with a drawn face, watery-blue eyes, a hooked nose, and a sweeping handle-bar mustache. He wore a low-crown black hat encircled with a silver hatband, from which protruded a small, red feather.

"My name is Amos Bodine," he announced. "And I'm lookin' for a man by the name of Cleo Wright."

There were only six others in the saloon, and Bodine studied each one of them. All but one returned his gaze. The one who did not was making a point of staring at his drink.

"You," Bodine said to the one who hadn't looked up. "What's your name?"

"Smith," the man replied. "John Smith."

Another man came in behind Bodine then, and the fact that Bodine didn't look around indicated that he knew who it was.

"He's lyin', Amos," the new man said. "I seen him at the trial before he broke jail. This here is Cleo Wright."

"Well, Mr. Cleo Wright," Bodine said, a wicked smile spreading across his face. "There's a reward out for you, did you know that?"

With a sigh, and a set of his shoulders, Cleo Wright

stepped away from the bar and faced Bodine. "Yeah," he said. "I know that."

"Tell you what," Bodine said. "You pay me the reward money, and I'll let you go."

"I don't have any money," Wright answered.

"Then I guess I'm just going to have to take you in. Unless you can stop me."

"Stop you? How am I supposed to stop you?"

"Well, you could draw against me," Bodine said. "You might get lucky. Or you can just show everyone in here what a sniveling, low-assed coward you are, then get down on your belly and slither out to your horse."

"What?" Wright asked with a gasp. "What are you asking me to do?"

"You heard me," Wright said. "You can either draw against me, or get down on your belly and slither across the floor like the cowardly snake that you are."

"No way in hell am I going to do that, mister!" Cleo said.

The smile had never left Bodine's face. "Then you are going to have to draw against me," he said in a sibilant tone.

The expression on Cleo Wright's face turned from one of anger to fear, then to resignation. With a shout of fury, Wright made a desperate grab for his gun.

Bodine's gun was out and firing before Wright was able to clear leather with his own pistol. Wright went down with a bullet in his heart.

Meeker, Colorado

Two men rode into town. One of the men was leading another horse, and draped across that horse was a body. As they rode down Main Street, several of the townspeople stopped what they were doing to watch, some coming out of the stores and buildings to stand on the side of the street.

The horses' hooves raised little clouds of dust and made hollow clopping sounds that echoed back from the buildings that lined the street.

In Dunnigan's Barber Shop, Ernie Peterson, who was waiting for a shave and a trim, happened to see the rider through the window.

"I'll be damn," Peterson said.

"What is it?" Dunnigan asked as he applied lather to the face of old Gil Tucker. Tucker was a veteran of the War of 1812.

"It's Amos Bodine," Peterson said.

"Bodine? The bounty hunter?"

"That's him all right," Peterson said.

Dunnigan left his customer and walked out onto the front porch, followed by Peterson and Gil Tucker. Tucker, whose face was half-lathered, was still wearing the barber apron Dunnigan had put around him.

"Who's that with him?" Dunnigan asked.

"You mean the one ridin' with him? Or the fella he's bringin' in?" Peterson replied.

"Both."

"I expect the one with him is a fella by the name of Colby. I've heard Colby is his partner. I don't have no idea who the one draped over the horse is," Peterson said.

"Yeah, well, they say that Bodine ain't none too particular," Dunnigan said. "If you're wanted, no matter what the reward is, he'll bring you in. And most of the time when he does bring someone in, he's dead."

When they passed by the saloon, Colby pulled over and dismounted, then tied his horse to the hitching rail.

"I'll be back in a few minutes," Bodine called to him.

"I'll be in the saloon," Colby called back.

* * *

By the time Bodine reached the sheriff's office, Sheriff Adams had already heard about his arrival and was standing on the front porch, waiting for him.

Bodine stopped in front, then rode back to the trail horse, leaned over to cut a rope, then gave the body that was draped over the saddle a push. The body landed on the dirt street, faceup, his arms thrown out to either side. His eyes were still open but opaque. His face had a bluish tint.

"Sheriff, I'm . . ." Bodine started, but Sheriff Adams finished for him.

"Amos Bodine. Yeah, I know who you are," Sheriff Adams said. He nodded toward the body on the ground. "Who is that?"

"His name is Wright. Cleo Wright," Boone said. He pulled a piece of paper from his pocket. "I got a dodger here says he's worth two hundred fifty dollars."

"Did you have to kill him?"

"Read what it says on the paper," Boone said. "It says dead or alive."

"I'm sure it does," Sheriff Adams said. He sighed. "That's not what I asked. I asked if you had to kill him."

"He drew on me," Bodine said.

"They always draw on you, don't they, Bodine?"

"I reckon they figure that's better'n goin' to jail."

"And it makes it easier for you to bring them in, doesn't it?"

"Some," Bodine admitted.

"How many have you killed, Bodine?"

"Twenty-five or thirty, I reckon," Bodine replied. "I really don't know, but I've never killed anyone that I didn't get paid for killin'."

"I'm sure you haven't."

"Speakin' of which, when am I goin' to get paid for this one?" he asked, nodding toward Cleo Wright.

"It'll be a day or two before I can get your money," the sheriff answered.

"That's fine by me, as long as I get it," Bodine said. "My partner, Colby, is already down to the saloon. If you need me, I'll be there. I can wait."

"You've got a partner now?"

"It's come in handy a time or two," Bodine replied. He turned his horse to ride away.

"Bodine?" Sheriff Adams called out.

Bodine turned back.

"Yeah?"

"Bodine, I don't want any trouble in my town," the sheriff said. "Do you hear me? I don't want any trouble in my town."

"Sheriff, let me get this straight. Are you sayin' that if I see a wanted man in Meeker, I can't go after him?"

"Yes—uh, no," Sheriff Adams replied.

"Yes or no what?"

"Just—just don't cause any trouble in my town," Adams repeated.

Chapter Twelve

When they rode into Meeker, Matt had a good look around. It had been several months since Matt had been in any town at all, and he had not really seen that many Western towns, so he had no real way of judging this one.

Someday, such towns would become the means of defining his life. Like mileposts, he would move from one town to another, each with a different name and with different people, but all with the same personality. And in some strange way that he could neither comprehend nor explain, he seemed to sense that even now.

The town was called Meeker, and it sat at the junction of Sulphur Creek and the White River. No railroad served the town, and its few streets were dotted liberally with horse droppings. The buildings of the little town were as washed out and flyblown up close as they had seemed from some distance.

The first building they rode by was a blacksmith's shop, and a tall and muscular man was bent over his anvil, working a piece of metal. The ringing of his hammer on steel was audible above everything else.

They rode by a butcher shop, a general store, a leather

goods shop, and an apothecary. Next to the apothecary was a building that had a sign reading:

ASSAY OFFICE

That was where they stopped.

"What is an assay office?" Matt asked.

"You know all the panning we've been doing this summer?" Smoke asked.

"Yes."

"Well, this is where it pays off. This is where we are going to get some money."

Swinging down from his horse, Smoke took the saddlebags down from his horse. "Let's go see how we did."

Matt followed Smoke into the little building. Smoke dumped the contents of his saddlebags out onto a counter. Matt knew that this was only a portion of what they had panned over the last three months. The rest of it was buried in cans around Smoke's cabin, with Smoke being careful to show Matt where each can was buried.

The man behind the counter was wearing a white shirt, buttoned to the neck. He was wearing a collar too, but the collar was askew. He had rimless glasses, which were raised to his forehead, but as he saw the nuggets that were dumped from the saddlebags, he moved the glasses down to his eyes, then positioned them with his forefinger.

"Oh, my," he said as he looked at the display before him. "Oh, my, oh, my, oh, my."

"Is that good, Smoke?" Matt asked. "Why does he keep saying oh, my?"

"You'll see," Smoke said.

The man with the glasses picked up a magnifying glass and looked more closely at the rocks.

"It's going to take me a while to figure how much all this is worth."

"Is it worth enough for you to advance my partner and me forty dollars apiece right now?" Smoke asked.

"Oh, heavens, yes," the assayer said. "It's worth much, much more than that."

"Give me a receipt for the ore, less eighty dollars," Smoke said. "We'll be back for the rest of the money later."

The assayer wrote out a receipt, then handed Smoke four twenty-dollar bills. Smoke gave two of the bills to Matt.

"No," Matt said, shaking his head and handing it back. "This is your money."

"Are you saying you didn't have anything to do with panning it? Are you saying you didn't feed and water the animals, you didn't chop firewood, you didn't bring in water, you didn't do any hunting?"

"Well, yeah, I did all that but . . ."

"No buts," Smoke said. "We're full partners in this operation."

From the assayer's office, they went to a café for lunch. Although he had spent three years eating in a dormitory, this was the first café that Matt had ever been in in his life.

A very large woman, seeing them come in, smiled broadly.

"Smoke Jensen, you old heartbreaker you," she said in greeting. "I see you survived another winter in the mountains."

"That I did, Julie, that I did," Smoke replied.

Julie looked at Matt. "Well, now, either Preacher has found some elixir that made him get really young, or you've got yourself a new partner. This sure don't look like Preacher."

"This is my friend Matt," Smoke said.

"Matt is ever' bit as good-lookin' as you are. You been hidin' somethin' from me, Smoke? Have you gone off and spawned a young'in of your own?"

"Afraid not," Smoke said. "But I wouldn't be ashamed to claim Matt as my own. He is a fine young man."

"I can tell that just by lookin'," Julie said. "Come on in and sit yourself down. What'll you have, Matt?"

"What will I have?"

"To eat," Julie said. "What do you want to eat?"

"I'm not particular," Matt said. "Whatever you've fixed for supper, I'll eat it."

"You have to be more specific than that," Julie said.

"Maybe this will help you," Smoke said, picking up a menu and showing it to Matt. "You can have ham, roast beef, fried chicken, pork chops, meat loaf."

"All that? Who could eat all that?" Matt asked incredulously.

Smoke chuckled. "You've never been in a café before, have you?"

Matt shook his head.

"You don't order all of it. You just order what you want."

"Anything I want?"

"Sure."

"I want fried chicken and apple pie," he said.

"You want potatoes with your chicken?" Julie asked.

Matt shook his head. "All I want is fried chicken and apple pie."

"Hon, that's not a very . . ." Julie began, but Smoke interrupted her.

"You heard him, Julie," Smoke said. "Bring him some fried chicken and apple pie."

At the next table someone got up and, as he was leaving, handed a newspaper to Smoke.

"Here's the latest paper, friend, if you would care to read it," he said.

"Thank you," Smoke replied. He read the paper for a few minutes, then glanced across the table toward Matt.

"The full name of the man you are looking for is Clyde Payson," he said.

"What? How do you know that?" Matt asked. "Is it in the paper?"

"See for yourself."

Smoke handed the paper to Matt.

DASTARDLY DEEDS IN CEDAR CREEK!

Bank Robbers Kill Teacher
and a Child.

Leave One of Their Own Dead.

On the fifth, *ultimate*, a band of bank robbers led by desperado Clyde Payson rode into the small town of Cedar Creek, Colorado. In a daring daylight robbery, the robbers relieved the Bank of Cedar Creek of its cash reserves, equaling at the time a little over six thousand dollars.

Told of their presence by an alert citizen, Marshal Jeremiah D. Cobb established wagon barricades at either end of the street, with the intent of preventing the robbers from getting out of town. However, the robbers managed to escape by riding through a school yard, which, at the time, was crowded with children at play.

Miss Margaret Miller, a beloved matron and longtime schoolteacher, as well as little Holly McGee, one of her second-grade students, were both killed in the gun battle that ensued. Also killed was Pete Lew, one of the robbers.

Clyde Payson is described as being a peculiarly ugly man. He is five feet nine inches tall, with a purple scar that starts at his forehead, disfigures the left eye, then proceeds unabated down his cheek and jaw-line until it pulls the left side of his mouth into a sneer.

One other member of the gang has also been identified as Garvey Laird. Laird is easily identified by the fact that, during the war, a minié ball diminished his left ear by one half. Readers are cautioned not to approach any of these men as they are very dangerous. Should one of them be seen, a county sheriff or United States marshal should be informed of their whereabouts. Marshal Cobb reminds readers not to inform him as he has no jurisdiction beyond the town limits of Cedar Creek.

"That's them!" Matt said, tapping the newspaper article with his fingers. "They are the ones who killed my ma, pa, and sister."

"If they stay this active, you won't have much trouble finding them," Smoke suggested. "Unless somebody else kills them first."

"I don't care who kills them," Matt replied. "As long as they are dead."

After the café meal, they went to a general store, where Matt bought three pair of jeans, three shirts, some underwear, socks, and boots.

"My, what a large purchase," the proprietor said. "It's almost as if you were starting from scratch."

"I am starting from scratch," Matt said without any explanation.

The shopping done, Smoke took Matt into one of the saloons.

"There's a way of entering saloons," Smoke explained. "And though you don't have any need to do so now, the time will come when it will serve you well. So you may as well learn how to do it."

"All right," Matt said.

Following Smoke's lead, Matt went into the saloon, then stepped immediately to one side with his back at the door.

"Always take a good look around," Smoke said, quietly.

"What are we looking for?"

"You'll know it if you see it," Smoke said.

Matt saw it almost as quickly as Smoke. A rather gaunt-looking man with a sweeping handlebar mustache was standing at the far end of the bar. He had seen them both in the mirror. He reached down and slipped his pistol out of his holster, then held it down out of sight, alongside his leg. He did it quietly and unobtrusively, and neither looked around nor made any sign of recognition. Had Smoke and Matt not been making it a point to study everyone in the saloon, neither of them would have seen it.

Because of their diligence, both saw it.

"Smoke," Matt hissed.

"I see it, boy," Smoke answered quietly. "Step away from me, over to the other side of the door. And keep your back to the wall."

Matt had only been with Smoke for about six months now, but he knew enough to do exactly as Smoke asked, doing so without question.

The man at the bar called out without turning toward Smoke.

"Mister, would your name be Jensen? Smoke Jensen?" the man from the bar called.

"That's me," Smoke replied.

"I've seen paper on you," the man said. "The paper says you are a murderer and a low-life son of a bitch."

These were challenging words, words that even Matt knew were killing words. Everyone at the bar knew so as well because, almost as one, they broke away from the bar and scrambled quickly to get out from between the two men.

"Are you the law?" Smoke asked.

"Nah, I ain't the law," the man replied. "The law can't collect rewards."

"I guess that makes you a bounty hunter."

"That's what I am, all right. And you are worth fifteen hundred dollars to me."

"No, I'm not," Smoke said. "The paper on me has been called back, so I'm worth nothing to you. Even if you could take me in."

"I don't plan on takin' you in. I plan on just killin' you right here, and havin' the sheriff vouch for it so's I can collect me that reward."

"What's your name?"

"Bodine," the man answered. "Amos Bodine. I reckon you've heard of me."

"Bodine, we don't have to do this," Smoke said. "You can just walk away now and nobody has to get hurt. I told you there is no reward."

"Well, now, maybe there is a reward and maybe there isn't," Bodine replied. "That still leaves you a murderin' low-life son of a bitch."

"Is there any way I'm going to be able to talk my way out of this?" Smoke asked.

Smoke's question surprised and disappointed Matt. Was Smoke scared? He would never have thought that Smoke would run scared.

Almost as soon as he thought it through, he felt ashamed of himself. Smoke had saved his life, and had kept him alive through the long, cold winter. What's more, Smoke had shared his gold secret with Matt. And right now, Matt still had about thirty dollars in his pocket, more money than he had ever held at any one time in his entire life. What an ingrate he was for questioning anything Smoke did.

At the bar, Bodine just shook his head. He still hadn't turned around to face Smoke.

"You ain't goin' to be able to talk your way out of this one, mister," Bodine said. "The reward says you are worth fifteen hundred dollars dead or alive, and I intend to collect."

"Then I expect it's time the killin' started," Smoke said dryly.

Bodine suddenly swirled away from the bar, his hand already coming up with a cocked pistol.

Smoke, reacting to the bounty-hunter's move, had his own pistol out so fast that it was a blur. He drew, fanned the hammer back, and fired in one fluid motion.

Matt saw Bodine gasp in surprise as the bullet from Smoke's gun plunged into his chest. Bodine staggered backward, then fell flat on his back on the floor of the saloon. His gun arm was thrown to one side, and the still-unfired pistol was in his hand.

Then, even as Bodine was falling, Smoke was firing a second time. Looking up, Matt saw someone tumble over the railing at the top of the stairs. The second man had been holding a rifle and the rifle fell before him, reaching the floor an instant before the man did. Matt had not even seen him until this moment, and he was amazed that Smoke had.

In the close confines of the barroom, the two gunshots were a sustained roar, like a sudden clap of thunder.

Smoke stood in place for a long moment, holding the discharged gun in his hand while a little stream of smoke drifted up from the end of the barrel.

"Holy shit!" someone said. "Did you see that?"

"And I thought Bodine was fast," another said.

"I need a drink," the first man said, and there was a mad rush to the bar.

"Matt, are you all right over there?" Smoke asked quietly.

"Yes, I'm fine," Matt answered in a small, awed voice.

"Get us a table," Smoke said. "I'll get you a sarsaparilla."

"I'd rather have a beer," Matt said.

"You might rather have a beer, but you are getting a sarsaparilla," Smoke said resolutely.

"Yeah, that's what I said. I'd like to have a sarsaparilla."

Smoke smiled. "I thought that was what you said."

Matt found a table and sat down.

"Did you see that?" someone asked at the next table.

"Of course I seen it. I was in here when it happened, wasn't I?"

"He beat Amos Bodine," the first man said, not to be denied telling the story, even though he was telling it to another eyewitness. "I tell you true, I didn't think anyone would ever be able to beat Amos Bodine."

"Hell, he beat Bodine and the man he was ridin' with."

"What's the name of the fella that shot Bodine?" one of the others asked.

"Jensen. Smoke Jensen."

The sheriff was in the saloon almost before the gun smoke drifted away. He saw the two men lying on the floor. Then he looked over at the table where Smoke was just rejoining Matt with a beer in one hand and Matt's pop in the other.

"Hello, Sheriff Adams," Smoke said.

Adams nodded toward the two dead men. "I see you got Bodine and Colby."

"Colby, huh? I was wondering who it was. I never got the chance to ask him his name," Smoke answered matter-of-factly.

Adams stared at Smoke for a moment; then he saw the

humor of the statement and he chuckled. "Well, it's too late to make friends now."

"What were they in town for?" Smoke asked. "Surely they weren't here just to kill me?"

Adams shook his head. "He just came in today, bringin' a body for claim. He would'a been gone by tomorrrow once the money come in. If you had waited one more day before comin' in, you two wouldn't have run in to each other."

"If not now, later," Smoke said. "People like Bodine don't seem to care much whether the reward poster is still good or not."

"I reckon not," Sheriff Adams said. He looked over at Matt, then stroked his chin as he studied him.

"Who'd you say this young man was?" he asked.

"I didn't say who he was. But he's my partner," Smoke said.

"The reason I asked is, I got a letter from the sheriff in Soda Creek. Seems a boy ran away from the Home up there."

"The Home?"

"The Home for Wayward Boys and Girls," Sheriff Adams said.

"You don't say," Smoke replied. "What about this boy that ran away? What did he do?"

"He ran away."

"No, I mean, why was he in the Home? Had he stolen from someone?"

"Oh, I don't know whether he stole anything or not. The letter didn't say anything about that. It just said that he ran away from the Home."

"You get a name for the boy that ran away?"

"The sheriff said his name is Matt."

Smoke chuckled. "You don't say. Well, now, that is a co-incidence. My partner's name is Matt. But he sure doesn't belong in a home for wayward boys and girls."

"No, I reckon not," Sheriff Adams said.

Smoke looked over at the two bodies. By now, Lennie Holman, the town undertaker, had arrived and was looking at the two men, gauging the size of the coffins he would have to make.

"Are you going to need me for a hearing or anything?" Smoke asked.

Sheriff Adams shook his head. "I don't think so. I know Bodine, and there's no doubt in my mind what happened here. Also, there are enough eyewitnesses to give me all the statements I need."

"Well, if you do need me, Matt and I are going to spend today and tomorrow in town."

"Enjoy your stay," the sheriff said. With a final nod, Sheriff Adams left the table, then went over to start talking to the eyewitnesses. There were many who saw it happen, and nearly all were anxious to tell their story.

"I don't mind telling you, I was a little nervous when you told the sheriff that my name was Matt."

"I had to tell him," Smoke said. "Otherwise, I might have tripped up and called you Matt. Best to get that part out in the open."

"And then when you said I didn't come from the home, well, I . . ."

"That's not what I said," Smoke interrupted.

"What?"

"I didn't lie. What I said was, 'My partner's name is Matt. But he sure doesn't *belong* in a home for wayward boys and girls.' I didn't say you didn't come from there."

Matt chuckled. "No, I guess you didn't." Matt turned the sarsaparilla up to his lips, then looked across the table toward Smoke. "You know, someday I hope to be as fast with a gun as you are," he said.

"Why? So you can kill Payson?"

"No," Matt said. "I mean, yes, I am going to kill Payson. But that's not the reason I want to be fast with a gun."

"What is the reason?"

"I don't know exactly. Maybe it is just because I would like to be really good at something."

Smoke smiled at his young friend. "That's a good enough reason," he said.

Chapter Thirteen

"And what do you think about this one, young sir?" the gunsmith asked, handing a pistol to Matt. The first place they had gone to after leaving the saloon was a gunsmith shop.

"It's a beauty," Matt said, holding the pistol gingerly in his hand as he looked at it. "What kind is it?"

"It is a Model 1861 Colt, manufactured at the Colt firearm factory in Hartford, Connecticut," the gunsmith replied.

"Take a look at the markings on the gun," Smoke suggested.

Matt studied the markings. On the barrel was stamped: "Address COL. SAML COLT New York U.S. AMERICA." The left front side of the frame was marked: "Colts/patent." The caliber marking, ".36 CAL," was stamped on the left rear side of the trigger guard.

"You like it?" Smoke asked.

"Yes," Matt replied.

"We'll take it," Smoke said to the gunsmith. "And a gun belt and holster rig."

"Yes, sir," the gunsmith said. "Would you like it wrapped, or in a box?"

Smoke looked at Matt and smiled. "I'm sure he would much rather wear it."

"Yes!" Matt said excitedly. "I would rather wear it."

"Then, wear it you shall, young sir," the gunsmith said, selecting a belt and handing it to Matt.

Matt put the belt on, then slipped the gun down into the holster.

"Let's see your draw," Smoke suggested.

Matt drew the pistol as fast as he could, and Smoke laughed.

"What is it?" he asked. "What did I do wrong?"

"Let's start with what you did right," Smoke said.

Matt smiled. "All right, what did I do that was right?"

"You didn't drop it," Smoke said.

"That's it? I didn't drop it?"

"That's it," Smoke said. "Everything else you did was wrong."

"Will you teach me?"

Smoke nodded. "Yeah," he said. "I'll teach you."

Smoke's cabin in the Gore Range of Colorado

"When you shot that bounty hunter, that was the fastest draw I ever saw," Matt said.

"Was it?"

"It sure was," Matt answered enthusiastically.

"How many fast draws have you seen?"

"Well—uh—I guess that is the only one I've ever seen," Matt admitted.

Smoke chuckled. "Then it isn't very hard to be the fastest, is it?"

"Are you the fastest?" Matt asked.

"I don't know," Smoke replied. "There are some out there who are very fast. Wild Bill Hickock, Payson Allison, Ian MacCallister, Angus Boone."

"I've heard of Hickock, Allison, and MacCallster," Matt said. "But I've never heard of Angus Boone. Who is he?"

"Some people call him the Gravedigger," Smoke said.

"Is he fast?"

"Very fast," Smoke said. "And he is one of those rare people who kills for the sake of killing."

"Why would someone do that?"

"Because he likes killing," Smoke said.

"Well, I wouldn't enjoy killing," Matt said. "But I do want to be fast."

"Being fast means nothing if you can't hit what you are shooting at," Smoke explained. "First thing we have to do with you is teach you how to shoot."

"I can shoot," Matt said. "I used to go squirrel hunting back when I was only eight or nine years old. I could hit them too."

"But you were using a rifle then, right? Or maybe a shotgun?"

"A shotgun," Matt admitted sheepishly.

"Well, that's pretty good, but now you have to learn to use a handgun, and that is very different. Are you willing to learn?"

"Yes."

"Good. Take off your holster and give it to me."

"What? Why?"

"Because you don't need it right now, and I don't even want you thinking about it. This is shooting, not fast draw."

"Whatever you say," Matt said, unbuckling his gun belt and handing it to Smoke.

"All right, show me what you can do," Smoke said. Looking around he found a rusty can, then stepped off about thirty yards and placed the can on a rock. "Shoot that can," he said.

Matt pulled the trigger. The pistol boomed and the bullet kicked up dirt well to the side of the rock where the can was sitting. It ricocheted across the meadow, making a loud whine.

"I missed," Matt said.

"Try again."

Matt fired a second time, with the same result.

"Here, let me see what we can do to help," Smoke said. Putting his hands on Matt's shoulders, he turned the boy to a position of about forty-five degrees from the target.

"Now, don't turn your body, but look at the target by turning your head and eyes only."

Matt responded.

"Bring the pistol up to eye level and sight on the target. Then, close your eyes, raise your pistol and arm straight up, and with your eyes still closed, bring your arm back down until it feels to you as if you are lined up with the target."

"Like this?" Matt asked, doing as instructed.

"Yes," Smoke said.

Matt let his arm come back down, then he opened his eyes. He was almost perfectly aligned.

"It's there!" he said excitedly.

"Good," Smoke said. "Now, spread your feet apart about the width of your shoulders. Keep your legs straight, but not stiff. Think you can do that?"

Matt tried it a few times, then looked at Smoke. "Yes, I can do it," he said.

"What are you going to do with your other arm?" Smoke asked.

"I don't know. What should I do?"

"Forget that it is there. It should be totally relaxed."

"All right," Matt said, again responding to Smoke's instruction.

"Now, again, look at your target by turning your head and eyes slightly without moving from the neck down. Once you are looking at it, raise your pistol so you can sight on the target. You should feel that the pistol is hanging from above, and not that you are pushing it up from below."

Again, Matt complied with Smoke's instructions.

"Are you aiming at the target now?"

"Yes."

"Shoot it."

Matt pulled the trigger. Again the pistol boomed and the bullet whined, but this time it knocked the can up into the air with a direct hit.

"Hey!" Matt shouted in excitement. "I did it!"

Smoke made Matt practice shooting every day for the next month. Matt was a natural shooter, and he hit the can so many times that, toward the end of his shooting, rather than reset the can, he just continued to shoot it, knocking it about the meadow.

Then, one day, Smoke came out to watch him. He stood there for a few minutes, nodded, then went back into the cabin. When he returned, he was carrying the pistol belt. He handed the holster rig to Matt.

"Put it on," he said.

"All right!" Matt replied excitedly.

"Empty your gun."

"Empty it?"

"I don't want you to shoot yourself in the leg while you are practicing."

Matt chuckled. "I don't want to shoot myself in the leg either," he said as he poked the cartridges out of the revolver. He put the empty gun back into his holster.

"I'm going to show you a draw," Smoke said. "First, I'll do it fast, then I'll do it slow, so you can see what I'm doing."

Smoke drew his pistol and fired, doing it with such blazing speed that, even though Matt was watching him, he was unable to see the actual draw. He saw only a quick jump.

"Now, I'll do it slow," Smoke said.

Smoke eased the pistol from his holster. As he was doing so, his left hand came across his body to fan back the hammer. He pulled the trigger when the gun came in line with the target. The gun had traveled just enough distance to clear the holster.

"You didn't bring the gun up to aim it," Matt said.

"No, I didn't," Smoke answered. "I aimed before I drew the gun."

Matt thought for a second, then nodded. "Yeah," he said. "Yeah, I know that doesn't sound like it makes sense, but I think I know what you mean."

"Matt, it all comes down to this," Smoke said. "The time is going to come when you will just think the gun into your hand, and the bullet into your target. The arm, the hand, the trigger finger are no longer there. They are just an extension of your mind. You think draw and shoot, and your mind will draw and shoot the gun for you."

"How do you do that?"

"Do you think about breathing?" Smoke asked.

"No, I just breathe."

"Think about breathing."

Matt took a few breaths, then laughed. "It's harder when you think about it."

"When you can draw and shoot a gun the same way you breathe, you'll be ready," Smoke said. "Now, let me show you something."

Smoke emptied Matt's pistol, and handed it to him. Then he emptied his own gun, checking each chamber in the cylinder again. He put his gun back in his holster.

"Point your gun at me," Smoke said. "When you see me start my draw, pull the trigger."

"Ha," Matt said. "Do you think I'm so slow that you have to give me that much of a head start?"

"Just do it," Smoke said.

"All right." Matt raised the pistol and aimed it at Smoke.

Smoke drew his pistol, fanned the hammer, and pulled the trigger before Matt could pull the trigger on his own gun.

"Wait, I wasn't ready," Matt said.

"We'll try it again," Smoke offered.

They did it several times, and Smoke beat Matt every time.

"How did you do that?" Matt asked.

Smoke chuckled. "Don't be so impressed," he said. "It was easy."

"Because I'm so slow?"

"No. You could be faster than I am, and I would still beat you."

Matt shook his head. "Wait a minute, that doesn't make sense. If I was faster than you, how would you beat me?"

"Remember when I said you had to think the gun into your hand?"

"Yes."

"Thinking about it takes longer than actually doing it," Smoke said. "See, when you saw me start my draw, you had to think to pull the trigger. But I had already thought about it. I had already thought the gun into my hand."

"That's amazing," Matt said.

"No, it's just a fact, but it might save your life some day."

"I see."

"All right, put your pistol back in your holster and start working on your draw," Smoke said.

"When can I load my pistol?"

"I'll let you know when."

For two weeks, Matt drew and pulled the trigger to an empty pistol. Then Smoke let him start drawing and shooting.

Before the first snow, Matt was good enough to perform a few shooting tricks. With tin cans put on posts that were set fifty yards apart, Matt stepped halfway between the two. He stood there, his gun in his holster, looking over at Smoke.

"Are you ready?" Smoke asked.

Matt nodded. "I'm ready," he said.

Smoke held a rock out over a pie pan. Matt watched Smoke's hand. When Smoke opened his hand to let the rock fall, Matt drew his pistol, shot the can off the post to the right of him, then whirled and shot the can off the post to the left.

After the sound of the second shot, the sound of the rock hitting the pie plate could be heard.

"You got both shots off in under a second," Smoke said, grinning broadly.

"Is that pretty good?" Matt asked.

Smoke nodded. "Yes," he said. "That's very good."

"How good?"

"What do you mean?"

"How many do you think are faster?"

"It doesn't matter how many are faster," Smoke said.

Matt looked confused. "What do you mean, it doesn't matter how many are faster?"

"It doesn't matter," Smoke repeated. "There may be some who are faster. There probably *are* some who are faster. But you have now reached the point to where the speed of your draw is no longer a consideration."

"What is?"

Smoke sighed, and ran his hand through his hair before he answered.

"I've held this for last, Matt. What I'm about to tell you is the final secret of the gunfighter. And, I'm sorry to say, it is a terrible secret."

"What is the secret?"

"At this level, being fast or accurate is not the differing

factor. At this level, everyone is fast and everyone is accurate. But not everyone is willing to kill."

"What?"

"The average man will pause—hesitate for just a heartbeat—before the pull of a trigger that he knows is going to kill," Smoke explained. "In a situation like that, the victory goes to the man who will not hesitate."

"Yes," Matt said. "Yes, I see what you mean."

"I hope you do see," Smoke said. "Because being able to see and understand that will keep you alive."

"How do you overcome it?"

"You have one thing going for you," Smoke said. "You have had it going for you from the beginning, and if you hadn't had it, I don't think I would have taught you how to use a gun at all."

"What? What do I have going for me?"

"You have already killed," Smoke said.

Matt was quiet for a moment before he spoke. "I'm not proud of that, Smoke."

"Nor should you be," Smoke answered. "Matt, the fact that you have killed is not a matter of pride. But it is a matter of survival."

"Survival?"

"Yes. I want you to think about it every day. I want you to know that if you have to do it, you can kill a man without a second thought."

"All right," Matt agreed.

"There's one more thing I want you to remember," Smoke said.

"What is that?"

"Remember our talk about knighthood?"

"Yes, I remember."

"Matt, you now have an awesome power. You have the

power of life and death. Only God, and the righteous, should ever have such power.

"You aren't God, so you must be righteous. Be a knight, Matt. Never abuse this power you now have."

"I won't."

"Swear to me, Matt," Smoke said. "Swear on the graves of your ma and pa that you will be a knight."

"I swear to you, Smoke. I will be a knight," Matt said.

Chapter Fourteen

Gehenna

The little town was hot, dry, and dusty. It had grown up in the middle of nowhere and now sat baking in the sun like a lizard. To the six riders approaching from the north, the collection of adobe and sun-bleached wooden buildings was so much a part of the land that it looked almost as if the town was the result of some natural phenomenon, rather than the work of man.

Out on the edge of town a sign read:

YOU ARE ENTERING

GEHENNA

Population Unknown

THE LAW AIN'T WELCOME.

IF YOU GOT NO BUSINESS HERE,

GET OUT — OR <u>GET SHOT</u>

On first glance, Gehenna looked like just about any other town in this part of the country, but that was on first glance only. A closer observation showed many differences.

Gehenna was a town that existed, not in spite of having no law, but because it had no law. It was a robber's roost, an outlaw's haven, and Clyde Payson, Garvey Laird, Clem Tyson, Bart Ebersole, Poke Lawson, and Syl Richards were drawn to it for just that reason.

"I'm so thirsty I'm spittin' dust," Clem said. "I aim to get me two beers an' drink 'em both down afore I even take me a breath." Clem smiled. "I aim to get me a good meal and a bottle of whiskey, then the best-lookin' whore in town."

Poke laughed.

"What's so damn funny?" Clem asked.

"There ain't goin' to be no good-lookin' whores in Gehenna."

"Why not?"

"'Cause whores that's still good-lookin' can make a livin' somewhere else. They don't have to come to a place like Gehenna."

"Then what the hell are we comin' here for?" Clem asked.

"We ain't here for the whores," Payson said. "We're here 'cause there's no law here."

"No law a'tall?" Syl asked.

"Only the law that we make," Payson said.

As the six men rode into town, not one person gave them a second look. Stopping in front of the single saloon, they dismounted.

A tall man dressed all in black stepped out onto the front porch and looked down at them.

"You're Payson, ain't you?" he asked. "Clyde Payson?"

"Yeah, you've heard of me?"

"I've heard of you."

Payson smiled and looked at the others. "What do you think, boys? I'm famous," he said.

"You've come here to stay away from the law?"

"That's right," Payson replied. Payson was still standing

beside his horse, so that it was between him and the man who was addressing them.

"It'll cost you a hundred dollars to stay here," the man said.

"A hundred dollars? Says who?" Payson asked angrily.

"Says me. You might say I'm the sheriff here. It's my job to collect taxes from those who come to enjoy our hospitality."

"You're the sheriff? I thought there wasn't no law here," Payson said.

The man spat a stream of tobacco, then wiped his lips with the back of his hand.

"Well, now, that ain't entirely true," he said. "We ain't got no courts or judges, or jails or such. But we do have me."

"And who are you?"

"The name is Loomis. Frank Loomis."

Payson was quiet for a moment before he answered. "Loomis. Frank Loomis," he said. "Yeah, I've heard of you. You used to be a sheriff, didn't you? Till you had a run-in with a U.S. marshal. You kilt 'im, I believe, and now you're a wanted man yourself. So, how come you're still sheriffin'?"

"It's a different kind of sheriffin' here," Loomis explained. "And I make a lot more money sheriffin' here than I did back in Colorado."

"Who pays you? The town?"

Loomis laughed. "No, the town don't pay me nothin'. I pay myself."

"I see. So the one hundred dollars you are asking for in tax, that's just to go to you, right?"

"You understand, I'm sure. If I'm going to pay myself to protect the town, then I have to charge a tax. I don't think a hundred dollars is askin' too much."

"What if I say I ain't goin' to pay it?" Payson asked.

"Then you aren't eligible for the protection of the town, so I'll ask you to just move on."

"What if I say I ain't goin' to pay it and I don't plan to move on?"

"If you've heard of me, then you know that I can back up what I say," Loomis said.

Unnoticed by Loomis, Payson had snaked his shotgun from the saddle holster. He now held the gun behind the horse to shield it from Loomis's view.

"Are you sayin' we ain't never goin' to be able to work this out?" Payson asked.

"Not unless you pay the one-hundred-dollar tax," Loomis said. He pushed his coat flap back, exposing his pistol. "Either pay, or git," he said menacingly. "You ain't got no other choice."

"No, I reckon there is another choice," Payson said. In a quick, smooth action, Payson raised the shotgun up, laid the barrel across the saddle, and pulled the trigger.

The gun roared and the horse reared. Loomis was so surprised by the sudden move that he never even touched his own pistol. The impact of a load of double-aught buckshot caught Loomis full in the chest and knocked him back through the batwing doors, taking one of them off the hinges. He wound up lying on the floor with his chest opened up so that his insides could be seen.

"Son of a bitch!" someone shouted from inside.

Payson stepped into the saloon right behind Loomis's body. He was carrying the shotgun with him, and a little curl of smoke was still streaming up from the end of the barrel.

"Anybody else want to talk about me payin' taxes?" Payson asked.

Nobody answered. In fact, nobody even looked at him.

"Yeah, I thought this might be the end of it," Payson said. He set the butt of the shotgun on the bar with the barrel pointed up. "Bartender, what do you have to drink in this place?"

"Beer and whiskey," the bartender answered.

"I'll have it."

"You'll have what, sir?"

"Beer and whiskey," Payson said.

"And we'll have the same," one of the five men who came in with him announced.

"Very good," the bartender said.

A moment later, the bartender returned with six empty whiskey glasses and a bottle of whiskey. He also had six mugs of beer.

"That'll be six dollars and fifty cents," the bartender said.

"Six fifty?" Payson gasped in amazement. "Six fifty for what?"

"Five dollars for the bottle of whiskey, and a quarter apiece for the beer."

"That's outlandish to charge so much," Payson complained. "I can get beer for a nickel anywhere else in the country. Why should I pay you so much for it?"

"Because you ain't anywhere else in the country," the bartender replied. "You're here. And here, beer is twenty-five cents."

Grumbling, Payson pulled enough money from his pocket to pay for the beer and the whiskey.

Payson tossed the whiskey down, then chased it with almost half the beer. He sat the beer glass down as well, and looked toward the body of the man he had just killed.

"What happens to him now? Does he just stay there and rot?"

"No," the bartender replied. "We learned just real quick that in a town like Gehenna we was goin' to need an undertaker. So we went out and hired us one."

"What about whores?" Clem asked. "You got 'ny whores?"

"Hell, yes, we got whores," the bartender said. "What good would a place like this be without whores?"

"Which one is the best-lookin'?" Clem asked.

"Hell, nearly ever' whore in town would make a train take five miles of dirt road," the bartender replied. "But I reckon Jolene is somewhat better-lookin' than most."

"Where's she at?"

The bartender didn't answer, but he pointed to a table in the back of the room.

There was someone sitting there, holding a whiskey bottle in one hand and a glass in the other.

"Jolene," the bartender called. "You got some business."

Jolene filled the glass one more time, then tossed the whiskey down before she walked up to the bar.

"You wantin' to ride me, cowboy?" Jolene asked.

"How much?"

"Two dollars."

"Two dollars? Damn, ain't that a little high?" Clem asked.

Jolene turned to go back to her seat at the back of the room.

"No, wait," Clem called. "I got two dollars."

"In that case, I got me a room upstairs," Jolene said, pointing toward the stairs at the back.

"Wait a minute," Clem said. He turned to the bartender. "Give me a bottle. If I'm goin' to have to pay two dollars, I plan to make it a party."

The bartender gave Clem a bottle in exchange for a five-dollar bill. Then, clutching the bottle by the neck, Clem followed Jolene up the stairs.

"Who's in charge around here?" Payson asked.

"If you mean do we have a mayor or something like that, we ain't," the bartender said.

"But somebody is in charge. Somebody always has to be in charge," Payson said.

"There was somebody in charge," the bartender replied. "But you just kilt him."

"Really," Payson said with a big smile. "Well, I reckon that sort of makes me the headman around here then, doesn't it?"

"I suppose so," the bartender said. "That is, until . . ."

"Until what?"

"Until the Gravedigger comes back."

"The Gravedigger? You mean Angus Boone? Boone is here?"

"Not all the time," the bartender replied. "But when he is here, he is in charge. Unless you want to challenge him."

"No, that's all right," Payson said. "The Gravedigger can be in charge while he's here, and I'll be in charge while I'm here."

"What if you are both here at the same time?"

"We won't be," Payson said.

Chapter Fifteen

Durango, Colorado

Two young men passing through the town stopped in front of the Sundown Saloon. Swinging down from their horses, they patted their dusters down.

"Donnie, you're as full of shit as a Christmas goose," one of them said. "There ain't nobody that lives on the moon."

"How do you know?" Donnie asked. "There ain't nobody ever gone up there to see that there ain't folks up there."

"Yeah, well, that's my point. There ain't nobody up there 'cause there ain't no way to get there."

"How did we get here?" Donnie asked.

"What?"

"How did we get here?"

"What do you mean, how did we get here? We've always been here."

"Well, they've always been there."

"No, they ain't."

"You know your problem, Bobby Joe? Your problem is, you ain't got no imagination."

"Yeah, well, right now I can imagine what a cool beer tastes like. And if we wasn't standin' out here in the road arguin' over whether or not there's people on the moon—which, if you ask me, is about the dumbest thing you can argue about—we'd be drinkin' a beer by now."

"You got that right," Donnie said, laughing. "It don't make no sense to be standin' out here jawin' when we could be inside drinkin'."

The two young men went into the saloon, then stepped up to the bar. The saloon was relatively quiet, with only four men at one table, and a fifth standing down at the far end of the bar. The four at the table were playing cards; the one at the end of the bar was nursing a drink. The man nursing the drink was dressed in black. A turquoise and silver band around his short-crowned black hat provided the only bit of color.

"What'll it be, gents?" the bartender asked.

"I want the coldest beer you've got," Donnie said.

"Every beer I have is the coldest one I have," the bartender replied.

Bobby Joe chuckled. "I'll have the same," he said.

"Two beers it is," the bartender replied. He turned to draw the beers.

"What brings you boys to Durango?" the bartender asked.

"Nothin' in particular," Donnie said. "We're just passin' through."

"We're up from Texas," Bobbie Joe said proudly.

The bartender put the beers in front of the two boys and they each picked up one.

"Yes, sir, the great state of Texas," Donnie added.

"Well, welcome to Colorado," the bartender said.

"Nothin' good ever come out of Texas," the man at the end of the bar said.

Using the back of his hand, Donnie wiped beer foam from his mouth. It was obvious that he had been irritated, and for the briefest of moments, that irritation reflected in his face. But he put it aside, then forced a smile.

"Hell, mister, Texas is a big state. You can't say you don't like Texas unless you've seen all of it. And I know you ain't seen all of it, 'cause no one has seen all of it."

"Is that how you get around people tellin' you they don't like your state?" the man in black asked.

Bobby Joe had not been a part of the conversation, but he was listening to it, and now he joined in.

"What the hell, mister? You trying to pick a fight or something?"

"Why?" the man in black asked. "If I was tryin' to pick a fight, would you be obligin' me?"

The way the man in black responded angered Bobby Joe even more.

"Hell, yes, I'd be willin' to oblige you," Bobby Joe said angrily. "Nobody up in these parts knows me, but if they did know me, they'd be quick to tell you that Bobby Joe Brubaker ain't a man you want to get on the wrong side of."

"You don't say," the man in black responded. Although Bobby Joe was getting angrier and angrier, and his voice getting louder and louder, the voice of the man in black was never more than a sibilant sneer.

Donnie recognized the growing danger before Bobby Joe did, and he reached out his hand to try and ease the situation.

"Easy, Bobby Joe. I'm sure he doesn't mean anything personal by that remark. Not everybody likes Texas, nor are they expected to."

"I just don't like being insulted by some son of bitch who doesn't know what he's talking about," Bobby Joe said.

"Let's just have our beers and get on our way," Donnie suggested.

"After you apologize," the man in black said.

"Apologize? You expect me to apologize?" Bobby Joe

said, so angry that his face was turning red. "Apologize my ass. What I'm going to do, mister, is wipe up the floor with your sorry ass!" Bobby Joe put up his fists.

The man in black smiled, a smile without mirth. "If we're going to fight, why don't we make it permanent?" he asked. He stepped away from the bar and flipped his jacket back, exposing a pistol that he wore low and kicked out, in the way of a gunfighter.

"Mr. Boone, I'm sure these boys would apologize to you if you would just give them a moment to reconsider," the bartender said. "There's no need to carry this any further."

"My God, Bobby Joe, back off!" Donnie said. "Don't you know who this is? This is the man they call the Gravedigger!"

Bobbie Joe realized now that things were beginning to go much further than he had intended, and he opened his fists and held his hands palm out in front of him.

"No, wait a minute!" he said. "We don't need to be doin' this. This is just a little dispute, it ain't worth either one of us dying over."

"Oh, it won't be *either* of us, sonny. It'll just be you," Boone said. "Both of you," he added, looking at Donnie, "for when the shootin' starts, I'm goin' to kill both of you."

"Uh-uh," Donnie said, shaking his head. "Neither Bobby Joe nor I have any intention of drawing on you. So if you shoot us, you are going to have to shoot us in cold blood in front of these witnesses."

"Oh, it ain't goin' to be in cold blood," Boone said. "You'll be drawin' on me. Both of you."

Donnie's knees grew so weak that he could barely stand, and he felt nauseous.

"Please, Mr. Boone, we don't want any trouble," Donnie said. "Why don't you just let us apologize and we'll go on our way?"

Boone shook his head. "I give you boys the chance to apologize. You didn't take it. It's too late now. Pull your guns."

Donnie and Bobby Jo looked at each other, then, with a scream from Donnie, they made ragged, desperate grabs for their pistols. They were slow, so slow that Boone had the luxury of waiting for just a moment to see which of the two offered him the most competition. Deciding it was Donnie, Boone pulled his pistol and shot Donnie first.

Bobby Joe, seeing his friend killed, and knowing that he was about to die, peed in his pants as Boone's second shot hit him in the neck. He pulled the trigger on his pistol, firing a shot into the floor before he collapsed and fell on top of Donnie.

Angus Boone put his pistol back in his holster, and was calmly sipping his whiskey by the time a few of the citizens of the town got up the nerve to look inside.

Smoke's cabin

By the time Matt was eighteen years old, he was six feet tall and strong as an ox. The older Matt got, the narrower was the difference between him and Smoke, in size, in quickness and accuracy with a handgun, and in just about any other attribute.

Sometimes, for fun, the two would wrestle, and the winner depended not on strength or skill, but on whoever happened to achieve a temporary advantage in leverage or position.

Also, the age difference between the two seemed less significant now, and the "fatherly" relationship had gradually changed into one of "big brother."

The two had continued to pan the streams and the streams had continued to be productive. For the entire time Matt had been with Smoke, they had buried the gold, each year taking just enough into town to buy goods and supplies for another year. But in the spring of Matt's eighteenth year, they took everything they had into town, having to enlist four pack animals to do so. When they cashed it out, it was worth a little over thirty thousand dollars, which was more money than the local bank had on deposit.

"We can have the money shipped from Denver," the assayer said.

"Can you write us a draft that will allow us to go to Denver to get the money ourselves?" Smoke asked.

"Yes," the assayer said. "Yes, of course I can do that. But you don't have to go to all that trouble. As I say, I can have the money shipped here."

"It's no trouble," Smoke said. "Denver's a big city. I think I'd like to have a look around. How about you, Matt?"

"I've never seen a big city. I'd love to go to Denver," Matt replied enthusiastically.

"Write out the draft," Smoke said.

"Very good, sir. And who shall I make this payable to?"

"Make it out to both of us. Kirby Jensen and Matt . . ." Smoke looked over at Matt. "I've never heard you say your last name."

"Smoke, just make the draft payable to you," Matt said.

"No, what are you talking about? This is your money too. You helped pan every nugget."

"You can pay me my share after you cash the draft."

"It might be easier if it is made to just one man," the assayer said.

Smoke sighed. "All right," he said. "Make it payable to Kirby Jensen."

The assayer wrote out the draft, blew on it to dry the ink, then handed it to Smoke.

"Here you are, Mr, Jensen," he said. "Just present this to the Denver Bank and Trust, and they will pay you the amount so specified."

Smoke held the bank draft for a moment and looked at it. "Hard to believe this little piece of paper is worth all that money," he said.

DENVER BANK & TRUST

Colorado Gold and Silver
Acceptance Company

June 19 18 *74*

PAY TO THE ORDER OF *Kirby Jensen* — $ *32,100* no/100

Thirty-two thousand one hundred & no/100 DOLLARS

Parker Allison – *Assayer*

"I assure you, sir, it is as good as gold," the assayer promised.

Smoke turned to Matt. "What do you say, Matt. You ready to see Denver?"

"I'm ready!" Matt answered eagerly.

Denver

Although there had been predictions that Denver would reach the magic number of 100,000 inhabitants by 1870, the actual growth of the city had fallen far short of the mark.

Editor William Byers, editor of the *Rocky Mountain News*, wrote an article about what he called the go-backers:

> Because they cannot shovel out nuggets like they have been accustomed to digging potatoes, they raise the cry that it is all a humbug and take the back track for home, where it is to be hoped that they will ever after remain.

Despite Byers's complaint, the city seemed exceptionally crowded on the day that Matt and Smoke arrived. It was certainly larger than any city Matt had ever seen, and as they rode down Wynkoop Street, they actually had to move aside frequently to allow coaches, carriages, and wagons to pass. Men and women walked briskly along the boardwalks on either side of the street, the women carrying parasols against the sun, the men wearing bowler hats and suits.

On one corner, some musicians were playing a fiddle, banjo, and guitar, accompanied by someone blowing into a jug. Several people had gathered around to hear them, and occasionally someone would drop a coin into an upturned hat.

There was a large banner stretched across the street. One corner of the sign had come loose and was flapping in the breeze, but it could still be read.

DENVER WELCOMES
THE DENVER PACIFIC RAILROAD
June 24, 1874

Shortly after they passed under the sign, they saw a building with a new sign proudly proclaiming it as the DENVER PACIFIC DEPOT.

"Have you ever seen a railroad train, Matt?" Smoke asked.

"No, I haven't," Matt said. "Have you?"

"I used to see them back in Missouri when I lived there as a boy during the war," Smoke said. "But I haven't seen one since."

"I'd sure like to see one," Matt said.

"According to the sign, the train will be here tomorrow," Smoke said. "How would you like to come down here tomorrow to watch?"

"Yes! Yes, I'd like to very much!" Matt said.

"Well, then, we'll just do that," Smoke said. "What do you say we go get our money, then get us a hotel room?"

"Sounds good to me," Matt agreed.

The Denver Bank and Trust was on the corner of Market and 17th Streets. Like most of the buildings in Denver, the bank was constructed of brick, and it was positioned in such a way that the entrance was at the corner of the building. Like nearly every other building in town, it was decorated in a festive mode with red, white, and blue bunting draped over the entrance.

Inside the bank, on the left wall, there was a Currier and Ives Print. The print was of two trains on parallel tracks. It looked as if the trains were racing each other. Smoke and steam streamed back from the engines and the great drive wheels were blurred in motion. There were people standing alongside the tracks waving at the engineers, who could be seen in the windows of their respective cabs, eyes staring ahead as they drove their iron steeds along the tracks.

Beside the Currier and Ives print was a large, printed sign.

The Denver Bank & Trust
Welcomes

THE DENVER PACIFIC RAILROAD

There were three tellers in the bank, and all three were wearing the caps of railroad conductors, as part of the celebration.

"Yes, sir, what can I do for you?" one of the tellers asked as Smoke stepped up to the window.

"Everyone seems excited about the arrival of the railroad," Smoke said.

"Yes, sir, we are indeed excited about it," the teller said. "By this time tomorrow, Denver will be a part of the railroad age. Why, did you know it will be possible to board a train right here in our own fair town and, within less than one week, be in San Francisco or St. Louis? What's more, it will only take two weeks to travel all the way to New York City."

"That is truly amazing," Smoke said. He took the draft from his pocket and slid it across to the bank teller. "I would like to negotiate this instrument, please," he said.

"Yes, sir, we'll be glad to take care of . . ." The teller stopped in mid-sentence as he looked at the size of the bank draft. "Uh—sir, this is a draft for over $32,000."

"Yes, I'm aware of that."

"But I don't know," the teller said.

"Is the draft not good?" Smoke asked. "Does Colorado Gold and Silver Acceptance Company not have enough money to cover it?"

"Oh, I'm sure they do," the teller said. "But they aren't who I'm worried about."

"Who are you worried about?"

"I don't know if we have that much money in our reserve," the teller said. "Wait here, please. I must talk to the bank manager."

The teller started to walk away with the bank draft in his hand.

"Uh-uh," Smoke said, pointing. "Leave that here."

"But Mr. Flowers will have to see it."

"You bring Mr. Flowers here to see it," Smoke suggested.

"Yes, sir," the teller said, handing the draft back to Smoke.

A few minutes later, the teller returned with a short, rotund man. Mr. Flowers had a flowing mustache that joined with his muttonchop sideburns. He had no chin whiskers.

"Mr. Jensen is it?" Flowers asked.

"Yes."

"This is quite embarrassing," he said. "But at the moment, we don't have enough funds on hand to honor the draft. However, if you will give us twenty-four hours, I believe we will be able to transfer some funds from some of the other banks in town. On the other hand, if you would like to do so, you could open an account in our bank and leave the draft for deposit. I would suggest that as the better solution."

Smoke shook his head. "No, thank you," he said. "You go gather up the money, we'll wait for it."

"Very good, sir. We'll have the money for you by tomorrow."

Chapter Sixteen

A long layer of blue tobacco smoke hung just beneath the ceiling of the Lucky Strike Saloon. Normally, there were as many as five or six poker games going on at the same time, but now there was only one. All the other games had stopped and the other players, the bar girls, and even the casual drinkers had been drawn to the action at the remaining game table.

Smoke had three piles of poker chips stacked in front of him, representing over fifteen hundred dollars in cash. He pulled out a long, thin cigar and lit it, examining the man across the table from him. The man had just taken a seat at the table, attracted by the size of the stakes.

"I'm told your name is Smoke Jensen," the man said.

"It is."

"Do you know who I am, Mr. Jensen?"

"Should I?"

"I'm a professional gambler, Mr. Jensen. My name is Kelly Smith. Does it make you nervous to be playing against a professional gambler?"

"No, not at all," Smoke replied.

"It should."

"Really? And why is that?"

"I have been watching you for the last several minutes, Jensen. You are a reckless player. You play with emotion, not with your mind." Smith put fifteen hundred dollars on the table. "I think I should give you a few lessons. But I warn you, they will be expensive."

"I've always heard that a good education is expensive," Smoke said. "But I do seem to have a winning streak going."

"Yes. Well, I'm here to stop that winning streak," Kelly Smith said.

"I do admire a man with confidence," Smoke said. He raked in the cards and started to shuffle them.

"No, don't use those cards."

Smith stuck his hand out to stop Smoke from shuffling the cards. "I'd like to play with a new deck of cards, if you don't mind," Smith said.

"I don't mind at all."

One of the bar girls standing nearby handed Smoke a new deck of cards, and he broke the seal, then dumped them on the table. They were clean and stiff and shining. He pulled out the joker, then began shuffling the deck. The stiff, new pasteboards clicked sharply. His hands moved swiftly, folding the cards in and out until the law of random numbers became king of the table. He shoved the deck across the table.

"Cut?"

Smith cut the deck, then pushed them back. He kept his eyes glued on Smoke's hands.

"Five card stud?" Smoke asked.

"That'll be fine."

Smith won five hundred dollars on the first hand, and a couple of hands later was ahead by a little over a thousand dollars. Smoke was ready to concede that his string of luck had run out. At that time, he was still almost a hundred dollars above what he had started with. He finished his beer.

"Well," Smoke said. "I guess your ambition wasn't misplaced. You've broken my streak. Perhaps I should quit while I have something left."

"You have a lot more money than you are showing on the table, Mr. Jensen," Smith said.

Smoke's eyes narrowed. "What are you talking about?" he asked.

"The whole town knows that you presented a bank draft today that was so large that the bank couldn't cash it. That is right, isn't it?"

"Mister, I figure whatever happens between me and the bank is my business," Smoke said.

"Well, seeing as they're having to raise the money from all the other banks in town, seems to me like it's everybody's business now," Smith said. He looked at the one hundred dollars Smoke had remaining. "What do you say we play one hand of showdown for what you have left on the table?"

Smoke sighed. "All right," he said.

"Let the woman deal," Smith said.

Smoke nodded and handed the cards to the bar girl, who was standing by.

She dealt five cards to each of them, and Smoke took the pot with a pair of fives.

"Again," Smith said.

Within three hands, Smoke was back up to eight hundred dollars.

"You've won three hands in a row. You can't possibly win a fourth," Smith said. "Do you have the guts to bet everything on another hand?"

"You know, Smith," Smoke said as the girl shuffled the deck, "there are only two of us playing at this table. Mathematically, that means the odds are fifty-fifty that I will win."

"So?"

"So I mean, the fact that I have already won three hands does not lessen the odds of me winning again."

Smoke did win with a pair of tens, and Smith threw his cards on the table in disgust. He slid the rest of his money to the center of the table. "I've got another thousand here," he said. "High card."

"All right, high card," Smoke said.

The bar girl fanned out the cards and Smith turned over a queen of hearts. He looked across the table and smiled triumphantly at Smoke.

"I've got you now," he said.

Smoke turned up a king.

"Well, it looks like my luck has returned," he said as he reached for the pile of money.

"You just ran out of luck, mister," Smith said, drawing his pistol and pointing it at Smoke. "Draw your gun."

"You may have noticed that I'm not wearing a gun," Smoke said easily.

"Hell, it don't matter whether you are armed or not. We hang card cheats here in Denver. I'll just shoot you and save the citizens the cost of a hangman."

There was a cold, ominous click of metal, then the barrel of a pistol was pushed against the back of Smith's head.

"Put your gun down."

"What?" Smith asked in a frightened voice. He lowered his pistol and tried to look around, but the gun barrel prevented him from turning his head. Beads of perspiration popped out on his upper lip. "Who are you? What are you gettin' mixed up in this for? This ain't none of your concern."

"My name is Matt. You just threatened to shoot an unarmed man, and that unarmed man is my friend. That makes it my concern. Now, put your pistol on the table, please."

Gingerly, very gingerly, Smith laid his pistol down. Smoke picked Smith's gun up, emptied all the cartridges, and then walked over to the stove, opened the door, and tossed the gun inside.

"Have a nice walk around town, did you, Matt?" Smoke asked as he slammed the door.

"Yes, I did."

"I'm going to cash in the chips. Then I suggest that we take our dinner at the most expensive restaurant in town."

"Good idea," Matt said. He let the hammer down on his pistol and returned it to his holster. It wasn't until after the gun was taken from his head that Smith turned to see who had accosted him. He saw a strongly built youth of seventeen or eighteen, with sun-bleached blond hair and bright blue eyes.

"Why you're—you're just a kid!" Smith sputtered. "You're going to get yourself into trouble playing a man's game. I should've taken you."

Smoke chuckled. "Mr. Smith, have you ever tried to pick up a bobcat by his back legs? That's exactly what you would have run into if you had tried anything with my partner."

"Really?" Smith said in obvious disbelief. "Well, I guess now we'll never know, will we?"

"And you'd better hope that you never have to find out," Smoke said. "Come on, Matt, let's go."

As Smoke and Matt left the saloon, they were poking money into all their pockets.

"I've never seen so much money," Matt said. "How much did you win tonight?"

"About twenty-five hundred, I think," Smoke replied. He laughed. "And if you think this is a lot of money, wait until tomorrow when we get our payoff at the bank."

* * *

The next day, the entire city of Denver turned out for the arrival of the first train. Most were dressed in their Sunday finest, there to greet the train on what they knew would be a great, historic day. Some were there to take advantage of the gathering, and there were several vendors working the crowd, selling pies, cakes, and candies.

One man had brought his patent medicine wagon up as close to the tracks as he could get them, and he was standing on the back of the wagon, shouting his pitch to the crowd. He was tall and thin, and wearing a black suit that was badly in need of a cleaning. His long, bony finger jabbed at the air as he spoke.

"Yes, ladies and gentlemen, I have come bearing a new miracle drug that will work wonders for all illnesses. If you suffer from ulceration of the kidneys, loss of memory, weak nerves, hot hands, flushing in the body, consumption, torpidity of the liver, hot spells, bearing down feelings, or cancer, this marvelous Extract of Buchu will be your salvation.

"And here is something else this drug will do that no other can. Young, unmarried ladies and gents, do you have an inability to control your own lustful thoughts? Did you know that such impure thoughts often lead to solitary practices against nature? And it is a well-known fact that such sinful practices lead to the diseases of dyspepsia, debility of thought, and insanity. If you are having a difficult time controlling such lascivious thoughts, Extract of Buchu will aid you.

"This miracle drug is available to you for one thin dime, yes, sir, one tenth of one dollar is all it takes to open the doors to health and energy."

"How about women?" someone shouted from the crowd. "If I drink a bottle of that stuff, will it make the women notice me?"

"Mister, you can drink a whole bottle of it if you want to. But if you do, then you had better start carrying a club around because you will need it to beat the women away from you."

The crowd laughed at the medicine man's response.

"Well, if that's the case, give me two bottles," the man replied. "I'll just get a bigger club."

Again, the crowd laughed.

Above the laughter of the crowd could be heard the distant sound of a train whistle.

"There it is!" someone shouted. "That's the train whistle! It's a-comin' down the track!"

Everyone moved toward the track, dangerously close to the brink of disaster as they waited for the train to come into view. Finally, it appeared around a distant curve, the sighting closely followed by the hollow sounds of puffing steam, like the gasps of some fire-breathing, serpentine monster. As if to add to the illusion, glowing sparks were whipped away in the black smoke clouds that billowed up into the bright blue sky.

As the train pounded by, Matt watched the huge driver wheels, nearly as tall as he was, and the white wisps of steam that escaped from the thrusting piston rods. The engine rushed by with sparks flying from the pounding drive wheels as glowing hot embers dripped from its firebox. Then came the cars, flashing by, slowing, and finally grinding to a halt with a shower of sparks.

Even after the train stopped, it was still alive with the rhythmic venting of steam and the popping and snapping of cooling gearboxes as it stood in the station. The crowd of over five thousand people who had gathered to watch this momentous event cheered loudly. The men lifted their hats and the women waved handkerchiefs to mark the start of a new era in Denver.

Matt did not think he had ever seen a more exciting thing

in his entire life than the arrival of the first train ever to roll into Denver, Colorado.

After meeting the train, Matt and Smoke went to the bank, where the teller proudly counted out the money. Smoke divided the money while they were still in the bank, giving Matt sixteen thousand and fifty dollars.

"That's a lot of money," Matt said.

"Yes, it is," Smoke agreed. "Most folks don't make that much money in twenty years of work, and here you are, only eighteen, with fifteen thousand dollars in your pocket. What are you going to do with it?"

Matt thought for a moment before he answered. "I'll figure something out," he said.

It was getting late in the evening, and Smoke and Matt were a good ten miles down the road from Denver, when they decided they would start looking for a place to camp for the night. Often, during the ride, Matt had leaned forward to touch the saddlebags that were thrown across his horse. It made him almost dizzy to think that he had so much money. It also made him feel guilty, because he knew this was more money than his father had made in his entire life.

If Matt's father had been able to come up with this much money, they would have never left the farm in Kansas, and Matt would just now be beginning to think of his own future.

Matt had been thinking about his future ever since they left Denver. It wasn't the first time he had considered such a thing. He knew he would not be able to stay with Smoke forever.

But now, with this money, the future was no longer frightening, nor even mysterious to him. He knew exactly what he was going to do.

Matt's thoughts were interrupted when four men, who

had been hiding in the bushes, suddenly stepped out into the road in front of them. All four were holding pistols, and the pistols were pointed at Smoke and Matt. The leader of the group was Kelly Smith, the man with whom Smoke had been playing cards the night before.

"You boys want to get down from them horses?" Smith asked.

Slowly, Matt and Smoke dismounted.

"Well, now," Smith said. "You didn't think I was really going to let you get out of town with all that money, did you?"

"What money?" Smoke asked.

"Why, the thirty thousand dollars you got at the bank today," Smith said. "The whole town is talkin' about it."

"Is that a fact?" Smoke asked.

"Oh, yes, it's a fact," Smith said. "You've got that money, plus the money you took from me in the card game last night."

"Well, now, Mr. Smith, if I had known you were going to be that bad of a loser, I'll be damned if I would have played poker with you," Smoke said. "And here you told me you were a professional gambler and all. I guess it just goes to prove that you can't always believe what people say."

Smith laughed, a dry, cackling laugh. "You're a funny man, Jensen," he said. "I'll still be laughin' when I'm in San Francisco, spending your money."

"What makes you think you're going to get my money?"

"Are you blind?" Smith asked. "There's four of us here, and we've got the drop on you."

"Oh, yeah, there is that, isn't there. I mean, you do have the drop on us," Smoke said almost nonchalantly. "By the way, Matt, do you remember that little trick I showed you?"

"I remember," Matt answered.

"Now would be a good time to try it out."

"Now?"

"Now," Smoke replied.

Even before the word was out of his mouth, Smoke and Matt both drew and fired two quick shots each. Kelly Smith and the three men who were with him were dead before they even realized they were in danger.

Matt waited until they were back at Smoke's cabin in the Gore Range before he spoke to Smoke.

"Smoke, I've been thinking," Matt said. "I'm eighteen now and . . ."

"You want to go off on your own," Smoke said, finishing Matt's sentence for him.

Matt nodded. "Yeah," he replied. "Don't get me wrong, it isn't that I don't like it here. You saved my life. More than that, you gave me a life. I've lived here nearly as long as I've ever lived anywhere, and, I reckon, for the rest of my life when I think of home, why, this is the place I'll be thinking of. But—it's just that . . ."

Smoke smiled. "You don't have to explain anything to me, Matt. It wasn't all that long ago that I was eighteen. And I was hell-bent to go out on my own as well. Truth is, if you weren't anxious to go—well, I might just be thinkin' I'd done something wrong in your upbringing."

"I'm glad you understand," Matt said.

"When are you leaving?"

"I thought I'd get started this morning."

Smoke nodded. "Seems about as good a time as any," he said. "Looks like you'll have good traveling weather for the next several days. You'll keep in touch, won't you?"

"I'll have to," he said. "You're all the family I've got."

Smoke nodded, but said nothing.

"Smoke, there's one more thing I want from you," Matt said.

"You can have it."

"You haven't asked what it is."

"It doesn't matter what it is," Smoke said. "If I have it, and you want it, then you can damn sure have it."

"When I first came here, you asked me what my last name was."

"Yeah, I recall."

"I didn't tell you."

"Yeah, I recall that as well."

"The thing is, you never asked me again."

"I figured your last name was your business," Smoke said.

"Only, now it's your business as well."

"What do you mean?"

"That's what I want from you, Smoke. If you don't mind, I'd like to take your name and use it as my own. I'd like the right to call myself Matt Jensen from here on out."

Smoke blinked a few times in surprise, then got up and walked over to look out through the window at the meadow by the cabin, the meadow where he had taught Matt to shoot, and ride, and use a rope and a knife.

"Smoke?" Matt said, addressing Smoke's back. "Smoke, if you don't want me to take your name, well, I'll surely understand. It's just that . . ."

"Matt, I would be honored for you to take my last name," Smoke said.

"You sure you don't mind?"

"Mind? I told you, I'd be honored. In fact, I can't think of anything that would honor me any more than to think of you using my last name."

"Thanks, Smoke. I appreciate that. I really do."

"You're welcome," Smoke replied as he continued to stare through the window. He didn't turn around, because he didn't think it would be good for the kid to see tears in his eyes.

Chapter Seventeen

The first thing Matt did after leaving the mountain cabin in the Gore Range was return to Soda Creek. He had not been in the town since he had run away from the Home for Wayward Boys and Girls five years earlier.

The town looked the same to him, and as he rode down the street he even recognized several of the town's inhabitants, though he knew that no one in town would recognize him. He recognized George Tate. Tate owned the feed store, and he was standing out front, supervising the unloading of a wagon. He waved at Andy Morrison, the barber, and saw the confused expression on Morrison's face as he waved back. He chuckled to himself, enjoying the sense of anonymity growing up had given him.

Matt stopped in front of McDougal's Saloon, dismounted, and stepped inside. He had worked in this saloon for the three years he was a resident of the Home, and McDougal had treated him, as he did all his employees, fairly.

Matt glanced toward a table in the right rear corner and, as he expected, there sat McDougal, drinking coffee and working on his books. It was as if Matt had left the day before, as if McDougal had not moved from that very spot in seven years.

"I'll have a beer, Frank," Matt ordered.

The bartender squinted as he looked at Matt. "Do I know you?" he asked.

"We've met, but you've no reason to remember me," Matt replied.

Frank chuckled and nodded. "No, I reckon not. That's the problem with a job like this," he said. "Hundreds of people have come through here over the years. And since there's only one of me, it's a lot easier for them to remember me than it is for me to remember them."

"I understand," Matt said.

Frank brought him a mug of beer and Matt took a swallow, then used the back of his hand to wipe away the foam.

"I'm trying to find someone who used to work here," Matt said. "This was about five years ago."

"Shouldn't be all that hard," Frank said. "Anyone that was workin' for us five years ago is still workin' for us. Except for a couple of the ladies. Flo got married and Jill went back to St. Louis. We've got us some new girls in."

"This was a boy," Matt said. "A young boy, about twelve or thirteen."

Frank nodded. "Oh, you must be talkin' about the orphans," he said.

"Yes."

"How would you know them?"

"I was one of them," Matt said.

Frank smiled broadly and pushed the money back across the bar. "This beer is on me. You must be Matt," he said.

Matt nodded. "That's me."

The smile left Frank's face. "And you'd be askin' about Eddie and Timmy? I reckon you haven't heard."

"Heard what?"

"They're dead," Frank said. "Both of them."

"How did it happen?"

"They drowned," Frank said. It happened real soon after you left. They was both found drowned in Muddy Creek."

"What were they doing there? It was too cold to swim."

"Most folks think they was killed by Connors and Simon. I know there was bad blood between them two boys and ever'one else in the Home. But the sheriff never could find no evidence that they done it, so there wasn't nothin' he could do about it."

"Do you think Connors and Simon did it?"

"I know they done it," Frank said. "They was both in here drunk one night, and they was laughin' and braggin' as how they had done it and got away with it."

"Did you tell the sheriff?"

"Yeah, I told him," Frank said. "But he said that me just overhearin' 'em talk while they was drunk wouldn't stand up in court."

Matt shook his head sadly. "Damn," he said. "I hadn't heard."

"Well, at least I'm glad to see you survived. Always thought you was a good kid," Frank said. He chuckled. "Never knew you would grow up so big, though. Are you going to stay around town for a while?" Frank asked.

"I'll probably spend the night here tonight, but won't stay any longer than that. I've got some things I need to do. I thank you for the information, Frank," Matt said. "And the beer," he added as he took the last swallow.

"My pleasure, Matt. It was good seeing you again," Frank said.

Leaving the saloon, Matt walked down the street to have supper in Lucy's Café. He had just finished when he saw a young boy come out of the kitchen carrying a tray. The boy began gathering up dishes from the table and he came over to Matt's table.

"Sir, if you are finished with your supper, I'll take your dishes," he said.

"Thanks, I'm finished."

"Uh, the biscuit?" the boy said. "Are you finished with it as well?"

Matt saw the hungry expression in the boy's face as he stared at the remaining biscuit.

"Do you want the biscuit?" Matt asked.

"Yes, sir. I get to eat all the leftover food if I want."

Matt drummed his fingers on the table for a second as he looked at the boy. He didn't know him, but he had seen this same expression in those he had known at the Home. This could have been Timmy or Eddie. It could even have been him.

"What's your name, boy?" Matt asked.

"Jules."

"Jules what?"

Jules shook his head. "They don't let us use last names."

"You're talking about Captain Mumford?"

"Yes, sir. Do you know him?"

"Yes, I know him."

"He's—he's a fine man, sir," Jules said hesitantly, frightened that Matt and Captain Mumford might be friends and allies.

Matt chuckled. "You have a funny idea of a fine man," he said.

Jules laughed as well, but he didn't say anything else. Instead, he went over to one of the other tables and started clearing it. He accidentally knocked one of the plates off the table and it fell in the diner's lap.

"You little son of a bitch!" the man at the table suddenly shouted in anger.

"Oh! I'm sorry, sir!" Jules replied. "I didn't mean to."

The diner stood up and started brushing off his clothes where some food had been spilled.

"Here's a napkin, sir!" Jules said, taking a napkin from the table and trying to hand it to the diner.

The diner pushed Jules away from him so hard that Jules fell on the floor. The diner took off his belt and doubled it.

"I'm going to tan your hide good," he said, drawing back his belt.

It happened so fast that nobody in the café saw it, but one moment the angry diner was raising his belt over his head, and the next, his belt was pinned to the wall, a knife sticking through it. The handle of the knife was still quivering back and forth.

"What the hell!" the diner shouted, looking around. "Who did that?"

"I did," Matt said, standing up and facing him.

The diner pointed at Matt. "Mister, you've just made a very big mistake. You don't have any idea who you are messing with," he said.

"Yeah, I know who you are, Connors. I could never forget anyone as ugly as you."

"What did you say?" Connors sputtered. "Mister, you'd better watch your mouth if you know what is good for you."

Matt shook his head slowly. "You don't want to brace me, Connors," he said calmly.

Connors made a grab for his gun, but because he was wearing no belt, he not only didn't get to his gun, his pants fell down around his ankles, and his pistol clattered to the floor.

"What the hell!" he shouted, reaching down to pull up his pants while everyone else in the café was laughing at him.

While Connors was pulling his pants back up, Matt moved over quickly, then kicked the gun all the way across the floor, where it wound up in the corner.

"I told you you didn't want to brace me," Matt said as he reached up to pull his knife from the belt that had been pinned to the wall. He handed the belt back. "You haven't learned a thing, have you, Connors? You're just as ornery now as you ever were."

"How is it that you know me? Was you in the Home? 'Cause I don't remember you."

"Sure you remember me," Matt said. "I'm the one who stole the ham that you got blamed for."

"You? You're the one that stole it? I thought Eddie and—I mean, I thought someone else stole it."

"Is that why you killed Eddie and Timmy?"

Connors's eyes narrowed to a squint. "I didn't kill nobody," he said.

"Connors," Matt said. "If I hear that you so much as touched one hair on Jules's head, you will answer to me," he said.

"Nobody threatens me," Connors said. "Do you hear me? Nobody threatens me."

"Oh, don't get me wrong, Connors," Matt said. "That wasn't a threat. That was a promise."

Chapter Eighteen

The next morning, Matt was awakened by the sounds of morning commerce in Soda Creek. Someone was using an ax and he could hear the thump each time the ax fell.

Thump, thump.

In counterpoint, and sounding on the offbeat of the ax, was the ringing of a blacksmith's hammer.

Thump—ring. Thump—ring.

Next door, one of the clerks of the general store was sweeping the porch, and the scratch of his broom could be clearly heard over the thump and ring of the ax and hammer.

Thump—ring—scratch, scratch. Thump—ring—scratch, scratch.

Finally, adding a coda to the cacophonous symphony, was the squeak of a wagon wheel as it passed down the street of the town.

Thump—ring—scratch, scratch—squeak. Thump—ring—scratch, scratch—squeak.

It was not by mere chance that Matt had come back to Soda Creek. In so doing, he felt as if he was closing one part of his life and starting a new chapter. And as a rite of passage, last night he had been with a woman for the first time. Matt turned his head to see the woman who was lying in bed with him.

She was on her back. Her head was turned away from him, and the bedcovers had slipped down from her left shoulder, exposing her left breast. Matt stared at the nipple, which was lighted by a bar of sunlight that spilled in between the bottom of the window shade and the top of the windowsill.

The woman was lying in such a way that her breast was nearly flat so that the globe of flesh Matt had seen last night—and had thoroughly explored—was now just a gentle curve that was topped by the taut nipple that gleamed in the single shaft of sunlight.

Quietly, and gently enough so that the woman wasn't aware of what he was doing, Matt lifted off the cover, then rolled it all the way down to the bottom of the bed. That action caused her body to be fully revealed so that Matt was able to see everything. He lay with his elbow bent and his head resting on his hand, studying her for a long time.

The woman chuckled. "Have you seen enough, honey?" she asked without turning her head or opening her eyes. "Because I'm getting cold."

"Oh!" Matt said, startled by her response. He had not known she was awake. "I'm sorry." He pulled the cover back over her.

The woman chuckled again. "You don't need to be sorry," she said, turning to look at him. "I'm not a virgin, you know."

Matt smiled. "Neither am I," he said.

"You mean, you are *no longer* a virgin, don't you? Last night was your first time, wasn't it?"

Matt nodded. "Yeah, it was."

The woman shook her head and clucked. "You don't recognize me, do you, Matt?"

Matt stared at her. It couldn't be. This woman looked ten to fifteen years older than he was, not a mere year or two older.

"My God," he said with an expulsion of breath. "Tamara?"

"I wondered when you were going to recognize me," Tamara replied. "Have I changed that much? I recognized you right away."

"No, it's not that, it's just that—well, I never expected to see you—here."

"You mean you didn't expect to see me whorin'," Tamara replied.

Matt didn't answer.

Tamara got out of bed and padded, naked, over to a chair where she had put her clothes the night before.

"What did you expect would happen to the girls at the Home?" she asked as she began dressing. "Mumford had us on the line by the time we were fifteen." She looked up at him and he saw tears sliding down her face. "I told you that. You do remember, don't you, Matt, that I told you that?"

Matt nodded. "Yes," he said. "I remember. I tried to take you with me."

Tamara's expression softened, and she shook her head.

"I know you did, honey. But I guess it just wasn't in the cards."

"If it hadn't been for you, I don't think I would have gotten away that night," Matt said. "You led them away from me and the boat."

"I know I did. And don't think that I didn't think about it a lot of times. I was sure you had died up in the mountains, and I figured that if you had, it would have been my fault."

"As you can see, I didn't die," he said. "And even if I had, it would not have been your fault. Like I said, I thank you for helping me out that night."

"And last night?" Tamara asked, a conspiratorial smile spreading across her face. "How about last night? Do you want to thank me for that as well?"

Matt chuckled and nodded. "Yeah," he said. "I want to thank you for that as well."

"Are you leaving town again?"

"Yes," Matt said. "I—have something to do."

"I know. I remember that you told me a long time ago. You are going to find the people who killed your parents, aren't you?"

"If I can."

"How do you know they are still alive?"

"I know one of them is still alive, because I've seen his name in the paper. It's Clyde Payson."

"Payson?" Tamara said. "Is that who you are looking for?"

"Yes," Matt said. He looked at Tamara with a curious expression on his face. "Tamara, do you know Payson?"

"Not exactly," Tamara said. "But I know where you can find him."

"How do you know that?"

"Men talk, honey," Tamara said. "I don't know, maybe it's a way of showing off, a way of saying they are dangerous, or they know someone who is dangerous. Most of it is just talk, but over the years I've learned how to tell what is true and what isn't."

"And they have told you where Payson is?"

"Sort of," she said. "He's running a town called Gehenna."

"He's running the town? What do you mean he's running it? Is he the mayor? Is he the sheriff?"

"He's both as far as I can determine," Tamara said. "Gehenna is what's called an outlaw town. There is no law there, and the only ones who live there are all wanted by the law. From the talk I've heard, the top outlaw there is Payson."

"Thanks," Matt said.

Tamara shook her head. "Payson is a really bad man. I've seen strong men start shaking with fear just at the mention of his name. I wish you would just ignore him now. Whatever he did has been done, and going after him won't bring your parents back."

"Believe me, Tamara, I know every argument there is as to why I should just forget about this and get on with my life," Matt said. "I know all the arguments because I have used them on myself. But I cannot put this down. I have to find Payson."

"Even if it gets you killed?"

"Even if it gets me killed," Matt said.

"You haven't changed a bit. Matt . . ." Tamara began. Then she looked questioningly at him. "What is your last name, Matt? If you recall, one of the things Mumford did was take our last names away from us. I never knew your last name."

Matt hesitated for just a moment. What name should he tell her? Should he say his birth name, which was Cavanaugh, or the name he intended to use for the rest of his life?

"Jensen," Matt said, making his choice. "My name is Matt Jensen."

"My name is Tamara Peabody." Tamara smiled. "And you may be the only one I've ever told that."

"Well, Tamara Peabody, would you like to have breakfast with me?"

"No, Matt, I can't," Tamara said.

"Why not?"

"I'm a whore, remember? It wouldn't do you to be seen with a whore."

"You're also my friend," Matt said. "I'll be hurt if you turn me down."

Tamara smiled. "All right," she said. "I'll have breakfast with you."

* * *

They drew a couple of stares when they went into Lucy's Café, but Lucy greeted them warmly, and that seemed to ease the situation with the rest of the customers. Within a few minutes, nobody was paying any attention to them at all and they were enjoying their breakfast.

Then Jules came up to the table and stood there for a moment until Matt noticed him.

"Good morning, Jules," Matt said, smiling broadly. He handed Jules a couple of biscuits and a couple of pieces of bacon.

"Thank you, no, I've eaten," Jules said. "That's not why I come over to your table."

"Oh?"

"The feller you had words with last night? The one you stopped from beatin' me with a belt? He's waitin' for you out in the street."

"Connors is waiting for me?"

Jules nodded. "He aims to kill you," he said.

"I see."

"If you want, you can leave through the back way. He won't see you 'cause the alley is all blocked off."

Matt shook his head. "No, if Connors is throwing a party for me, it would be rude not to show up."

"Matt, no, don't go out there," Tamara said. "I've seen Connors before. He works at the stamp mill, guarding the gold shipments. He's really good with a gun."

"I have to go, Tamara," Matt said as he pulled his pistol and checked the loads. He slipped the pistol back in his holster. "If I don't go out there and face him now, like as not he'll shoot me in the back."

In a town as small as Soda Creek, news of an impending gunfight traveled faster than the telegraph. The street that had been so busy with commerce that it had awakened Matt earlier was now deserted, except for Connors, who stood in the middle of the street about one hundred feet away. Men and women were scurrying down the boardwalks, stepping into buildings to get out of the line of fire while taking observers' positions in the doors and windows so as to be able to see everything. Even the horses had been moved off the street, as nervous owners feared they might be hit by a stray bullet.

"I didn't think you'd come out," Connors called.

"Yeah, you would've liked that, wouldn't you?" Matt said. "I would've sneaked out the back, you would look big in front of the rest of the town."

Suddenly, a bullet fried the air just beside his ear, hit the dirt beside him, then skipped off with a high-pitched whine on down the street. The sound of a rifle shot reached him at about the same time, and Matt dropped and rolled to his left, his gun already in his hand. That was when he got a quick glimpse of the rifleman. But it was a quick glance only, as the rifleman ducked behind the Chinese laundry.

By now, Connors had his own pistol out. He fired but missed, his bullet crashing harmlessly into the wooden front stoop of Lucy's Café.

From a prone position on the ground, Matt fired at Connors and hit him in the knee. Connors let out a howl and went down.

The rifleman fired again, this time sending a bullet through the crown of Matt's hat. This time, Matt got a close enough look at him to see that it was Simon.

"Connors! Connors, are you hit?" Simon called.

"Yes!" Connors answered, his voice reflecting the pain of a busted kneecap.

Simon fired again, and the bullet came so close that Matt could feel the concussion of its passing.

Matt was lying out in the open, so he got up and ran across the street, bending low and firing as he went. He dived behind the porch of the barbershop, then rose and saw that he had a perfect shot at Simon, who had moved into position behind a watering trough. He fired, saw Simon drop his rifle into the watering trough, then fall back.

By now, Connors had managed to improve his own position, and he fired again at Matt. His bullet sent splinters of wood into Matt's face.

Matt stared across the street, trying to find an opening for a shot. Then he smiled. Connors had improved his position by getting out of the street and behind a wooden bench in front of a dressmaker's shop. What he didn't realize, though, was that the large mirror in the window of the dressmaker's shop showed his reflection, and from across the street, Matt watched as Connors inched along on his belly to the far end of the bench. Matt took slow and deliberate aim at the end of the bench where he knew Connors's face would appear.

Slowly, Connors peered around the corner of the bench to see where Matt was, and what was going on. Matt cocked his pistol and waited. When enough of Connors's head was exposed to give him a target, Matt squeezed the trigger. The pistol roared and bucked in his hand, and a cloud of smoke billowed up, then floated away. When the cloud cleared, Matt saw Connors lying facedown in the dirt with a pool of blood spreading out from under his head.

Chapter Nineteen

Matt was well armed. He carried a throwing knife that he wore on a scabbard that hung just behind his right shoulder, a bowie knife hanging from his belt on his left hip, a .44 double-action Colt on his right hip (though he still kept his .36 Navy Colt stuck down in a saddlebag), and a Winchester .44-40 rifle. He also had a rain slicker, an overcoat, two blankets, two spare shirts, two extra pairs of socks, two pairs of trousers, and two sets of underwear.

But perhaps most significant of everything that he carried was the fifteen thousand dollars Smoke had given him when they divided up. That money was still in its original bank packets, rolled up in oilskin and kept in a secret sleeve on the inside of his saddle blanket.

Matt didn't know the name of the town he was approaching, but it didn't matter. He didn't know today's date, but that didn't matter either. He was looking for Clyde Payson and Garvey Laird, and until he found them, not much else mattered.

Since leaving Soda Creek almost six months ago, he had heard other references to the town of Gehenna, though some referred to it as Purgatory, and others called it Perdition. It was the various names by which it was known that was making the town hard to find.

Of course, the fact that it was a lawless town and a sanctuary for outlaws also made it hard to find. It was on no maps, and many thought it might just be a myth.

Matt was reasonably certain that the town did exist, and he was sure he would locate it. When he did find it, and Payson and Garvey, he knew that the advantage would be all his. He was sure he would recognize them, while they would never connect the six-foot-tall, broad-shouldered, powerful man he had become with the runny-nosed skinny little boy he had been when they encountered him on the trail.

It was mid-morning, and the sun was halfway through its transit to high noon, as Matt approached the town, which was no more than a cluster of buildings clinging to the side of a hill. Shimmering sunlight bounced off the roofs and flashed back from the windows.

This appeared to be a mining community, and a little higher up, above the buildings of the town, zigzagging wooden trestles filigreed the face of the mountain. White wisps of steam escaped from the vents of the press mill, and its cylinder steam pipe boomed loudly, as though the place were under a cannonade. Boiling out of the high smokestack was a large plume of black smoke, its sulfurous odor permeating the entire valley.

Matt's horse, Spirit, realizing that he was near the end of a long journey, picked up the pace slightly as they approached into town.

A kiosk in the middle of the street advertised The Pickax Saloon, and even though it was not yet noon, Matt found the idea of a cool beer appealing. He would have a beer, but not before he had taken care of his horse. Smoke had inculcated that in him a long time ago, not from sentimentality or from affection for the critter, but from practicality—that the health of his horse could mean the difference between surviving and dying.

A few minutes later, with Spirit boarded at the livery, Matt crossed the street and walked down the boardwalk passing a handful of buildings until he came to The Pickax Saloon. A large sign touting the establishment hung over the boardwalk, squeaking an invitation as it rocked in a gentle breeze. Right under the swinging sign was another sign, nailed to the wall alongside the door. This was a big picture of a beer mug, golden yellow at the bottom, white foam at the top. It was actually for those who couldn't read, but it also had the effect of appealing to those who could, for Matt literally licked his dry lips as he passed it on his way inside.

Remembering to enter the saloon the way Smoke had taught him, he pushed through the batwing doors, then stepped to one side and placed his back against the wall as he studied the establishment.

There were eight people in the saloon, the bartender, six men customers, and one woman. Three of the men, wearing coveralls and hats with unlit lanterns, were sitting together at one of the tables. These were obviously miners. The other three men were at a different table. These men were wearing jeans and flannel shirts. They were also wearing cowboy-style hats, and all were wearing pistols with bullet-studded belts. The one woman in the place was sitting in a chair by a piano. The piano was silent and looked as if it had not been played for some time.

The woman, seeing someone new come into the bar, smiled broadly and walked over to meet him. Matt guessed that she was in her early thirties, though her face was older and her eyes were ancient.

"Buy me a drink, mister?" she asked.

"Sure," Matt said.

"My name's Sue," the woman said. "What's yours?"

"Matt."

"You ever been here before, Matt?"

"I don't know."

"You don't know?"

"I don't know where here is," Matt replied honestly.

"Why, this is The Pickax Saloon," Sue said.

"What's the name of the town?" Matt asked.

"The town is called Slick Rock," Sue said.

"No," Matt said.

Sue looked confused by his reply. "No?"

"You asked if I had ever been here before. The answer is no, I've never been to Slick Rock."

Sue laughed.

"How do we get those drinks?"

"Give me the money, I'll get them," Sue offered.

"I want a beer."

Matt sat at one of the tables and waited as Sue walked over to the bar, spoke to the bartender, then stood there for a moment waiting for him to fill her order.

"You come to Slick Rock lookin' for work, mister?" one of the miners called over to him.

"Not at the moment," Matt answered.

"But you are lookin' for somethin', right?"

"Yes, I'm looking for a town."

"Hell, mister, Slick Rock is a town," the miner said. The others laughed.

At that moment, Sue returned carrying a mug of beer and a small glass. It looked like whiskey in the glass, but Matt would have been willing to bet that it was tea. He didn't care; he knew that Sue's job was getting customers to buy drinks. If she could drink tea rather than whiskey, it would keep her sober, and it would be more profitable.

"What's the name of the town you are lookin' for?" one of the miners asked.

"I'm not sure," Matt replied.

Again, the miners laughed. "Well, mister, if you don't even know the name of the town, you are going to have one hell of a time finding it."

"Yeah," Matt answered. "It seems to be working out that way. The thing is I've heard three names for the town. I've heard Gehenna, Purgatory, and Perdition. I just don't know which one is right."

"I've heard of that place," one of the miners said. "From what I hear, it's filled with nothing but bad characters."

"Yes, that's what I'm looking for," Matt replied.

"The town is called Gehenna," the miner said. "But it's an outlaw town. Are you what folks would call an outlaw, mister?"

"I reckon that depends on who is doing the telling," Matt replied.

"Are you a bounty hunter?"

"No."

"Then why would you want to go to a place like that?"

"I've got business with a couple of people I was told might be there," Matt said.

"Who would they be?"

"Clyde Payson and Garvey Laird," Matt said, speaking loudly and clearly.

There was almost an audible gasp in response to the names.

"I've never heard of either one of them," the talkative miner said, the tone of his voice changing drastically.

"Me neither," one of the others said.

"That's funny," Matt said.

"What's funny?"

"When I said the names, a couple of you acted as if you had heard them before."

"Well, whatever, it ain't none of our business," the talkative miner said. "And if you're smart, you'll quit looking for them. They're dangerous characters, both of them."

"Oh? I thought you said you had never heard of either of them."

"I haven't," the miner said. "But if they are hanging out in a place like Gehenna, you don't want to find them."

"I thank you for your concern," Matt said. "But I have a score to settle with the two of them, so I do intend to find them."

Out of the corner of his eye, Matt noticed that the other three men in the saloon got up and left.

"Those three didn't even talk to me," he said to Sue. "They must not be very friendly."

"Don't worry none about them," Sue said. "They're drifters, all three of them. In and out of here all the time. They say they are cowboys, but there ain't nobody ever seen 'em work anywhere. But now me, I can be very friendly, if you know what I mean. I've got a room upstairs just in case you'd like to see how friendly I can be. It wouldn't cost you too much."

Matt looked at her. Tamara was six months ago, and there had been very few others since. Most of the experiences had been temporarily satisfying, but in almost every case it left him with an empty feeling that he couldn't quite explain. He knew that it would probably be like that until he found one woman to settle down with. But he knew also that he would not be fit for any one woman until the thing that drove him was taken care of. Still, the idea of putting down the search, maybe for a short time, did hold some appeal for him.

Sue knew men and could read them the way Matt could

read a trail. When she saw the flicker of interest in Matt's eyes, she smiled seductively. The effect of her smile was instantaneous. Now her features weren't quite as hard as he thought, and her eyes were not nearly as old.

"So, how about it?" she asked.

"Oh, I don't know," Matt said. "It seems a little early in the day to . . ."

Sue put her hand on his. "I promise you, you won't be sorry," she said.

There was something in the expression on her face and in the tone of her voice that made Matt think that she was talking about more than just sex.

"All right," he said. He drank the rest of his beer, then wiped his mouth with the back of his hand. "Where do we go?"

"Like I said, I have a room upstairs."

Matt was sitting in a chair, pulling on his boots. Sue was still in bed, with the cover pulled up to her chin.

"If all men were like you, I wouldn't mind this job," Sue said.

"Yeah, I'll bet you say that to everyone," Matt teased.

"No," Sue said seriously. "No, I don't. You are different. You were more . . ."

"Don't say I was more skilled," Matt said, waving his hand. "To tell the truth, I barely knew what I was doing."

"No, I wasn't going to say you were more skilled. I was going to say something that is much better than skill. You have a tenderness about you, a feeling for others. With most men, I'm just here to be ridden, like a horse or something. I'm a tool. But you not only knew that I was here, you acted as if you really cared about what I felt."

"It seemed like the thing to do," Matt replied.

"You have known people like me before, haven't you?"

"You mean other women?"

"No. I mean whores. You have known a whore, not just as a whore, but as a person."

Matt thought of Tamara, and nodded. "Yes," he said.

"Did you love her?"

Matt started to say no, but he hesitated. He was not "in love with" Tamara. But she was a part of his youth, and he couldn't deny that he loved her.

"Yes," Matt said. "I love her."

"I knew it," Sue said, smiling broadly. She reached across the bed to touch him, and as she did so, the sheet fell down, exposing her bare breast. "You are a good man."

"Thanks."

"Mr. Jensen?"

Matt chuckled. "How close do we have to get before you call me Matt?"

"Matt," Sue said. "Do you remember those three men who left the saloon while you were talking with the miners?"

"Yes."

"Look out for them."

"Look out for them?"

"They are from Gehenna, and they know Clyde Payson."

"How do you know?"

"They've been here before," Sue said. "I've heard them talking."

"Do you know where Gehenna is?"

Sue shook her head. "No, I don't, but it can't be too terribly far from here."

"That's what I'm thinking," Matt replied.

"Matt, I mean it when I say be careful of them. You are looking for Payson, which means that all these men would have to do to get on Payson's good side is to kill you."

"I'll be on the lookout," Matt promised. "Thanks for the warning."

"I wish I could talk you into giving up your hunt for Payson. It would be a lot safer."

"I'm sure it would," Matt agreed. "But I'm afraid I can't just put this down."

"I know," Sue said. "But I had to try and talk you out of it. I had to try."

Chapter Twenty

Leaving The Pickax Saloon, Matt walked across the street to have his lunch in the Palace Café. After that, he visited the other saloons in town trying to find out if anyone had any information he could use. He discovered a long time ago that he could get more information in casual conversation than by direct questioning.

Matt had learned a lot about Payson during his search. He'd learned that Payson was a cold-blooded killer. But then, he already knew that because he had witnessed it firsthand. He'll learned also that Payson had built up a network of support, partly because people were afraid of him, and partly because he paid people to protect him.

Matt was standing at the bar in a saloon called the Brown Dirt Cowboy when the sheriff came up to talk to him.

"Would you be Matt Jensen?" the sheriff asked.

"Yes," Matt answered. "But there's no paper on me, Sheriff. If this is about that fracas back in Soda Creek, it was ruled justifiable homicide."

The sheriff smiled. "No, this isn't anything about that. I've got a letter for you. Come on down to my office."

Matt looked confused. "You have a letter for me? That's

impossible. Who would know that I'm here? Are you sure it's for me?"

"I guess that depends on whether or not you know a fella named Smoke Jensen," the sheriff replied.

A big smile spread across Matt's face. "What? Yes! Yes, I know him!" he said. "What about him?"

"He's the one who sent you the letter."

"But I don't understand. How did you get the letter?"

"My name is Tate Casey," the sheriff said. "Smoke and I are friends." He stuck his hand out and Matt took it. "He sent the letter to you inside a letter he sent me. In my letter, he said he had a feeling you might show up. Come on down to my office. I'll give it to you."

"Thanks," Matt said.

A deputy was sitting at a desk in the sheriff's office when Matt and Casey went in.

"Johnny, take a round for me, would you?" Casey asked.

"Sure thing, Tate," Johnny answered, getting up and taking his hat down from a peg. There were three jail cells in the back of the building. Only one was occupied and its occupant was on the cot, snoring loudly.

"Who've you got back there?" asked Casey. "Mr. Fitz-simmons?"

"Yes, sir. He was passed out drunk in front of the millinery. He should be wakin' up soon."

"Poor man," Casey said to Matt. "His wife had just bought a new hat and was coming out of the millinery when a runaway team and wagon ran over her, killing her. Fitzsimmons took it hard, and has been a drunk ever since. Two or three times a week, we find him passed out right where his wife was killed."

"And you lock him up?"

"For his own safety," Casey said. "Soon as he sleeps it off, we feed him a meal, then we let him go."

Matt nodded. "Makes sense," he said.

Sheriff Casey opened the middle drawer of his desk, then pulled out an unopened envelope and handed it to Matt.

"Here is your letter, and as you can see, I haven't read it," he said. "Although, technically I could have read it, I suppose, without breakin' any laws, since this was in a letter that was sent to me. But I didn't figure it would be right to read another man's mail."

"Thanks, Sheriff," Matt said as he opened the envelope. "I appreciate that."

Pulling the letter from the envelope, Matt unfolded it and began to read.

Dear Matt,

After you left, I joined up with Preacher again to help him move a herd of half-broken mustangs and Appaloosa. We took them south into the wild country, crossing the Colorado River and keeping west of the Uncompahgre Plateau.

That was when we first picked up the scent. There is no other smell like that of charred flesh, so we had us a notion of what we were about to run into before we actually saw them.

Then we saw them. One man was tied by his ankles, hanging from a limb over a fire. His head and shoulders were blackened cooked meat. The bodies of the others were pretty well hacked up, one was tied to the wheel of a wagon. All of them had died hard.

Then we found a young woman hiding in the bushes. Somehow, she'd managed to get away from the Indians. Her name is Nicole, and it turns out that I've taken her for my wife.

Here, Matt looked up in surprise. "I'll be damned," he said. "Smoke has got himself married!"

Sheriff Casey chuckled. "Yeah, he told me that too. Surprised the hell out of me, I have to tell you."

Matt went back to the letter.

Anyhow, the main purpose of this letter was to tell you I got myself married to about the prettiest thing you ever saw. But also, to tell you about Sheriff Casey.

If you are reading this letter, Matt, then I reckon you are sitting in the sheriff's office right now. He's a good man, but I know something about him that not many people do know. I know he used to ride the outlaw trail. Now I tell you this, not to say anything bad about the sheriff, but so you might understand that someone like Casey, who has been on the outlaw trail, might be just the man to help you find Payson.

Ask him to tell you what he knows. Say it would be a personal favor to Smoke Jensen. Tell him if he is able to help you, I'll figure that the Spring Hill matter is all squared away. He'll know what you're talking about.

> *Your friend,*
> *Smoke*

Matt folded the letter and put it in his pocket.

"Thanks for giving me the letter," he said.

"Well, I'm glad you came through Slick Rock so I could give it to you. I've had the letter for six weeks or so. I wasn't sure you would show up, but Smoke says you are looking for the people who killed your parents."

"That's right."

"I hope you find them."

"Smoke seems to think you can help," Matt said.

Casey looked surprised. "He thinks I can help find the people who killed your parents? How would I do that?"

"He also said to tell you that if you do help me, the Spring Hill matter would be closed."

"Oh, he said that, did he?"

"Yes. What is the Spring Hill incident?"

Casey ran his hand through his hair and looked at Matt for a long moment. Then he took a deep breath.

"I was young," he said. "About your age, I reckon. I had been raised on a farm back in Missouri and figured there had to be more to life than plowing fields behind a mule. So I came West, and no sooner got here than I met a fella by the name of Amos Meeker.

"Well, sir, it turns out that Amos Meeker was the lead dog of a bunch of what I thought at the time to be really fun people to be with. Like me, they were young, restless, and obviously looking for something more out of life than they were getting. Fact is, I figured we were all riding the same-color horse."

Casey walked over to the stove, where a blue-steel coffeepot sat. Using a folded cloth to protect his hands from the heat, he poured two cups of coffee. He handed one cup to Matt before he continued his story.

"Then one day, they asked me if I would like to come along on a real adventure with them. Here, all this time, I thought we were having real adventures, hunting, fishing, sparking the ladies, that sort of thing. But Meeker scoffed at it, said what we had been doing was nothing. According to Meeker, if I wanted some real adventure, I should come along with them while we robbed a stagecoach."

Casey took a swallow of his coffee and grew silent for a moment.

"So, did you hold up a stagecoach?"

Casey nodded. "Yes, I am ashamed to say that I did. In fact, I reckon we must've hit ten or twelve stagecoaches over the next couple of months. And we were beginning to get pretty well known for it too. To be honest with you, it was sort of exciting. I thought, what was the harm? Nobody was getting hurt, and we always had enough money for whiskey, beer, and women.

"Then came Spring Hill. That was when Meeker decided we were wasting time robbing stagecoaches. He said we should rob a bank because that was where the real money was. So that's what we did—or rather, that's what we set out to do."

Casey continued with the story, telling it in such vivid and dramatic detail that it wasn't hard for Matt to believe he was there, watching the drama unfold, rather than listening to it.

There were two tellers and six customers in the bank when Meeker, Casey, and four other would-be bank robbers stepped in with guns drawn.

"Oh, my God! It's a holdup!" one of the tellers shouted in fear.

"That's right, mister, this is a holdup," Meeker said. Meeker waved his gun. "Now, open your safe and give me all the money you have."

The teller shook his head. "No," he said. "I can't do that."

"What do you mean you can't do that?"

"That money doesn't belong to the bank. It belongs to the good people of Spring Hill. I won't give it to you."

Without another word, Meeker shot the teller. There were two women in the bank, an older woman and her eighteen-year-old daughter. They both screamed.

"Now, you," Meeker said, pointing the gun at the other

teller. "Are you going to open that safe for us? Or do I have to kill you too?"

The teller was shaking so hard that he could scarcely speak. "No, no, please don't kill me," he pleaded. Then, thinking of a possible way out of his situation, the teller smiled, almost triumphantly.

"You can't kill me," he pointed out. "If you kill me, there won't be anyone left that knows the combination," the teller said. "Then what would you do?"

"You've got a point there," Meeker said, glaring angrily at the teller. Then, inexplicably, he smiled and pointed his gun at the young woman. "But I've got me another idea," Meeker said. "If you don't open that safe in one minute, I'll kill her."

"Meeker, no, I won't let you do it!" Casey shouted, jumping toward him and wrestling for his gun.

"Get away!" Meeker shouted.

The two men struggled over the gun until it discharged. Casey went down with a bullet in his hip.

Casey's attempt to take Meeker's gun failed in its original objective, but had an unexpected effect when it so distracted everyone that two of the male customers in the bank were able to draw their own guns.

"Meeker! Them two has drawed on us!" one of the bank robbers called out in panic.

Guns roared and smoke filled the room as men and women shouted and cursed in fear and anger. When the smoke cleared, three of the bank robbers were lying dead on the floor and a fourth was wounded. In addition, the bank teller, a man named Foster, was dead.

Meeker and the one surviving bank robber had managed to dash out of the bank, and were now galloping away, the sound of their horses' rapid hoofbeats permeating the town.

The robber on the floor, bleeding from a bullet wound in his thigh, was Tate Casey.

Within a matter of moments, several of the town's citizens, having heard the commotion, charged into the bank. Seeing four dead men, one of whom was the teller, the townsmen grew incensed. They pointed to Casey.

"He was one of them!"

"Hang him!" someone shouted.

"I'll get a rope!" another yelled.

"Hold it! Nobody is going to hang anybody!" the older of the two men who had fought the robbers off shouted.

"Mister, you ain't from here, so maybe you don't know. But the teller them robbers killed was one of the best men in this town."

"Mr. Foster taught Sunday school!" another said of the teller.

"I say we hang the bastard!"

There was the deadly click of a pistol being cocked. "And I say that if anyone touches this man, I'll kill him."

"What the hell, mister? Are you one of them?"

"No!" the young woman shouted, pointing to the two armed customers. "These two men ran the robbers off." She pointed to Casey. "And this man saved my life."

"Well, if we ain't goin' to hang this fella, what are we going to do with him?" someone said, pointing to Casey.

"You aren't going to do anything with him. He's coming along with us," the man with the gun said. Then, to Casey, he said, "Do you think you can sit a horse?"

"I think so," Casey answered.

"Then let's go."

The younger of the two men helped Casey to his feet, then, with Casey's arm around his shoulder, started toward the door.

"Hold it. You ain't takin' him out of here!"

"Yes, we are," the older of the two men said. "And if anyone sticks their head out the door to try and stop us, I'll shoot them."

The two men helped Casey out of the bank and onto a horse; then the three of them rode away.

Casey finished the story at the same time he finished with his cup of coffee. He wiped his coffee cup out, then hung it on a nail for future use.

"Here I was, a stagecoach robber and a bank robber, yet those two men took me back to a cabin in the mountains," he said. "And once we got there, why, the older one took the bullet out of my leg with all the skill of a surgeon. They tended me till I was nursed back to health.

"I figured it was all over then. I figured they were going to find someplace to turn me in to the law for the reward, and to tell the truth, I wasn't plannin' on fightin' 'em off. I'd had enough runnin'. I was ready to take my medicine."

"So did they turn you in?" Matt asked.

Casey shook his head. "No, sir, they didn't do nothin' of the sort. What they done was make me promise to leave the outlaw trail. I told 'em that was just what I was plannin' on doin'. So, they let me go, and I've been on the straight and narrow ever since." The sheriff looked pointedly at Matt. "What I've just told you could ruin me," he said. "The only person in town that knows about my past is my wife."

"I think everyone deserves a second chance," Matt said. "Let me guess. The two men were Preacher and Smoke, right?"

Casey nodded. "That's them, all right."

"Have you ever wondered about the young woman? What may have happened to her?" Matt asked.

Casey chuckled. "I don't have to wonder what happened to her. Anytime I get curious, I just go home."

"Go home?"

"Yep. I married her," Casey said with a little chuckle. "I told you that the only one in town who knew about my past was my wife."

"That's quite a story," Matt said.

Casey nodded. "And every word the gospel. All right, Matt, what is it you are wanting to know?"

"I'm looking for the town of Gehenna. Have you ever heard of it?"

"Yeah, I've heard of it."

"Do you know where it is?"

"Matt, are you sure you want to go there?"

"Yeah, I do want to go there," Matt insisted. "Do you know where it is?"

"Yes, I know," Casey answered. The sheriff walked over to the wall where a map of Colorado hung.

"It's right here," he said. "On Tabequacha Creek."

"Thanks," Matt said. "I might just be wasting my time, but right now it's all I have to go on."

"You said you are looking for Clyde Payson, right?"

"Yes."

Casey nodded. "Then that's where you need to go. Payson may not be there now, but I know that he has been there. And that's as good a place to start looking for him as any."

Matt felt a charge of excitement. This was the strongest lead he had gotten yet.

"Thanks!" Matt said enthusiastically. He put his empty coffee cup down and started for the door. "And thanks for the coffee," he called back.

"Matt?"

Matt stopped and looked back toward Casey. Casey was standing there with a worried expression on his face.

"I don't have to tell you that Payson is a killer, because you already know that," Matt said. "But I'm not sure you fully understand just what sort of a person he really is. Don't expect to just be able to call him out, because men like Payson don't understand things like honor, or fair play."

"I know," Matt said.

"I'm sure you do," Casey replied. "I just felt like I should tell you anyway."

"I appreciate it," Matt said.

As Matt swung into his saddle, then rode out of town, he thought about Casey's story. Like Matt, Casey's life had been immeasurably affected by Smoke Jensen. Smoke's life had been influenced by Preacher, and Preacher's own life had been shaped by the mountain men who had found him when he was but a boy himself.

Contemplating that gave Matt a sense of continuity. He had lost one family when they were murdered by Payson and his associates. But now, in a very real sense, he felt that he was part of a new family, consisting of Preacher, Smoke, and indirectly, even Casey.

It was a good feeling knowing that he was not alone in the world.

Chapter Twenty-one

Bud and Fred Pease were brothers. Pug Cooper was their first cousin, and the three were on top of a mesa overlooking the trail by which anyone heading to Gehenna from Slick Rock would have to come. Bud and Fred were lying on their stomachs, keeping an eye on the trail below. Cooper was standing a few feet behind them, relieving himself.

"Ha!" Cooper laughed.

"What are you laughin' at?" Bud asked.

"I just pissed me a grasshopper offen that branch there," Cooper said. "Knocked him clear across that rock."

"Get back over here and help us keep watch. If he comes through before dark, I don't want to miss him," Bud said.

Cooper came back toward the edge of the mesa, still buttoning his pants.

"What makes you think he's comin' anyway?" Cooper asked.

"You heard 'im, same as me'n Fred did," Bud replied. "He said he was lookin' for Payson."

"So what if he is? It ain't none of our concern," Cooper said.

"Yeah? Well, it won't hurt to be gettin' ourselves on

Payson's good side," Bud said. "To say nothin' of we'll prob'ly get a reward for killin' this fella."

"If he don't come before nightfall, what're we goin' to do?" Cooper asked.

"Yeah, Bud. If he don't come before nightfall, what are we goin' to do?" Fred repeated.

"We ain't got to worry none about that," Bud answered. "Here he is a'comin' now."

It was too far away to know who was sitting the horse, or even to be able to see the horse. The only thing Bud saw was the golden gleam of a little feather of dust, glowing brightly in the setting sun. Bud didn't need to see the horse or the rider. He knew that this was the man they were waiting for. Nobody else would be coming this way.

"Get ready," Bud said, jacking a round into the chamber of his rifle. "Whenever I give you the word, fire."

The other two jacked rounds into their rifles as well, then Cooper lay down and all three waited for the rider to come into range.

Matt couldn't see them, but he didn't have to. He knew they were there, and he knew they were on top of the mesa. The problem was that the mesa was at least half a mile across, and they could be anywhere on top. There was no way he could get to them without putting himself in their line of fire.

"Well, Spirit, if I can't go to them, I'll just bring them to me," he said, reining to a stop.

"What the hell is he doin'?" Cooper said. "Why don't he come on?"

"I don't know, unless he knows we are here," Bud said.

"How could he know we are here? He doesn't even know about us," Fred said.

Bud stroked his chin. "Some folks just know things," he said.

Cooper raised his rifle to his shoulder. "Well, I'm going to take a shot at him."

"No!" Bud said, pushing Cooper's rifle down. "He's way out of range. You'd just give us away if you shot at him now."

"What do you mean, give us away? I thought you said he already knew about us?"

"He might know, and he might not," Bud said. "But there's no sense in just tellin' him we are here."

"So, what are we going to do? Are we just going to ride on, or what?" Cooper asked.

"I'll be damn," Bud said

"What? What is it?"

"He's gathering firewood," Bud said. "He's going to camp there for the night."

"Why would he camp there?" Fred asked.

"Why not? There's a creek there. He has water, grass for his horse, dried wood for his fire." Bud chuckled. "I don't know why I didn't think of this in the first place."

"Think of what? Us camping there?"

"No," Bud said. "Us waiting until he camped."

After nightfall, Matt banked the fire so that it would continue to burn, pushing out a little bubble of golden light into the darkness. Then, finding a partial log that was about his size, he spread out his bedroll, draped a blanket over the log, put his hat at the top and his boots at the bottom. Stepping away from it, he looked at his handiwork. From as close as ten feet, it looked exactly like someone sleeping.

That accomplished, Matt slipped away from his encampment, and slid down into a small depression. From there, he had a perfect view of the fire, and the dummy in the bedroll.

He waited.

It was at least an hour before he heard anything.

"Damn it!" someone hissed.

"Shut up! You want to give us away?" another voice said, also in a hiss.

"I just stepped into a cactus, I've got needles in my leg."

"Leave 'em be."

"They hurt."

"Leave 'em be. Wait till we kill this son of a bitch, then you can take all the time you want to pull 'em out."

"Will you two shut up?"

"Has he moved any?"

"No, he's still there, sleeping as sound as a log."

When Matt heard someone say he was sleeping as sound as a *log,* he had to bite his lip to keep from laughing out loud.

The three men stepped into the bubble of light and looked down at the sleeping roll.

"Hey, Bud, there's something funny here," Fred said.

"What do you mean?"

"He ain't movin' or nothin'. Hell, he ain't even breathin'."

"Don't you boys know better than to come into a camp uninvited?" Matt said, standing then.

"What the hell! Shoot! Shoot!" Bud shouted.

Suddenly, the night was lit by muzzle flashes as the three men started shooting at Matt. The three men fanned their pistols, getting off several shots, though they were shooting wildly. Flashes of light continued to illuminate the night as the guns roared and bullets whistled through the darkness.

Matt's return fire was much more deliberate, one shot for each of his adversaries. One shot for each man was all it took, as all three of them went down with fatal bullet wounds. After making certain that all three were dead, Matt pulled them over to one side of the encampment; then he went to sleep.

The next morning, in the light of day, Matt went through the pockets of each of the men. In the pocket of one of them, he found a pencil-drawn map. The map showed the location of the town of Gehenna, verifying the directions given him by Sheriff Casey.

Matt buried the three of them in a shallow grave, back-tracked their trail until he found their horses, hobbled on top of the mesa.

"Well, here you are," Matt said. He walked up to the three animals and patted them on the forehead. They seemed grateful for the attention, and nuzzled him.

"It's not your fault your owners were a bunch of no-count bastards," he said as he untied the rope that was hobbling them. He gave the horses swats on their rumps, and all three took off running.

Matt watched them gallop free. He knew that if they stayed in the wild, there was plenty of grass and water for them in the valley. If they wandered into a ranch somewhere, they would be well taken care of. Either way, he had done as much as he could for them. He walked over and rubbed Spirit behind the ear.

"Don't worry about them, Spirit," Matt said. "They'll be fine."

Spirit bobbed his head up and down as if he understood what Matt was telling him.

Matt chuckled, then mounted Spirit to continue his journey, now bolstered by the fact that he had two separate sources that pointed to the same location.

The town was small and flyblown, a dried-up cow plop in the middle of sagebrush and shimmering heat waves. What breeze there was was coming from the south and it felt as if it was coming from the furnace of a locomotive.

Matt stopped to look at the sign, then smiled when he realized that, at long last, he had found the place he had been looking for.

YOU ARE ENTERING

GEHENNA

Population Unknown

THE LAW AIN'T WELCOME.

IF YOU GOT NO BUSINESS HERE,

GET OUT — OR <u>GET SHOT</u>

As Matt rode down the street, he looked around at the town. There was only one street to the town, flanked on either side with a few leaning shacks that were thrown together from rough-hewn lumber, the unpainted wood turning gray and splitting. There was no railroad serving the town, no stagecoach service either. There were no signs of any kind to show that Gehenna was connected to the outside world. The little town may as well have been on the moon. It was a self-contained little community, inbred and festering.

Matt looked at the buildings. There was a rooming house, a livery stable with a smithy's shop to one side, a general store, and a saloon. He did not see any houses, nor was there a school, or a church. There was a saloon.

As he passed the saloon, a woman stepped out on the porch, smiled, and waved at Matt. Matt was surprised to see that the woman was naked from the waist up.

Although Matt had been in several towns throughout the West by now, he had never before been in a town like this.

This town differed from all the others because he could see no signs of normal, domestic life here. In addition, the only women he saw were soiled doves, and they moved up and down the street freely, garishly made-up and outlandishly dressed, or in some cases, like the woman he had seen in front of the saloon, nearly undressed. He saw more than one bare breast over the course of his traverse through town.

Without commerce, most towns would be sleepy, almost deserted during the day, coming alive only at night. But though it was only mid-afternoon, Matt could already hear the sounds of revelry. There was only one saloon, but it was more than loud enough to make up for the fact that it stood all alone.

And the sounds were different, not only louder, but more out of control. There was no music, but there were screams, shouts, raucous laughter, and gunfire. Matt didn't know whether the gunshots were being fired in anger, or were part of the overall boisterous condition that prevailed.

The saloon in Gehenna had no name.

"What the hell does it need a name for?" Willie Simpson replied every time he was asked why. "The only thing you need to know is that you can get whiskey and beer here and, seeing as this is the only saloon in town, then it doesn't need a name."

Willie Simpson owned the saloon. He had never owned anything before, but he had managed a few saloons, and though he had no particular criminal past, he had been fired on at least two previous occasions for stealing from his employer.

Despite a past record of cheating his employers, Willie had never been prosecuted and never been put into jail. There had been several close calls, though, and those close calls had closed all the doors to him as far as honest employment was concerned. That being the case, there was nothing left for him but to come to Gehenna and trade with outlaws. What he had thought might be a hand-to-mouth existence proved to be a very profitable operation, cashing in on the misdeeds of others. Outlaws had no choice. They would pay Willie's inflated prices for rotgut whiskey, or they didn't drink.

Gehenna was a robbers' roost, a place of haven for men on the run. Fully three-fourths of the residents of the town were outlaws, and the remaining population made their living by serving the outlaws. Not one person in town was of sterling reputation.

Dismounting in front of the saloon, Matt stepped up on the porch, paused for a moment, then pushed his way inside. Never was the lesson on how to enter a saloon more needed than here. He moved over to the wall and stood there for a moment.

"You son of a bitch! You was holdin' that card out!" someone shouted angrily from one of the tables where a card game was in progress.

"Are you calling me a cheat?"

"Yes, you double-dealing bastard, I'm calling you a cheat!"

The accusation was followed almost immediately by the sound of a gunshot as the man who had been called a cheat drilled the other player through the chest.

The man who did the shooting was wearing a suit and vest, and no holster rig. But he was holding a smoking .41-caliber derringer in his hand. The man who had challenged him was wearing two pistols, neither of which did him any good as both were still in their holsters.

The sudden shooting interrupted the flow of conversation and laughter for but a moment. Then, when everyone realized that the excitement was over, they returned to the business at hand, leaving the dead man sprawled out on the floor.

"You was right to shoot 'im, Pippin," one of the other players said. "You wasn't cheatin'. It's sons of bitches like Miller there who cause trouble for ever'one else. Hell, if they don't know the rules, they got no business comin' to Gehenna."

"Hey, Willie, get us a new bottle of whiskey," Pippin called to the bartender.

Willie put the bottle on the bar. "Annie, take this to him," he said, calling to one of the bar girls.

Annie came over to retrieve the bottle.

"Now, mister, what can I do for you?" Willie asked, running a soiled rag over the bar just in front of where Matt was standing. There was a sour smell to the rag.

"Beer," Matt said.

"Twenty-five cents."

"Damn expensive, isn't it?"

"Find a cheaper beer in town," Willie said, and some of the others laughed.

"I'll take this one," Matt said, putting a quarter on the bar.

Willie drew a mug of beer and set it in front of him.

"You on the run, boy?" one of the men standing at the bar asked.

"Mister, I don't figure that's any of your business," Matt answered.

"Oh, it's my business all right," the man said, turning to face Matt. "You see, there's only two kinds of people come to a place like Gehenna. Those who are on the run, and bounty hunters. Now which are you?"

"I don't know," Matt replied. "I guess it depends on how much you are worth."

"What?" the man at the bar replied, surprised by Matt's answer.

"I could always use a little extra money," Matt said. "If you're worth enough, I might be tempted to do a little bounty hunting."

By now, several others in the bar had overheard Matt and

the man at the bar, and they stopped their own conversations to see where this was going.

"Nah," Matt said dismissively. "Somebody like you couldn't be worth more than twenty-five dollars or so. You aren't worth it."

"Ha! He's got your number, Aimes!" someone said, and several others in the bar laughed.

"Why, you snot-nosed punk! I'm going to wipe up the floor with you!" Aimes said, rushing down the bar toward Matt.

Aimes was bigger and heavier than Matt, and figured to use his size and experience. But that same size and experience made him overconfident and as he charged Matt, Matt just stood there until the last second. Then, like a matador avoiding a charging bull, Matt stepped to one side. As Aimes rushed by him, Matt stuck out his foot and tripped Aimes, helping him along by an open-handed blow to the back of Aimes's head.

Aimes went down, crashing into a nearby chair. He got up on his hands and knees, shook his head, then stood up and looked back at Matt. He smiled at him, then raised his fists.

"Sonny, I was just going to play with you a bit," he said. "But now I'm going to hurt you, and I'm going to hurt you really bad."

Aimes rushed toward Matt trying to catch him with a powerful swing of his right hand. Matt leaned back at the waist avoiding the blow, then counterpunched with a hard, straight left jab. He scored well, but Aimes shook it off and swung again.

By now, people had come in from the street to watch the fight. Nobody had a favorite, nobody cared who won; they just wanted the entertainment of watching it.

The fight was one-sided in that Matt seemed able to score

anytime he wanted, but so far, Aimes was brushing Matt's blows off as if they were totally ineffectual.

Then Matt hit Aimes on the nose, and he felt it go under his hand. The nose began bleeding, but even that didn't stop Aimes. He continued to smile as he swung at Matt, his teeth now red with blood. Aimes finally connected with a punch, and though Matt managed to deflect most of it, it still retained enough force to knock him down.

With a triumphant yell, Aimes picked up a chair and raised it over his head, preparing to crash it down on Matt.

Quickly, Matt rolled out of the way, then kicked out with his right foot, catching Aimes on the side of his knee. With a yell of pain and surprise, Aimes went down, then lay on the floor, groveling and grabbing his knee.

Matt stood up, looked down at him, then walked over to the bar to resume drinking his beer.

"You son of a bitch! I'm going to kill you!" Aimes yelled.

Turning, Matt saw Aimes clawing for his gun. Matt threw the beer mug and hit Aimes right between the eyes. He went out like a light.

"You should'a killed him," Willie said.

"No need to kill him now," Matt said. "I can kill him anytime I want."

Chapter Twenty-two

Matt recognized Poke Lawson and Syl Richards the moment they came into the saloon. He didn't know their names, but he remembered their faces. Poke and Syl had been with Clyde Payson on the day Payson killed his parents and his sister. He stared at them, holding the stare until Poke became aware.

He looked over at Matt.

"You starin' at me, mister?" Poke asked.

"Yes."

"I don't like bein' stared at."

Matt didn't respond, but neither did he look away.

"Did you hear me? I said I don't like you starin' at me."

Matt still didn't respond.

"You got somethin' stuck in your craw, boy?" Poke asked, growing more frustrated.

"Poke, what's got you all riled?" Syl asked.

"What do you mean what has me riled?" Poke asked. "Look at him, Syl. The son of a bitch just keeps starin' at us."

Now Syl turned away from the bar as well so that both he and Poke were facing Matt.

"Why are you starin' at us?" Syl asked.

"You were with him that day, weren't you?" Matt said. "Both of you were."

"We was with who? Boy, I don't know what the hell you are talking about," Syl said.

"You were with Clyde Payson and Garvey Laird."

"You are gettin' me riled, boy," Poke said. "What about Clyde Payson and Garvey Laird?"

"Do you know where they are?"

"Yeah, I know where they are. What's that to you?"

"I intend to kill them," Matt said. "Both of them."

Both Poke and Syl laughed. "You?" Poke said, pointing at Matt. "You are going to kill Payson and Laird?"

"That's right."

"What makes you think you can kill them?" Syl asked. "Why, you're so young you still got snot runnin' out of your nose."

"How old do you have to be to kill someone?" Matt asked.

"What do you mean how old do you have to be to kill someone?" Poke asked. "That question don't make sense."

"Say you are nine years old," Matt said. "Say you are nine years old and a group of low-life, yellow-bellied bastards come up on your wagon, and they kill your ma, your pa, and your sister."

A hint of recognition began to flicker across the faces of Poke and Syl.

"And say you grab your pa's rifle and get into the rocks, then kill two of the bastards who killed your family. Is nine years old too young to kill?"

"Son of a bitch!" Poke shouted, suddenly realizing what Matt was talking about. "You're that brat!"

"That's right. I'm that brat," Matt confirmed.

Both Poke and Syl made desperate grabs for their guns.

Matt waited patiently until Poke and Syl had cleared the holsters with their guns.

Seeing that they had the jump on Matt before he even started his draw, Poke and Syl smiled in triumph.

The smile was short-lived, however, because before they could bring their guns to bear, Matt had his pistol out and fired twice.

The smiles were replaced by looks of shock as the two men realized that they had been shot. Poke tumbled forward, Syl fell backward. Both men were dead before they hit the floor.

Matt held the smoking pistol in his hand for a moment, then looked around the room to see if anyone else was about to challenge him.

"Son of a bitch!" Willie said, pouring himself a whiskey. "I ain't never seen nothin' like that."

"You're as fast as Angus Boone," one of the others said.

"Ain't nobody as fast as Angus Boone," one of the others said.

"I believe this fella is."

"Better not let the Gravedigger hear you saying that."

"Where is Clyde Payson?" Matt asked the bartender.

"I . . . I don't know!" Willie answered. "I admit that he does come in here from time to time, but I ain't seen him in a couple of weeks now."

Matt put his pistol in his holster, then turned his back to the bar and faced the others who were in the saloon. All were wearing looks of amazement over the shooting demonstration they had just seen.

"My name is Matt Jensen and I'm looking for Clyde Payson and Garvey Laird," Matt said.

"Mister, maybe you didn't notice, but we don't welcome the law in Gehenna. And we don't help 'em out none either."

Matt smiled. "I'm not the law," he said. "This is personal."

"Even if we know'd where he was, ain't nobody goin' to be dumb enough to tell you where to find him. I figure if he wants to get hisself found, he'll let you know where he is."

Clem Tyson and Bart Ebersole had seen the whole thing. They were sitting at a table in the back of the room when it started, and Clem started to get involved, but Bart reached out to stop him.

"This here ain't our fight," Bart said. "This is about somethin' that happened before we ever joined up with Payson."

"Yes, but don't we owe . . . ?" Clem began, but Bart interrupted him.

"We don't owe anybody nothin'."

A moment later, seeing the ease with which Matt put down both Poke and Syl, Clem was glad that Bart had stopped him.

"What do we do now?" Clem asked.

"Now we go see Payson and tell him this young punk is after him," Bart replied.

"I thought you said this wasn't our fight."

"If Payson is willin' to pay us to take a hand in it, then it will be our fight," Bart said.

Salcedo

Clyde Payson stuck his hand up under the skirt of a passing bar girl, grabbed the cheek of her butt, and squeezed.

The bar girl squealed, then laughed out loud. "Now, honey, it's not nice to get a girl all hot and bothered like that unless you intend to do something about it," she said.

"Ha, Payson, what do you think? Damn if I don't think she's in love with you," Garvey said.

"She's not in love with me," Payson said. "She's in love with the two dollars it would cost to take her up to her room."

Garvey and a couple of others who were nearby laughed out loud. They were still laughing when Clem Tyson and Bart Ebersole pushed through the front door. The two men came directly for Payson's table.

"Damn, boys, look at you," Payson said. "You look like you been rode hard and put away wet."

"They's someone after you, Payson," Bart said.

Payson laughed. "I expect there's a lot of people after me. There is a reward out, you know." He pointed to Bart and Clem. "Only, it isn't just me. The reward is for you two, Garvey, and Poke and Syl."

Clem shook his head. "It ain't for Poke and Syl," he said.

"What do you mean, it ain't for Poke and Syl? They were in Cedar Creek same as the rest of us."

"This don't have nothin' to do with Cedar Creek," Clem said. "This has somethin' to do with a wagon you'n Poke and Syl come across some years back, afore me'n Bart joined up with you."

Payson shook his head. "A wagon? What wagon? I don't know what you're talkin' about."

"Yeah, well, the man that's lookin' for you knows what he is talkin' about. And Poke and Syl know'd too, just before they was killed."

"Killed? Wait a minute, are you sayin' Poke and Syl are dead?"

"Deader'n a cow turd in the sun," Bart said.

"Who killed them? Did you get a name?"

"Yeah, his name was Jensen. Matt Jensen. And according to what Poke and Syl said just before they was killed, this here fella was at some wagon you all jumped afore me'n Clem joined up with you."

Payson shook his head. "Jensen? Jensen? No, I don't remember jumpin' no one named Jensen."

"From the way they was talkin', this fella was nine years old. He grabbed a rifle and run into the rocks, then killed two of your men."

"Son of a bitch!" Payson said, striking his open palm with a closed fist. "It's the brat! He's still alive! But his name is Cavanaugh. What's he callin' hisself Jensen for?"

"Who knows? Maybe he was adopted and changed his name. Whatever it is, he's alive, and he wants to kill you."

"Oh, he wants to kill me, does he?" Payson replied. He pulled his pistol and rotated the cylinder, checking each chamber. "Well, we'll just see about that."

"He's good, Payson," Bart said.

"Yeah? How good?"

"Fastest I ever seen," Bart said. "Except for maybe Boone."

"He's faster'n Boone," Clem said.

"What makes you say that?" Payson asked.

"Well, for one thing, he waited till both Poke and Syl had their guns drawed before he even started to draw his own gun," Clem said.

"Yeah," Bart said. "This fella just stood there, calm as you please, while Poke and Syl went for their guns. He waited till they had them both drawed before he pulled his own gun."

"Like this," Clem said, using his hand, but without a gun, to demonstrate. "Only it was about three times faster."

"All right, boys, you've made your point. He's fast. What am I supposed to do about it? You think I should run?"

"Might not be a bad idea," Clem said.

"Ain't no way I'm going to run," Payson replied.

"There's something you got to consider," Bart said.

"What's that?"

"This fella has seen you before. He knows what you look

like. He could be right up on you before you even know'd you was in danger."

"I've seen him before too," Payson said.

"Yeah, when he was nine years old. I didn't see him then, but I'm pretty sure he don't look the same. As fast as he is, and you not knowin' what he looks like and all, I reckon he can kill you just about anytime he wants."

Payson poured himself a drink. With shaking hands, he lifted the glass to his lips. "Then what the hell am I supposed to do about it?" he asked.

"There is a way," Bart suggested.

Payson tossed the drink down. "What is the way?" he asked.

"You could offer money to anyone who found him for you."

"Well, now, that don't make a hell of a lot of sense, does it? I mean, I don't want the son of a bitch to find me, so why would I pay someone to find him?"

Bart smiled. "Well, not find him exactly. What I meant was, maybe you could pay somebody to kill him for you."

"If he is as fast as you say he is, where'm I goin' to find someone who is willin' to do that?"

"Me'n Clem will do it," Bart said.

"I thought you was tellin' me how fast he is. How are you and Clem goin' to go up against him if he's as fast as you say he is?"

"He is fast," Bart said. "But me'n Clem got an advantage over you, because we know what he looks like. And while he knows what you look like, he don't know us from Adam. He won't be lookin' out for us."

Payson smiled. "Yeah," he said. He nodded. "Yeah, that's right, ain't it? All right, I'll give you hunnert dollars to kill him."

"Apiece," Bart said. "There's two of us."

"No, one hundred dollars for the two of you. How you divide it up between you is up to you."

"A hunnert dollars apiece, or you can handle him yourself," Bart said.

Payson sighed, then ran his hand through his hair. "All right, a hunnert dollars apiece," he said. He pointed his finger at Bart. "But do it quick. I don't like the idea of thinkin' about that son of a bitch lurking around somewhere."

"He'll be dead within the week," Bart promised.

Chapter Twenty-three

Cobb's Station

Matt rode up to the hitching rail in front of the saloon, dismounted, looped the reins around the hitching rail, and went inside.

The shadowed interior of the saloon gave the illusion of coolness, though it was an illusion only. The air inside was hot, still, and redolent with the sour smells of beer and whiskey and the stench of a dozen sweating, unwashed bodies.

Matt walked over to the bar and put a nickel down.

"Beer," he said.

"You just passin' through?" the bartender asked as he set the beer on the bar.

"Sort of."

"Sort of?"

"I'm lookin' for someone."

"You're lookin' for someone, huh? Are you the law? Or are you a bounty hunter? If you are the law, I'll tell you what I know. If you are a bounty hunter, you'll get no information from me," the bartender said.

Matt shook his head. "I'm not the law or a bounty hunter," he said. "This is personal."

"Who are you lookin' for?"

"I'm looking for two people actually. One named Clyde Payson, the other Garvey Laird."

"I'll be damn," the bartender said. "You're him, aren't you?"

"Him?"

"Matt Jensen," the bartender said. "That would be your name, wouldn't it? Matt Jensen?"

"Yes, it is," Matt said, squinting his eyes. "How do you know my name?"

The bartender chuckled. "Well, hell, Mr. Jensen. You've done got famous, didn't you know that?"

"No, I don't suppose I did know it."

"Well, they ain't here."

"What?"

"Them folks you're lookin' for," the bartender said. "They ain't here."

"Would you know if they were here?"

The bartended nodded. "I reckon I'd know, seein' as they've both been here before. Payson has a scar here." He made a motion across his face with his hand. "And the oth-er'n has half an ear gone."

"That's them."

"The story I've heard is that they kilt your ma and pa and you're out for revenge."

"That's right," Matt said, taking another swallow of his beer.

"Well, like I say, they ain't here now, but I hope you find 'em," the bartender said.

"Thanks."

Another customer stepped up to the bar requiring the bartender's attention, so he stepped way. As he did so, Matt turned his back to the bar and slowly surveyed the interior of the saloon. It was typical of many he had seen. Wide, rough-hewn boards formed the plank floor, and against the wall behind the long, brown-stained bar was a shelf of whiskey bottles, their number doubled by the mirror they stood against. Half a dozen tables, occupied by a dozen or more men, filled the room, and tobacco smoke hovered under the ceiling in a noxious cloud.

"You got anything to eat?" Matt asked when the bartender came back a moment later.

"Ham and taters," the bartender answered.

"Good enough," Matt replied. He nodded toward an empty table. "I'll be over there."

"I'll tell the kitchen," the bartender said.

"Thanks."

As the bartender left to see to his order, Matt moved over to the table to await his food. When he did so, one of the other saloon patrons left, then walked resolutely to another saloon at the far end of the street. There, two men were sitting at a table at the back of the room. They looked up as the man approached their table.

"What are you doing here, Les? Did the cards start running bad for you?"

"Bart, Clem, it's him," Les said.

"Him who?"

"Matt Jensen. He's here in Cobb's Station. He's down at the Horse Shoe."

Bart squinted at Les. "How do you know it's him? What's he look like?"

"He's a big fella, tall, with wide shoulders, narrow at the hip," Les said. "It's him, I tell you."

"You ain't never seen him before. That description could fit dozens of men."

"Maybe. But the barkeep recognized him," Les answered. "He called him out on it, and Jensen didn't deny it."

"Is he still down at the Horse Shoe?"

"He was when I left, and I figure he still is, seein' as he just ordered his supper."

"You think it's him for real?" Clem asked.

"Well, me'n you have both seen him before," Bart said. "If it ain't him for real, we'll know soon enough."

"What are we goin' to do if it is him for real?"

"We're goin' to get ourselves that two hunnert dollars," Bart said.

"The only way we can do that is by killin' him."

"That's the plan," Bart said. "There's three of us, and only one of him."

"Look here, you are the ones who are lookin' for him. Not me," Les said. "All I agreed to do was keep an eye open for him and if I seen him, come let you know. You said you would give me ten dollars. Ain't no way I'm goin' up against this man for ten dollars, even if there is three of us. Which there ain't goin' to be, 'cause I ain't goin' to do it."

"What if we give you fifty dollars?" Bart asked.

"So, what you're sayin' is, you want me to take the same risk as you and Clem, but you'll each get seventy-five dollars and I'll get fifty?"

"Well, yeah, but we are the ones that come up with the idea," Bart said.

"Fifty dollars ain't enough to get myself kilt over. Just give me my ten dollars now and I'm out of it."

"All right, but if it ain't him, you don't get your money," Bart said.

"I want the money now," Les said.

"Why should I give you any money before I know whether or not it is actually Matt Jensen?"

"'Cause if it ain't Matt Jensen, all you got to do is come down here and get your money back," Les said. "On the other hand, if it is him and he kills you, then I won't get my money."

"Yeah, well, I ain't givin' you no money now. So you just better hope we kill him instead of him killin' us," Bart said.

"Yeah? Well, to tell you the truth, I don't have much hope for that," Les said.

"How are we goin' to do it?" Clem asked. "Do you have a plan?"

"Yeah, I have a plan," Bart said. "We're going to call the son of a bitch out."

"Call him out? What are you talkin' about? Ain't no way I'm going to call him out. You seen the way he handled Poke and Syl," Clem said.

"He know'd who Poke and Syl was," Bart said. "And they didn't know who he was. And they was both standin' right together. Only now the shoe is on the other foot. We know who he is, but he don't know who we are. And we ain't goin' to be standin' together."

"Yeah, well, which one of us is goin' to call him out?" Clem asked.

Bart sighed. "It was my idea," he said. "I'll do it."

"You sure you want to do that?" Clem asked. "Go up ag'in him by yourself? You seen what happened to Poke and Syl."

"Oh, don't you worry none about that. I'm callin' him out by myself, but I ain't goin' to fight him by myself. You're goin' to be right there with me, only he ain't goin' to know it," Bart said, smiling.

"Yeah," Clem said. "Yeah, that plan might work."

Matt was halfway through his supper when he saw the two men come into the saloon. He probably wouldn't have paid any attention to them at all, had it not been for their strange behavior. They were obviously together, but as soon as they came in they split up, one going to one end of the bar and the second going to the other end of the bar.

It also seemed to Matt as if they had looked at him longer than mere curiosity about a stranger would dictate. Lessons learned from Smoke had not created in Matt the ability to perceive danger long before it was apparent. It had merely enhanced the natural instinct for survival with which Matt had been born.

To most, the fact that two men came in together, then took up positions at opposite ends of the bar, would mean nothing. But Matt became instantly aware of danger. He moved the chair back from the table and positioned himself so he could watch both men. He watched as each of the men ordered a beer, then stood at the bar, nursing his drink.

After about five minutes, Matt finished his supper. Neither of the men had tried anything, so he was beginning to think that the perceived danger was just his imagination. He walked back up to the middle of the bar and ordered another beer.

"Would you be the fella they call Matt Jensen?" the man at the right end of the bar asked.

Matt almost felt relieved that his instinct had not been a false alarm.

"I am," he replied.

"Well, Mr. Matt Jensen, my name is Bart Ebersole, and I'm callin' you out," the man at the bar said.

With that announcement, there was a sudden repositioning of all the other patrons at the bar, and even in the main part of the saloon, as everyone hurried to get out of the way should shooting begin. Matt noticed, however, that the man at the left end of the bar, the one who had come in with Bart Ebersole, had not left his position.

"Are you sure you want to go through with this, Mr. Ebersole?" Matt asked.

"Oh, yeah, I'm sure," Bart said.

"May I ask why?"

"Yeah, you can ask why. I'm told you are looking for Clyde Payson. Is that right?"

"I am," Matt said. "What does that have to do with you?"

"Let's just say that Payson is my friend, and I wouldn't want to see anything happen to him."

"Mister, if Clyde Payson is your friend, all I can say is you have a piss-poor choice of friends," Matt said.

"Now, Clem!" Bart shouted as he started his draw.

Matt sensed, more than saw, Clem drawing his gun behind him.

For just a moment, Matt was not in a saloon in a festering Western town facing down two armed and determined men. Instead, he was in the little valley alongside Smoke Jensen's mountain cabin, standing between posts that were set fifty yards apart. There was a tin can on each of the posts, and Smoke Jensen was standing to one side, holding a rock over a pie pan.

"Are you ready?" Smoke asked.

Matt nodded. "I'm ready," he said.

Smoke opened his hand to let the rock fall and Matt drew his pistol. . . .

But Matt wasn't in that peaceful meadow, shooting at tin cans. He was in a saloon, standing between two armed men who wanted to kill him and who had stacked the deck in their favor by positioning themselves to either side of him.

Although it was Bart who shouted the order to draw, Matt sensed that Clem had begun his draw even before the call. Matt whirled to face the man behind him, surprising Clem, who thought that Matt was unaware of him. Matt fired before Clem could get off a shot. Then, as Clem's gun clattered to the floor, and blood began pooling in the hands Clem clasped over his wound, Matt whirled toward Bart. Bart was able to get off a shot, but he missed. Matt did not. Matt's bullet hit Bart right between the eyes and he fell back against the bar, then tumbled forward.

After the final crash of gunfire, there was a long, pregnant moment of absolute silence, broken only by a measured tick-tock, tick-tock from the swinging pendulum of the clock that hung on the back wall by the scarred piano.

"Holy shit," someone said quietly. A few of the others laughed nervously.

Slowly, the patrons started back toward the bar. "This here one is dead," someone said of Bart.

"Yeah, this one too," one who was standing over Clem said.

"Here," the bartender said, sliding some money across the bar.

"What is that for?" Matt asked.

"Your drinks and your supper are free," the bartender said. "Mister, you don't know it, but you just made this place famous. There will be folks comin' from all over to see where Matt Jensen took down two men who were standing on opposite sides of him. You're going to make me a ton of money."

"Thanks," Matt said, pushing the money back. "But I'd rather have some information on where to find Payson."

The bartender paused for a moment, then let out a sigh. "You might try the town of Salcedo," he said. "I heard he was there."

Chapter Twenty-four

Salcedo

Payson looked at his cards, then pushed a chip into the middle of the table. Not until then did he look up at the man who was standing beside him.

"What did you say your name was?"

"Les. Les Clemmons."

"Well, Les Clemmons, that's quite a tale you're telling me. You say that Bart and Clem are dead and . . ."

"I'm not just saying it. It's true. They are both dead. And they owe me ten dollars."

"Well, now, if they are dead and they owe you ten dollars, it looks like you are going to have a hard time collecting, doesn't it?" Payson called the bet on the table.

"Three aces," Garvey said, turning his cards up, then reaching for the pot.

"Full house, fives over threes," Payson replied, showing his hand as he raked in the pot.

Les cleared his throat. "I thought I might be able to collect the ten dollars from you," he said.

Payson laughed out loud. "Now, what makes you think that?"

"Because I know that Matt Jensen is coming here to look for you."

"And you think I should pay for that information?" Payson asked. "Hell, ever'body who has ever heard of Matt Jensen knows that he is lookin' for me'n Garvey. Why should I pay you for information that I already know?"

"Do you know that he is coming right here to Salcedo?" Les asked.

"No, I didn't know that," Payson answered.

"Do you know what he looks like?"

"No."

"So in other words, he could be right here in this very room, right now, and you wouldn't even know it, would you?"

Even now a new hand was being dealt, and Payson was picking it up one card at a time. He looked up at Les.

"What do you mean? What are you talking about?"

"Just what I said. He could be here right now and you would never know the difference. I could be Matt Jensen."

With that remark, Payson got up from the table so quickly that the chair tumbled over behind him. The sudden movement caught the attention of everyone else in the room, and all looked toward Payson to see him pull his gun.

"No! No! Hold it! Hold it!" Les shouted quickly, frightened that he might have pushed the game too far. "I ain't Matt Jensen!" he said, holding his hands, palms out, in front of him. "I was just tryin' to make a point, is all."

"Yeah? Well, you've got a hell of a way of makin' a point," Payson said angrily. He was still holding the pistol.

"My point is, you don't know what he looks like, and I do," Les said. "I figure that ought to be worth some money to you."

"That's worth nothing to me," Payson said. He put his pistol back in his holster. "But since you know what he looks like, maybe you can do something that will be worth money to me."

"What?"

"Find some way to make the son of a bitch go away," Payson said.

"Make him go away? What do you mean? How am I supposed to do that?"

"I don't care how you do it," Payson said. "Just do it, then come talk to me about money."

"How much money are you willin' to pay?"

"One hundred dollars," Payson said.

Les shook his head. "That ain't enough. You was going to give Bart and Clem two hundred dollars."

"But I didn't."

"That's because they didn't get the job done," Les said. "If I don't get the job done, you don't have to give it to me either. But if I do get the job done, I'm going to want two hundred dollars."

Payson nodded. "All right. Get the job done. It'll be worth two hundred dollars."

Halfway between Cobb's Station and Salcedo was the town of El Gato. One could almost say that El Gato was two towns, one half American, and one half Mexican. The north side of the town was the American side, while the Mexican population was concentrated on the south side.

Ripsawed lumber buildings made up the American town, while in the Mexican section of town, adobe buildings were laid out around a dusty plaza.

Les Clemmons rode into the south side of town, aware that he was being stared at by people who wondered what an Anglo was doing there. He tied his horse off at a hitch rail in front of Rosita's Cantina. A woman's high, clear voice was singing, and that and the accompanying guitar music spilled out through the beaded doorway. Les pushed through the hanging beads, then stepped inside.

He wasn't concerned about being accepted here. He knew that Americans often came to the Mexican side for tequila, or women, or even to eat the spicy Mexican food. Because of that, he raised little attention as he stepped up to the bar and ordered tequila. Pouring salt on his hand, he licked it off, then tossed down the fiery liquid as he examined the patrons of the cantina. He had an idea how he was going to collect the two hundred dollars from Payson, and the idea started here.

A woman, wearing a red dress that was cut so low that her breasts threatened to spill out, came up to him. She was dark and sultry-looking, and she smiled up at him.

"Do you want a woman, Señor? *La mayoria de los anglos que vienen a Rosita's vienen para buscar a una mujer.*"

"Maybe most of the Anglos come looking for women, but I'm looking for men."

The woman got a shocked look on her face. "You don't like women? You like men?"

"What?" Les asked. Then he realized what she was saying. "No! No, it's nothing like that. I need to hire some men to do a job for me."

"What kind of job?"

"I need someone who is very good with a knife. A *cuchillo,*" he said, using the Spanish word to make certain she understood.

"I think you want Manuel maybe," the woman said.

"Is Manuel in here?"

"Sí." She pointed. "That is Manuel."

Manuel was standing at the far end of the bar. He was almost a head taller than most of those around him. His hat was pushed back so that Les could see his face. He was standing alone, and the expression on his face gave a hint as to why. He looked like someone who was angry with the world.

Manuel also had a large bowie knife protruding from a sheath that he wore across his chest. Only someone who was very good with a knife would dare to wear it in such a fashion.

"Thanks," Les said. He finished his drink, put it down, then walked over to confront Manuel.

"Manuel?"

"How do you know my name?" Manuel asked.

"How I know your name doesn't matter," Les said. "What matters is the fifty dollars I am willing to pay you, if you are interested."

"*Sí,* I am interested."

"You haven't asked what the job is."

"You will pay fifty dollars?"

"Yes."

"I do not care what the job is, Señor. If you will pay fifty dollars, I will do it."

"We need to find one more person," Les said.

Matt had come into El Gato earlier in the day and, after boarding his horse, spent most of the afternoon in the saloon, playing cards and listening in on conversations for any clues that might help him find Clyde Payson. It was dark when he finally left the saloon and started down the street toward the hotel.

There were no street lamps in this small town, but a full moon and a few dim squares of light splashing through open windows kept the street from being in total darkness. Back in the saloon Matt had just left, the piano player was hard at work, his discordant and cacophonous attempt at music spilling out into the street.

From the shadows of the Mexican quarters on the south

side of town, a strumming guitar and a trumpet competed with each other, and though they were playing different songs, they somehow seemed to blend together.

He heard a dog's insistent yap.

A baby's cry joined the mix.

"That's him," Les whispered to the two Mexicans he had hired.

"That's the gringo you want killed?" Manuel asked.

"Yes."

"Why would a gringo pay me to kill another gringo?"

"Can you do it?"

"*Sí,* it will be easy."

"Then do it. It doesn't matter why."

Matt felt the assassins coming for him before he heard them, and he heard them before he saw them. Two men suddenly jumped from the dark shadows between the buildings, making wide slashes with their knives. But that innate sense that allowed him to perceive danger when there was no other sign had saved his life, for he was moving out of the way at the exact moment the two men were starting their attacks. Otherwise, their knives, swinging in low, vicious arcs, would have disemboweled him.

Despite the quickness of his reaction, however, one of the knives did manage to cut him, and as Matt went down into the dirt, rolling to get away from them, the flashing blade opened up a long wound in his side. The knife was so sharp and wielded so adroitly that Matt barely felt it. He knew, however, that the knife had drawn blood.

One of the assassins moved in quickly, thinking to finish Matt off before he could recover. But Matt twisted around on the ground, then thrust his feet out, catching the assailant in the chest with a powerful kick and driving him back several feet. The second one darted in on the heels of the first, but by now Matt had managed to pull his own knife and he held it out low, with the blade parallel to the ground, letting his attacker impale himself on it.

He heard the attacker grunt in pain and surprise, then give out a long, life-surrendering sigh. Matt twisted the knife in him so that, as the attacker fell, his own weight against the knife opened him up.

"Mamá de Dios, usted me ha matado, señor," the Mexican said, trying to hold his guts in as he collapsed in the dirt. "You have killed me," he repeated in English.

The first attacker, thinking he had the advantage, made another wide, slashing thrust. He was good, skilled and agile, but Matt managed to twist away from him. As he twisted away from his assailant, Matt's knife was not in position to counterthrust, but his left hand was. Matt thrust his left hand out, using stiffened fingers to gouge out both eyes.

"Aiiyee!" the assailant screamed, dropping his knife and reaching up to his face. Mucus and eye matter streamed through his spread fingers, and Matt knew that he had blinded him. This fight was over.

Matt's assailant stood in the middle of the street, screaming in pain and terror.

"Soy ciego! Soy ciego!"

By now several of the townspeople, having heard the commotion, had come out into the street to see what was going on. They had watched in awe as Matt defended himself against two attackers.

"What's that Mexican fella sayin'?" one of the onlookers asked.

"He says he is blind."

"I'll be damned."

* * *

Across the street, in the darkness afforded by the unlit shadows, Les stood between the apothecary and the leather-goods store. Jacking a round into his rifle, he raised it to his shoulder and aimed at Matt, but before he could pull the trigger, those who had poured into the street crowded around, blocking his target.

"Damn it!" Les said under his breath. "Get out of the way!"

More people arrived, pouring out of other saloons, and even coming from the houses. With a sigh of disgust, Les lowered his rifle.

"I'll give you this, Matt Jensen," he said under his breath. "You are one hard son of a bitch to kill."

Matt felt the nausea beginning to rise. Bile surged to his throat. Light-headed now, he turned and staggered back toward the saloon. He was barely aware of those who had come into the street to watch the fight, barely aware of them moving aside, like the sea parting for Moses, as he walked back to the saloon. Reaching the front of the saloon, he grabbed the overhang pillar for support and pulled himself up onto the plank porch, then pushed in through the door to stand in the brightness. It was not until he was inside, in the bright light, that the severity of his wound could be seen.

One of the bar girls, seeing the bloody apparition standing there, screamed. All conversation came to a halt, and a dead silence hung over the saloon as if it were something palpable. Everyone stared at him, their eyes wide and their mouths open in shock.

Matt stood just inside the doorway, ashen-faced and holding his hand over a wound that spilled bright red blood between his fingers. He looked around the room for just a moment, then with effort, walked over to the bar.

"Whiskey," he ordered.

"Mr. Jensen, you better let a doctor look at that wound you got there," the bartender said. By now Matt's side was drenched with blood from his wound, and the blood was beginning to soak into the wide-plank floor.

"I'll be fine," Matt said. Then his eyes rolled back in his head and he crumpled to the floor, passed out cold.

Chapter Twenty-five

When Matt awakened, he experienced a moment of confusion as to where he was. But when he moved, a sharp stitch in his side reminded him of what had happened the night before and he reached down to feel the bandage. He was gratified to see that there had been no more bleeding since last night.

Matt looked around at his surroundings. He knew that he was in a hotel room, but he wasn't quite sure how he got there. He didn't know exactly what time it was, but he could tell by the texture of the sunlight streaming in through the window that it was still fairly early in the morning. He also saw his clothes, clean and neatly folded, lying on a chair by the window.

He thought back to last night and remembered the knife fight he had had with the two Mexicans. He didn't know who they were, nor did he know why they had attacked him, though he suspected it might have something to do with Clyde Payson. He had heard that Payson had put out a reward for him, and the incident last night seemed to validate that.

Matt was startled when the door to his room opened. Thinking his gun belt and pistol were hanging from the headboard of the bed, he reached for his weapon.

It wasn't there!

He was about to get out of bed, despite the pain in his side, when the person who opened the door stepped into his room.

It was Tamara!

"Tamara!" he gasped in surprise. "What are you doing here?"

"You're awake!" she said happily.

"Well, yes. It's morning. I normally wake up in the morning," Matt replied. "But you didn't answer my question. What are you doing here?"

"Why, I'm here to take care of you, of course," Tamara answered. "I came as soon as I heard you had been wounded."

The expression on Matt's face reflected his confusion. "How could that be possible?" he asked. "I was just wounded last night."

"Last night?" Tamara said. She laughed. "Silly boy. Do you actually think you were wounded last night?"

"Yes, of course. I had just come out of the saloon when a couple of . . ." Matt stopped in mid-sentence.

Suddenly a jumbled series of scenes began tumbling through Matt's mind.

He recalled the fight.

He remembered going into the saloon.

A worried-looking doctor had cleaned his wound and sewn it shut.

Some men carried him to the hotel room.

Sometime during all this, Tamara showed up, and now, as he thought back on it, he could recall seeing her face many times, worried as she sat on the edge of the bed, looking down at him, sometimes washing his face with a damp cloth, other times stroking his cheek. Sometimes she kissed him.

He looked up at her, and saw that she had been watching him go through the thought process.

"How long have I been here?" Matt asked.

"Ten days."

"Ten days?" Matt gasped. "Have I been out all that time?"

"Not entirely," Tamara said. "You've been in and out of it, and a few times you have even recognized me."

"Really? Have we—uh—have we been together?" Matt asked.

Tamara laughed. "You haven't exactly been in the mood," she said. "Why do you ask? Are you in the mood now?"

"I might be," Matt said.

"Oh, my," Tamara said. "Then I would say you are just about fully recovered."

Tamara walked over to the door, opened it, looked outside, then closed and locked it. When she returned to the bed, she began removing her dress. She lay it neatly on a chair, then stepped out of her petticoat. Next came the camisole, exposing her rather small but well-formed breasts.

"You know, when I first started in this business, the way I was able to get through it was to imagine that the man I was with was you," she said.

"How did that help?" Matt asked. "You remembered me as a twelve-year-old boy."

"Maybe it was my fantasy of what you would become," Tamara said. "And I was right, because look at you now."

Smiling, Tamara started to step out of her bloomers.

Suddenly, there was the tinkling sound of broken glass as something whizzed through the window, followed by a solid "thock," like the sound of a hammer hitting a nail.

Tamara pitched forward, even as a mist of blood was spraying out from the back of her head.

"No!" Matt shouted in a loud, grief-stricken voice.

* * *

Across the street from the hotel, on the roof of the hardware store behind the false front, Les saw the woman step into his line of fire just as he pulled the trigger.

"No!" he said, ironically matching Matt.

"Son of a bitch! What did you move for!" Les asked, jacking another round into the rifle. He fired a second time.

Matt heard the second bullet come through the window and slam into the wall behind the bed. This bullet missed him by no more than an inch.

Rolling out of bed, Matt looked around for his pistol, then saw that it was on the chair under his clothes. He crawled over to the chair, pulled his pistol, then crawled to the window.

When Matt looked down onto the street, he saw two men standing in front of the tobacco store. They had obviously heard the shots fired, and were looking up. One was pointing toward the roof of the hardware store.

Yes, he thought. That made sense. The hardware store was directly across the street from the hotel. If someone wanted to shoot into the second floor of the hotel, that would be the best place to shoot from.

At first, Matt saw nothing. Then, something caught his attention on the wall of the feed store that was next to the hardware store. The morning sun was at exactly the right angle to project shadows from the roof of the hardware store, and there he saw the shadow of the shooter.

Using the shadow as a guide, Matt aimed at the false front. He knew that it consisted of thinly cut boards, and he aimed at a point where he calculated the shooter to be. He fired three times in quick succession.

He didn't need the shadow to know he had been successful. He saw the shooter fall off the roof, then land hard on the ground, where he lay without moving. Moving away from the window, he went back into the room to check on Tamara.

There was nothing to check. Tamara was dead.

Salcedo

Clyde Payson threw a whiskey bottle against the wall of the saloon.

"What the hell?" he shouted in anger. "Is he a ghost or something? Is there nobody who can kill him?"

"I can kill him," someone said.

Payson looked toward the door at the man who had just come into the saloon. He was dressed all in black, except for a turquoise and silver band around his short-crowned black hair.

"Boone?" Payson said.

Boone nodded.

"Don't get me wrong. I would welcome anyone killing him. But why do you want to kill him?"

"Because I can," Boone said.

Payson chuckled. "Because you can," he said. He nodded. "Yes, yes, I really believe you can kill him. And if you want to kill him just because you can, well, that's a good enough reason for me."

"And for the one thousand," Boone added.

"What? What one thousand dollars?"

"The thousand dollars you are going to pay me to kill Matt Jensen," Boone said.

"I don't know," Payson said. "One thousand dollars is a lot of money."

"How much is your life worth to you?" Boone asked.

"What do you mean?"

"If I don't kill Matt Jensen, he will kill you. Isn't your life worth one thousand dollars to you?"

"Yes, of course it is. But where am I supposed to get one thousand dollars?" Payson asked.

"That's your problem."

"What if you kill him, and I haven't been able to come up with one thousand dollars?"

"Then it will still be your problem, because I will kill you," Boone said in a matter-of-fact voice.

Payson thought for a moment, then nodded. "All right," he said. "Kill him."

Chapter Twenty-six

Salcedo

"Yeah, he was here," the bartender told Matt. "Matter of fact, he hung around here for several weeks. But he left a few days ago."

"Do you know where he went?"

"Why should I tell you that?" the bartender replied. "If I tell you where he went and word gets back to Payson that I told you, why, my life wouldn't be worth a plugged nickel."

"It won't make any difference if word gets back to him," Matt said.

"Why would you say that?"

"Because I'm going to kill him."

"So you say. But people have been trying to kill him for a lot of years, and he ain't dead yet," the bartender said.

At that moment a boy, no older than twelve, came into the saloon.

"Here, what you doing here, boy?" the bartender scolded. "This is no place for kids."

"Is there a Mr. Matt Jensen in here?" the boy asked.

"I'm Matt Jensen," Matt said.

"He said if you don't come, he will shoot another one."

"What? Who said that? What do you mean, he will shoot another one?"

"Another kid," the boy said. "Like he shot me," the boy added in a voice that was strained with pain. It wasn't until then that Matt noticed the boy was holding his hand over his arm. Blood was just beginning to ooze through his fingers.

"Quick! Somebody get a doctor," Matt said. He pointed to the bartender. "You, give me a clean towel and a bottle of whiskey."

"What the hell?" the bartender said. "Who did this to you, kid? Who shot you?" the bartender asked as he pulled a clean towel from under the bar.

"Angus Boone shot me," the boy said. Matt was the first one to him, and he sat the boy down in a chair. "Boone is down at the school. Mr. Jensen, he said he was going to shoot someone every ten minutes until you come out into the street to meet him."

"Boone!" someone said. "Did you say Boone shot you?"

"Yes, sir. Angus Boone."

"That's the fella they call the Gravedigger," another said.

The boy looked at Matt. "He's callin' you out, Mr. Jensen. He said he would meet you in the middle of the street."

"You ain't a'goin' to do that, are you, Jensen?" one of the patrons asked. "I mean, this is Angus Boone we are talking 'bout. Nobody is crazy enough to go up against Angus Boone, face-to-face."

"Looks to me like Jensen don't have much choice," the bartender said. "If he don't, Boone will shoot another kid."

"Oh, I doubt that. Not even Boone is that mean."

"Yeah, he is that mean," Matt said as he poured whiskey onto the boy's wound, then wrapped the towel around it. "He shot this boy just to prove that he would do what he said he was going to do. What's your name, son?"

"Cole," the boy answered. "Cole Virdin."

"Cole, you are a brave young man," Matt said. The doctor arrived then, his rapid arrival facilitated by the fact that his office was just next door. He was walking quickly and carrying his bag.

"God in heaven," he said when he saw Cole. "What kind of mad man would shoot a boy?"

"It's Boone, Doc," one of the patrons told him. "Angus Boone. He's down at the school and he says he's goin' to shoot a kid ever' ten minutes unless Matt Jensen meets him on the street."

Matt pulled his pistol and checked all the chambers; then he put his pistol back in his holster.

"You aren't actually going to go out in the street and meet him, are you?" the doctor asked.

"Doesn't look to me as if I have any choice, unless you want to start treating a bunch of kids for gunshot wounds," Matt said. "And he might even kill the next one."

The doctor sighed. "You are right," he said. "I guess you've got to do it."

Matt smiled. "I was sort of hoping someone would talk me out of it," he said in an attempt at a joke. No one laughed.

Matt looked back at Cole. "Any of your family still at the school?" he asked.

"Yes, sir, my sister is," Cole answered.

"I hope your sister knows what a brave young man you are," Matt said.

Matt pushed through the batwing doors and walked outside. He started up the street toward the school, which was at the far end of the street from the saloon.

As soon as Matt left the saloon, several other patrons left as well, and they started running up the boardwalks along either side of the street, spreading the word.

"There's going to be a shoot-out!"

"Boone has called Matt Jensen out!"

"Boone and Jensen are meetin' head to head!"

The crowd of onlookers grew larger as Matt walked toward the school, though the spectators were all very careful to stay well back from the street.

"Boone!" Matt shouted. "Angus Boone!"

All eyes were on the school building at the far end of the street.

"Boone, it's Matt Jensen. You asked for me. Here I am!"

The front door of the schoolhouse opened, and Boone stepped out onto the front stoop. He stood there for a moment, then started walking toward Matt.

"Well," Boone said. "I've got to hand it to you, Jensen. I didn't think you would face me."

"You were shooting kids," Matt replied. "I didn't have much choice."

Boone chuckled. "Yeah, I thought that might get your attention."

"I have a question," Matt said.

"Go ahead and ask," Boone replied. "I wouldn't want to see a man die without getting his curiosity satisfied."

"Why?"

"Why what?"

"Why are you calling me out?" Matt asked. "Surely you aren't just trying to satisfy yourself that you are faster than I am."

"That question never crossed my mind," Boone replied. "I know I'm faster than you."

"Then why this?"

"You are looking for a man named Clyde Payson, aren't you?"

"Yes."

"Mr. Payson is paying me one thousand dollars to make sure you go away."

Matt whistled. "A thousand dollars?"

"A thousand dollars," Boone said.

"That's a lot of money. He must be running scared."

"I reckon you could say that he is running scared," Boone said. "You seem pretty determined to kill him. And from what I've heard, you have already taken care of several people he has sent out to stop you."

"That's right."

"And to think that it's all going to come to an end right here on Front Street in the little town of Salcedo," Boone said.

Matt had been watching Boone very closely, all the while monitoring half-a-dozen different things: the tone of his voice, the rhythm of his breathing, the look in his eyes, and the set of his shoulders. As a result, he was aware the instant Boone started his draw.

Matt started his draw at the same instant, and he had his pistol out and the hammer back by the time Boone had his own gun out. Matt pulled the trigger an instant before Boone, hitting Boone in the chest as Boone pulled the trigger on his gun.

Boone's shot went into the dirt. He tried to raise his gun hand for a second shot, but suddenly found that his arm weighed several hundred pounds. He dropped his gun into the dirt, slapped both hands over the wound, then sank to his knees.

"Who would have believed it?" he said aloud. He coughed, and his lips were spattered with blood. "Who would have . . . ?" He fell forward, facedown, into the street.

"Son of a bitch!" someone said loudly. "Did you see that? Son of a bitch!"

Matt stood over Boone's body for a long moment, making certain that he was dead, then kicking Boone's gun away. He returned his pistol to his holster and walked back to the saloon, trailed by half the town. He was followed into the saloon as well; then the tension broke as everyone started shouting at once, ordering drinks and giving eyewitness reports on what they had seen to other eyewitnesses who had seen the same thing.

"Where's the boy?" Matt asked the bartender. "Where's Cole?"

"The doc took him home," the bartender replied.

"Is he going to be all right?"

"The doc said he thought he would be."

"Good."

"I didn't think you could do it," the bartender said. "I seen it all through the window. I sure didn't think you could do it."

The bartender put a beer in front of Matt. "It's on the house," he said.

"Thanks," Matt said, lifting the beer to his lips.

"Dolores Mountains," the bartender said.

"What?"

"You're lookin' for Clyde Payson?"

"Yes."

"He has a cabin up in the Dolores Mountains, about ten miles east of here. Just follow Disappointment Creek until it ends. His cabin is the only one there."

"You are sure he's there?"

The bartender nodded. "Yes, I'm sure," he said. "He and Garvey hired our bouncer as a bodyguard."

"A bodyguard?"

"Yes. He has two bodyguards actually. Ben, who worked here as a bouncer, and a fella by the name of Elmer Gleeson. Gleeson used to be a deputy sheriff till he got hisself fired for stealin'."

"Gleeson sounds like Payson's kind of man," Matt said.

"Yeah, well, Ben ain't no better. I fired Ben for stealin' from drunks."

"I appreciate you telling me where to find him," Matt said.

"If I hadn't seen the way you handled Boone, I never would've told you. But I figure you might just be the kind who could handle Payson and his bodyguards. And if it turns out that you can't, well, just don't let him find out I'm the one who told you."

"He won't find out," Matt promised.

Chapter Twenty-seven

Ben Rogers and Elmer Gleeson were standing at the last bend in the creek when they saw the rider approaching.

"Who's that comin'?" Gleeson asked, cocking the rifle and lifting it to his shoulder.

"No, no, hold your fire," Ben said. "That's Lew. He's bringin' us provisions."

Gleeson nodded and lowered his rifle. They watched Lew as he rode in. He nodded to them, then proceeded on up to the little cabin that was some fifty yards back from where the lookouts were stationed.

Garvey opened the door to the cabin and let Lew in. Payson was lying on one of the bunks with his hands laced behind his head.

"Did you bring whiskey and vittles?" Payson asked.

"Yeah, it's all in this rucksack," Lew said.

"How much?"

"Twenty dollars?"

"Twenty dollars?" Payson said angrily, sitting up quickly. "What do you mean twenty dollars? You can't have more'n five dollars worth of goods in that sack."

"Five dollars in town, twenty dollars out here," Lew said.

"When this is all over, there's goin' to be some settlin' up done," Payson said. "You understand me? There's goin' to be some settlin' up."

"Yeah, I understand you," Lew said.

"What's happenin' with Boone and Jensen?" Payson asked. "Have you heard anything?"

"No."

"You will soon," Payson said.

"And once Boone kills Jensen, we'll be taking care of people who tried to cheat us," Garvey said, glaring at Lew.

"You want the vittles and whiskey or not?" Lew asked.

"I asked you to bring 'em out here, didn't I?"

"Twenty dollars," Lew said again.

"Give him twenty dollars, Garvey," Payson said.

"We ain't got hardly any money left," Garvey complained.

"Give him twenty dollars," Payson said again. "Right now, we got no other choice." He pointed to Lew. "I will remember this," he said.

Lew took the twenty dollars, then remounted and started out of the little valley. Ben and Gleeson waved at him as he passed, and he stopped to speak to them.

"You boys here protecting Payson, are you?" he asked.

"No, we're just out here fishing," Ben answered, and Gleeson chuckled.

"Well, you can tease if you like, but I'd sure as hell never put my life on the line for any son of a bitch like Payson."

"Ha! We're just here to collect the money is all," Gleeson said. "Haven't you heard? Boone is goin' after this Matt Jensen fella. Once Boone gets done with him, our job will be over."

"Once Boone gets done with him, huh?" Lew said. He laughed.

"What is it? What are you laughing about?"

"Matt Jensen killed Boone in a shoot-out this morning."

"What? Impossible! I don't believe it. Who told you that?"

"Nobody told me," Lew said. "I seen it myself. They faced each other on the street, Boone went for his gun first, and Jensen still beat him. Killed him with one shot."

"What the hell? What kind of man is this Matt Jensen?" Ben asked.

"He's not the kind you want to mess with," Lew said. "Especially for some son of a bitch like Payson."

"You know what, Gleeson, he's right," Ben said. "What are we doing out here?"

"We can't leave now, we haven't been paid yet," Gleeson replied.

"What good is the money going to do us if we're dead?" Ben asked. "And even if he don't kill us, he'll kill Payson. How are we going to collect from a dead man?"

Gleeson looked back toward the cabin, then over toward the horses. He nodded. "You're right," he said. "Let's get the hell out of here."

From his position on a hill, looking down at the head of Disappointment Creek, Matt watched the brief confab between Lew, Ben, and Gleeson. Then he saw Ben and Gleeson go over to their horses, mount them, and ride away with Lew. That left the cabin undefended, except for whoever was inside.

"Jerky and hardtack," Garvey complained. "We paid twenty dollars for jerky and hardtack."

"It'll keep us from starvin' to death," Payson said. "And

we won't have to be here much longer. I figure Boone is going to kill Jensen pretty soon now; then it'll all be over."

"What if Jensen kills Boone?"

Payson laughed. "Are you joking? There's not a man alive who could kill Boone."

"Yeah, well, that's good for us now," Garvey said. "But what are we going to do when Boone comes after us wantin' his thousand dollars?"

"I've got a thousand dollars," Payson said.

"What? Where did you get a thousand dollars?"

"You remember the bank we robbed back in Cedar Creek?"

"Yes, of course I remember."

"I held a thousand dollars back from the split."

"What? You mean you cheated the rest of us?" Garvey said angrily.

"Hold on, hold on there!" Payson said, holding up his hand. "I held it back for an emergency," he said. "This is an emergency. If I didn't have the money, Boone would kill us both."

Garvey paused for a moment, then he nodded. "Yeah," he said. "Yeah, I guess you're right."

"Damn right I'm right." Payson took a strip of jerky, then cut it lengthwise into two pieces. "Take this out to Ben and Gleeson."

Nodding, Garvey took the two strips of dried meat, then started up the creek bank toward the bend where the two guards had been posted. When he didn't find them where he expected them to be, he looked around for a moment, then called out to them.

"Ben! Gleeson! I've got your lunch here!" he shouted. "Ben! Gleeson! Where are you? Why aren't you where you are supposed to be?"

"They've run out on you, Garvey!" Matt called.

"What? Who's there?"

Matt stood up on the rock, then looked down at Garvey.

"You know who I am," Matt said. "I've changed a little since the last time you saw me, but you know who I am."

"No!" Garvey shouted in terror. He turned and started running back toward the cabin. "He's here! He's here!" he shouted. "Payson, he's here! Matt Jensen is here!"

Matt climbed down from the hill, then walked, almost casually, toward the cabin. He heard the glass break, then saw a rifle stick out through the window. The rifle barked, and a bullet whizzed by. Matt jumped down behind a rock outcropping.

Matt fired at the cabin a couple of times. Then he followed a ravine that took him around behind the cabin. He heard periodic firing coming from the cabin, and realized that they were still shooting at the rock where he had been.

When he reached the back of the cabin, he crept up to the back door. There were no windows back here, so he knew he couldn't be seen.

"What happened to the son of a bitch?" he heard one voice ask. "Where did he go?"

"He's still behind that rock," the other voice answered.

"How come he ain't showed hisself?"

"He's waitin' for us."

"Yeah? Well, the son of a bitch can wait till hell freezes over. We got enough vittles and water to wait him out."

"We just goin' to stay here?"

"You want to go out, you go out. I'm just going to stay here. Hell, there's two of us, and only one of him. We can take turns sleeping, he can't. We got the advantage."

"Yeah," the other voice said. "Yeah, you're right. We'll just wait him out."

Matt jumped up to grab the eaves that protruded just over the door. Then, using them as the pivot point, he swung out, then back in, bending his legs at the knees as he did so. He thrust his legs forward, and kicked the door open.

"What the hell!" Payson shouted, turning around.

"Drop it!" Matt said, pointing his gun at the two men. "Both of you!"

Payson dropped his gun and Garvey followed suit.

"Now what?" Payson asked. "Are you going to shoot us?"

"I had planned on it," Matt replied. "But shooting you is too good for you. I think I'd rather take you back and watch you hang."

"It's a long way back," Payson said. "Do you expect us to just go along quietly?"

"Whether you go quietly or not, it makes no difference to me," Matt said.

"It makes no difference, huh?" Payson said. "Well, maybe there's something you haven't thought about. You've got to sleep sometime. What makes you think we won't run away?"

"Good question," Matt said.

Suddenly, and totally unexpectedly, Matt fired two shots, hitting each man in the knee. They cried out in shock and pain, and started hobbling around.

"You crazy sonofabitch, you shot us in the knee!" Payson said.

"Yeah, I did," Matt answered calmly. "Let's get going now."

County Courthouse, Cedar Creek, Colorado

"Here ye, hear ye, hear ye! The sentencing is about to be announced. All rise for the Honorable Felix J. Crane, pre-sidin'," the bailiff shouted. "Everybody stand respectful."

The Honorable Felix J. Crane came out of a back room. After taking his seat at the bench, he adjusted the glasses on the end of his nose, then cleared his throat.

"Would the bailiff please bring the accused before the bench?"

The bailiff, who was leaning against the side wall, spat a quid of tobacco into the brass spittoon, then walked over to the table where the defendants, Clyde Payson and Garvey Laird, sat next to their court-appointed lawyer.

"Get up, you two," he growled. "Present yourself before the judge."

Payson and Garvey were handcuffed, and had shackles on their ankles. They limped up to stand, as best they could on busted knees, in front of the judge.

"You two have been tried by a jury of your peers, and found guilty of the murders of Miss Margaret Miller, a beloved teacher of our children, as well as little Holly McGee, one of her students. For these two murders, you are sentenced to hang by your neck until you are dead," Judge Crane said. He cleared his throat, then looked over at Matt Jensen, who was present in the courtroom.

"Mr. Jensen, I regret that we could not find these two despicable creatures guilty of the murder of your family. While I have no doubt as to your veracity, the court has only your account of the incident, and that account is your memory from when you were nine years old. However, though we could not find them guilty for that particular crime, I hope you can find some comfort in knowing that these two men will hang. And they will hang because you have brought them to justice."

"I am satisfied, Your Honor," Matt said. He looked at Payson and Garvey. "You two will be dead," he said. "And dead is dead."

"You go to hell, Matt Jensen!" Payson shouted. "Do you hear me? You go to hell!"

"Silence that man!" Judge Crane said, banging his gavel.

The bailiff signaled two deputies, and they stepped up quickly to gag Payson.

"It is interesting that you would mention hell, Mr. Payson," Judge Crane said. "Because, although I do not have the power to sentence you to hell, I will soon be passing you on to a higher judge who does have that power. And there is no doubt in my mind but that you will suffer eternal torment for the misery you have caused others during your stay on earth.

"This court is adjourned."

As Matt rode away from Cedar Creek, he felt a sense of closing the book on the part of his life that he had shared with his mother, father, and sister.

"Pa," he said, speaking aloud. "I hope you know that I meant no disrespect to you by droppin' your name and takin' up the name of Jensen. Finding the son of a bitch that killed you, Ma, and Cassie gives me some rest now, and I hope it does for you as well."

It was getting colder, and Spirit blew clouds of vapor that drifted away in feathery wisps. Matt headed south. He didn't care much for the cold.

J. A. Johnstone on William W. Johnstone:
"When the Truth Becomes Legend"

William W. Johnstone was born in southern Missouri, the youngest of four children. He was raised with strong moral and family values by his minister father, and tutored by his schoolteacher mother. Despite this, he quit school at age fifteen.

"I have the highest respect for education," he says, "but such is the folly of youth, and wanting to see the world beyond the four walls and the blackboard." True to this vow, Bill attempted to enlist in the French Foreign Legion ("I saw Gary Cooper in *Beau Geste* when I was a kid and I thought the French Foreign Legion would be fun") but was rejected, thankfully, for being underage. Instead, he joined a traveling carnival and did all kinds of odd jobs. It was listening to the veteran carny folk, some of whom had been on the circuit since the late 1800s, telling amazing tales about their experiences which planted the storytelling seed in Bill's imagination.

"They were honest people, despite the bad reputation traveling carny shows had back then," Bill remembers. "Of course, there were exceptions. There was one guy named Picky, who got that name because he was a master pickpocket. He could steal a man's socks right off his feet without him knowing. Believe me, Picky got us chased out of more than a few towns."

After a few months of this grueling existence, Bill returned home and finished high school. Next came stints as a deputy sheriff in the Tallulah, LA. Sheriff's Department, followed by a hitch in the U.S. Army. Then he began a career in radio broadcasting at KTLD in Tallulah, Louisiana, that would last sixteen years. It was here that he fine-tuned his storytelling skills. He turned to writing in 1970, but it wouldn't be until 1979 until his first novel, *The Devil's Kiss*, was published. Thus began the full-time writing career of William W. Johnstone. He wrote horror (*The Uninvited*), thrillers (*The Last of the Dog Team*), even a romance novel or two. Then, in February 1983, *Out of the Ashes* was published. Searching for his missing family in the aftermath of a post-apocalyptic America, rebel mercenary and patriot Ben Raines is united with the civilians of the Resistance forces and moves to the forefront of a revolution for the nation's future.

Out of the Ashes was a smash. The series would continue for the next twenty years, winning Bill three generations of fans all over the world. The series was often imitated but never duplicated. "We all tried to copy *The Ashes* series," said one publishing executive, "but Bill's uncanny ability, both then and now, to predict in which direction the political winds were blowing, brought a dead-on timeliness to the table no one else could capture." *The Ashes* series would end its run with more than thirty-four books and twenty million copies in print, making it one of the most successful men's action series in American book publishing. (*The Ashes* series also, Bill notes with a touch of pride, got him on the FBI's Watch List for its less than flattering portrayal of spineless politicians and the growing power of big government over our lives, among other things. "In that respect," says collaborator J. A. Johnstone, "Bill was years ahead of his time.")

Always steps ahead of the political curve, Bill's recent thrillers, written with J. A. Johnstone, include *Vengeance Is Mine, Invasion USA, Border War, Jackknife, Remember the Alamo, Home Invasion, Phoenix Rising, The Blood of Patriots, The Bleeding Edge,* and the upcoming *Suicide Mission.*

It is with the Western, though, that Bill found his greatest success and propelled him onto both the *USA Today* and *New York Times* bestseller lists.

Bill's western series, co-authored by J. A. Johnstone, include *The Mountain Man, Matt Jensen the Last Mountain Man, Preacher, The Family Jensen, Luke Jensen Bounty Hunter, Eagles, MacCallister* (an *Eagles* spin-off), *Sidewinders, The Brothers O'Brien, Sixkiller, Blood Bond, The Last Gunfighter,* and the upcoming new series *Flintlock* and *The Trail West.* Coming in May 2013 is the hardcover western *Butch Cassidy, The Lost Years.*

"The Western," Bill says, "is one of the few true art forms that is one hundred percent American. I liken the Western as America's version of England's Arthurian legends, like the Knights of the Round Table or Robin Hood and his Merry Men. Starting with the 1902 publication of *The Virginian* by Owen Wister, and followed by the greats like Zane Grey, Max Brand, Ernest Haycox, and of course Louis L'Amour, the Western has helped to shape define the cultural landscape of America.

"I'm no goggle-eyed college academic, so when my fans ask me why the Western is as popular now as it was a century ago, I don't offer a 200-page thesis. Instead, I can only offer this: The Western is honest. In this great country, which is suffering under the yoke of political correctness, the Western harks back to an era when justice was sure and swift. Steal a man's horse, rustle his cattle, rob a bank, a stagecoach, or a train, you were hunted down and fitted with a hangman's noose. One size fit all.

"Sure, we westerners are prone to a little embellishment and exaggeration and, I admit it, occasionally play a little fast and loose with the facts. But we do so for a very good reason—to enhance the enjoyment of readers.

"It was Owen Wister, in *The Virginian* who first coined the phrase '*When you call me that, smile.*' Legend has it that Wister actually heard those words spoken by a deputy sheriff in Medicine Bow, Wyoming, when another poker player called him a son-of-a-bitch.

"Did it really happen, or is it one of those myths that have passed down from one generation to the next? I honestly don't know. But there's a line in one of my favorite Westerns of all time, *The Man who Shot Liberty Valance*, where the newspaper editor tells the young reporter, 'When the truth becomes legend, print the legend.'

"These are the words I live by."

Turn the page for an exciting preview!

The Family Jensen
HARD RIDE TO HELL

by
USA TODAY BESTSELLING AUTHORS
William W. Johnstone
with J. A. Johnstone

The Epic New Series from the authors of
The Mountain Man

The Jensen clan is William W. Johnstone's epic creation—
God-fearing pioneers bound by blood on an untamed
and beautiful land. Once more, Preacher, Smoke,
and Matt are reunited in a clash of cultures and
a brutal all-out fight for justice. . . .

HELL TO PAY

Smoke Jensen and his adopted son Matt are cooling
their heels in Colorado when they are called to the Dakotas.
Preacher, the legendary mountain man, is in the midst of
a vicious struggle. Someone has kidnapped a proud Indian
chief's daughter and grandchild. When the kidnapping
turns to murder, and Preacher vanishes after clashing
with a ruthless Union colonel turned railroad king,
Matt sets out to infiltrate the Colonel's gang of killers;
Smoke seeks out the only honest citizens in the crooked
town of Hammerhead. It will take brave men to blow
Hammerhead wide open and force the Colonel and
his gunmen on a hard ride into a killing ground.

And the Family Jensen will make sure there is hell to pay . . .

On sale May 2013, wherever Pinnacle Books are sold!

Chapter One

The two men stood facing each other. One was red, the other white, but both were tall and lean, and the stiff, wary stance in which they held themselves belied their advanced years. They were both ready for trouble, and they didn't care who knew it.

Both wore buckskins, as well, and their faces were lined and leathery from long decades spent out in the weather. Silver and white streaked their hair.

The white man had a gun belt strapped around his waist, with a holstered Colt revolver riding on each hip. His thumbs were hooked in the belt close to each holster, and you could tell by looking at him that he was ready to hook and draw. Given the necessity, his hands would flash to the well-worn walnut butts of those guns with blinding speed, especially for a man of his age.

He wasn't the only one with a menacing attitude. The Indian had his hand near the tomahawk that was thrust behind the sash at his waist. To anyone watching, it would appear that both of these men were ready to try to kill each other.

Then a grin suddenly stretched across the whiskery face of the white man, and he said, "Two Bears, you old red heathen."

"Preacher, you pale-faced scoundrel," Two Bears replied. He smiled, too, and stepped forward. The two men clasped each other in a rough embrace and slapped each other on the back.

The large group of warriors standing nearby visibly relaxed at this display of affection between the two men. For the most part, the Assiniboine had been friendly with white men for many, many years. But even so, it wasn't that common for a white man to come riding boldly into their village as the one called Preacher had done.

Some of the men smiled now, because they had known all along what was coming. The legendary mountain man Preacher, who was famous—or in some cases infamous— from one end of the frontier to the other, had been friends with their chief Two Bears for more than three decades, and he had visited the village on occasion in the past.

The two men hadn't always been so cordial with each other. They had started out as rivals for the affections of the beautiful Assiniboine woman Raven's Wing. For Two Bears, that rivalry had escalated to the point of bitter hostility.

All that had been put aside when it became necessary for them to join forces to rescue Raven's Wing from a group of brutal kidnappers and gunrunners.* Since that long-ago time when they were forced to become allies, they had gradually become friends as well.

Preacher stepped back and rested his hands on Two Bears's shoulders.

*See the novel *Preacher's Fury*

"I hear that Raven's Wing has passed," he said solemnly.

"Yes, last winter," Two Bears replied with an equally grave nod. "It was her time. She left this world peacefully, with a smile on her face."

"That's good to hear," Preacher said. "I never knew a finer lady."

"I miss her. Every time the sun rises or sets, every time the wind blows, every time I hear a wolf howl or see a bird soaring through the sky, I long to be with her again. But when the day is done and we are to be together again, we will be. This I know in my heart. Until then . . ." Two Bears smiled again. "Until then I can still see her in the fine strong sons she bore me, and the daughters who have given me grandchildren." He nodded toward a young woman standing nearby, who stood with an infant in her arms. "You remember my youngest daughter, Wildflower?"

"I do," Preacher said, "although the last time I saw her, I reckon she wasn't much bigger'n that sprout with her."

"My grandson," Two Bears said proudly. "Little Hawk."

Preacher took off his battered, floppy-brimmed felt hat and nodded politely to the woman.

"Wildflower," he said. "It's good to see you again." He looked at the boy. "And howdy to you, too, Little Hawk."

The baby didn't respond to Preacher, of course, but he watched the mountain man with huge, dark eyes.

"He has not seen that many white men in his life," Two Bears said. "You look strange, even to one so young."

Preacher snorted and said, "If it wasn't for this beard of mine, I'd look just about as much like an Injun as any of you do."

Two Bears half-turned and motioned to one of the lodges.

"Come. We will go to my lodge and smoke a pipe and talk. I would know what brings you to our village, Preacher."

"Horse, the same as usual," Preacher said as he jerked a thumb over his shoulder toward the big gray stallion that stood with his reins dangling. A large, wolflike cur sat on his haunches next to the stallion.

"How many horses called Horse and dogs called Dog have you had in your life, Preacher?" Two Bears asked with amusement sparkling in his eyes.

"Too many to count, I reckon," Preacher replied. "But I figure if a name works just fine once, there ain't no reason it won't work again."

"How do you keep finding them?"

"It ain't so much me findin' them as it is them findin' me. Somehow they just show up. I'd call it fate, if I believed in such a thing."

"You do not believe in fate?"

"I believe in hot lead and cold steel," Preacher said. "Anything beyond that's just a guess."

Preacher didn't have any goal in visiting the Assiniboine village other than visiting an old friend. He had been drifting around the frontier for more than fifty years now, most of the time without any plan other than seeing what was on the far side of the hill.

When he had first set out from his folks' farm as a boy, the West had been a huge, relatively empty place, populated only by scattered bands of Indians and a handful of white fur trappers. At that time less than ten years had gone by since Lewis and Clark returned from their epic, history-changing journey up the Missouri River to the Pacific.

During the decades since then, Preacher had seen the West's population grow tremendously. Rail lines criss-crossed the country, and there were cities, towns, and settlements almost everywhere. Civilization had come to the frontier.

Much of the time, Preacher wasn't a hundred percent sure if that was a good thing or not.

But there was no taking it back, no returning things to the way they used to be, and besides, if not for the great westward expansion that had fundamentally changed the face of the nation, he never would have met the two fine young men he had come to consider his sons: Smoke and Matt Jensen.

It had been a while since Preacher had seen Smoke and Matt. He assumed that Smoke was down in Colorado, on his ranch called the Sugarloaf near the town of Big Rock. Once wrongly branded an outlaw, Smoke Jensen was perhaps the fastest man with a gun to ever walk the West. Most of the time he didn't go looking for trouble, but it seemed to find him anyway, despite all his best intentions to live a peaceful life on his ranch with his beautiful, spirited wife, Sally.

There was no telling where Matt was. He could be anywhere from the Rio Grande to the Canadian border. He and Smoke weren't brothers by blood. The bond between them was actually deeper than that. Matt had been born Matt Cavanaugh, but he had taken the name Jensen as a young man to honor Smoke, who had helped out an orphaned boy and molded him into a fine man.

Since Matt had set out on his own, he had been a drifter, scouting for the army, working as a stagecoach guard, pinning on a badge a few times as a lawman. . . . As long as it kept him on the move and held a promise of possible adventure, that was all it took to keep Matt interested in a job, at least for a while. But he never stayed in one place for very long, and at this point in his life he had no interest in putting down roots, as Smoke had done.

Because of that, Matt actually had more in common with Preacher than Smoke did, but all three of them were close. The problem was, whenever they got together trouble seemed to follow, and it usually wasn't long before the air had the smell of gunsmoke in it.

Right now the only smoke in Two Bears's lodge came from the small fire in the center of it and the pipe that Preacher and the Assiniboine chief passed back and forth. The two men were silent, their friendship not needing words all the time.

Two women were in the lodge as well, preparing a meal. They were Two Bears's wives, the former wives of his brothers he had taken in when the women were widowed, as a good brother was expected to do. The smells coming from the pot they had on the fire were mighty appetizing, Preacher thought. The stew was bound to be good.

A swift rataplan of hoofbeats came from outside and made both Preacher and Two Bears raise their heads. Neither man seemed alarmed. As seasoned veterans of the frontier, they had too much experience for that. But they also knew that whenever someone was moving fast, there was a chance it was because of trouble.

The sudden babble of voices that followed the abrupt halt of the hoofbeats seemed to indicate the same thing.

"You want to go see what that's about?" Preacher asked Two Bears, inclining his head toward the lodge's entrance.

Two Bears took another unhurried puff on the pipe in his hands before he set it aside.

"If my people wish to see me, they know where I am to be found," he said.

Preacher couldn't argue with that. But the sounds had gotten his curiosity stirred up, so he was glad when someone thrust aside the buffalo hide flap over the lodge's entrance. A broad-shouldered, powerful-looking warrior strode into the lodge, then stopped short at the sight of a white man sitting there cross-legged beside the fire with the chief.

"Two Bears, I must speak with you," the newcomer said.

"This is Standing Rock," Two Bears said to Preacher. "He is married to my daughter Wildflower."

That would make him the father of the little fella Preacher had seen with Wildflower earlier. He nodded and said, "Howdy, Standing Rock."

The warrior just looked annoyed, like he wasn't interested in introductions right now. He looked at the chief and began, "Two Bears—"

"Is there trouble?"

"Blue Bull has disappeared."

Chapter Two

Blue Bull, it turned out, wasn't a bull at all, not that Preacher really thought he was. That was the name of one of the Assiniboine warriors who belonged to this band, and he and Standing Rock were good friends.

They had been out hunting in the hills west of the village and had split up when Blue Bull decided to follow the tracks of a small antelope herd while Standing Rock took another path. They had agreed to meet back at the spot where Blue Bull had taken up the antelope trail.

When Standing Rock returned there later, he saw no sign of Blue Bull. A couple of hours passed, and Blue Bull still didn't show up. Growing worried that something might have happened to his friend, Standing Rock went to look for him.

This part of the country was peaceful for the most part, but a man alone who ran into a mountain lion or a bear might be in for trouble. Also, ravines cut across the landscape in places, and if a pony shied at the wrong time, its rider could be tossed off and fall into one of those deep, rugged gullies.

"You were unable to find him?" Two Bears asked when his son-in-law paused in the story.

"The antelope tracks led into a narrow canyon, and so did

Blue Bull's," Standing Rock replied. "The ground was rocky, and I lost the trail."

The young warrior wore a surly expression. Preacher figured that he didn't like admitting failure. Standing Rock was a proud man. You could tell that just by looking at him.

But he was genuinely worried about his friend, too. He proved that by saying, "I came back to get more men, so we can search for him. He may be hurt."

Two Bears nodded and got to his feet.

"Gather a dozen men," he ordered crisply. "We will ride in search of Blue Bull while there is still light."

Preacher stood up, too, and said, "I'll come with you."

"This is a matter for the Assiniboine," Standing Rock said, his voice stiff with dislike. Preacher didn't understand it, but the young fella definitely hadn't taken a shine to him. Just the opposite, in fact.

"Preacher is a friend to the Assiniboine and has been for more years than you have been walking this earth, Standing Rock," Two Bears snapped. "I would not ask him to involve himself in our trouble, but if he wishes to, I will not deny him."

"I just want to lend a hand if I can," Preacher said as he looked at Standing Rock. He didn't really care if the young man liked him or not. His friendship for Two Bears and for Two Bears's people was the only things that really mattered to him here.

Standing Rock didn't say anything else. He just stared back coldly at Preacher for a second, then turned and left the lodge to gather the search party as Two Bears had told him to.

The chief looked at Preacher and said, "The hot blood of young men sometimes overpowers what should be the coolness of their thoughts."

"That's fine with me, old friend. Like I said, I just want to help."

As they left the lodge, Preacher pointed to the big cur that had come with him to the village and went on, "Dog there is about as good a tracker as you're ever gonna find. When we get to the spot where Standin' Rock lost the trail, if you've got something that belonged to Blue Bull we can give Dog the scent and he's liable to lead us right to him."

Two Bears nodded.

"I will speak to Blue Bull's wife and make sure we take something of his with us."

Several of the warriors were getting ready to ride. That didn't take much preparation, considering that all they had to do was throw blankets over their ponies' backs and rig rope halters. Preacher had planned to spend a few days in the Assiniboine village, but he hadn't unsaddled Horse yet so the stallion was ready to go as well.

The news of Blue Bull's disappearance had gotten around the village. A lot of people were standing nearby with worried looks on their faces as the members of the search party mounted up. Two Bears went over to talk to one of the women, who hurried off to a lodge and came back with a buckskin shirt. She was Blue Bull's wife, Preacher figured, and the garment belonged to the missing warrior.

Two Bears swung up onto his pony with the lithe ease of a man considerably younger than he really was. He gave a curt nod, and the search party set out from the village with the chief, Standing Rock, and Preacher in the lead.

Standing Rock pointed out the route for them, and they lost no time in riding into the hills where the two warriors had been hunting. Preacher glanced at the sky and saw that they had about three hours of daylight left. He hoped that would be enough time to find Blue Bull.

Of course, it was possible that nothing bad had happened

to Blue Bull at all, Preacher reflected. The warrior could have gotten carried away in pursuit of the antelope and lost track of the time. They might even run into him on his way back to the village. If that happened, Preacher would be glad that everything had turned out well.

Something was stirring in his guts, though, some instinctive warning that told him they might not be so lucky. Over the years Preacher had learned to trust those hunches. At this point, he wasn't going to say anything to Two Bears, Standing Rock, or the other Assiniboine, but he had a bad feeling about this search for Blue Bull.

Standing Rock pointed out the tracks of the antelope herd when the search party reached them.

"You can see they lead higher into the hills," he said. "Blue Bull followed them while I went to the north. He wanted to bring one of the antelope back to the village."

"Why did you not go with him?" Two Bears asked. "Why did you go north?"

Standing Rock looked sullen again as he replied, "I know a valley up there where the antelope like to graze. I thought they might circle back to it."

Two Bears just nodded, but Preacher knew that his old friend was just as aware as he was of what had really happened here. Standing Rock had thought he could beat Blue Bull to the antelope by going a different way. Such rivalry was not uncommon among friends.

"Did you see the antelope?" Two Bears asked.

Standing Rock shook his head.

"No. My thought proved to be wrong."

Two Bears's silence in response was as meaningful and damning as anything he could have said. Standing Rock angrily jerked his pony into motion and trotted away, following the same path as the antelope had earlier.

Preacher, Two Bears, and the rest of the search party

went the same way at a slower pace. Quietly, Two Bears said, "If anything happened to Blue Bull, Standing Rock will believe that it was his fault for not going with his friend."

"He wants to impress you, don't he?" Preacher said. "Must not be easy, bein' married to the chief's daughter."

"He is a good warrior, but he does not always know that."

Preacher nodded in understanding. He had always possessed confidence in himself and his abilities, and he had learned not to second-guess the decisions he made. But he had seen doubts consume other men from the inside until there was nothing left of them but empty shells.

Eventually Standing Rock settled down a little and slowed enough for the rest of the search party to catch up to him. The antelope herd had followed a twisting path into the hills, and so had Blue Bull as he trailed them. Preacher had no trouble picking out the unshod hoofprints of the warrior's pony.

The slopes became steeper, the landscape more rugged. In the distance, the snow-capped peaks of the Rocky Mountains loomed, starkly beautiful in the light from the lowering sun. They were dozens of miles away, even though they looked almost close enough to reach out and touch. Preacher knew that Blue Bull's trail wouldn't lead that far.

The tracks brought them to a long, jagged ridge that was split by a canyon cutting through it. Standing Rock reined his pony to a halt and pointed to the opening.

"That is where Blue Bull went," he said. "The tracks vanished on the rocks inside the canyon."

"Did you follow it to the other end?" Two Bears asked.

"I did. But the tracks of Blue Bull's pony did not come out."

"A man cannot go into a place and not come out of it, one way or another."

Standing Rock looked a little offended at Two Bears for pointing that out, thought Preacher, but he wasn't going to say anything. For one thing, Two Bears was the chief, and for another, he was Standing Rock's father-in-law.

"Let's have a look," Preacher suggested. "We can give Dog a whiff of Blue Bull's shirt. He ought to be able to tell us where the fella went."

The big cur had bounded along happily beside Preacher and Horse during the search. He still had the exuberance of youth, dashing off several times to chase after small animals.

They rode on to the canyon entrance, where they stopped to peer at the ground. The surface had already gotten quite rocky, so the tracks weren't as easy to see as they had been. But Preacher noticed something immediately.

"Some of those antelope tracks are headed back out of the canyon," he said to Two Bears. "The critters went in there, then turned around and came out. They were in a hurry, too. Something must've spooked 'em."

Standing Rock said, "There are many antelope in these hills. Perhaps the tracks going the other direction were made at another time."

Preacher swung down from the saddle and knelt to take a closer look at the hoofprints. After a moment of study, he shook his head.

"They look the same to me," he said. "I think they were all made today, comin' and goin'."

He knew that wasn't going to make Standing Rock like him any better, but he was going to tell things the way he saw them to Two Bears. He had always been honest with his old friend and saw no need to change that policy now.

"What about the tracks of Blue Bull's pony?" Two Bears asked.

"He went on into the canyon," Preacher said. "Can't see that he came back out, so I agree with Standin' Rock on that.

The way it looks to me, Blue Bull followed those antelope here and rode up in time to see 'em come boltin' back out. He was curious and wanted to see what stampeded 'em like that. So he rode in to find out."

"It must have been a bear," Standing Rock said. "Blue Bull would not have been so foolish."

"Blue Bull has always been curious," Two Bears said. "I can imagine him doing as Preacher has said." He looked at the mountain man. "As you would say, old friend, there is one way to find out."

"Yep," Preacher agreed. "Let Dog have Blue Bull's scent. If there's anybody who can lead us right to him, it's that big, shaggy varmint."

Chapter Three

Two Bears took out the shirt Blue Bull's wife had given him from the pouch where he had put it and handed it to Preacher. Preacher called Dog to him, knelt beside the big cur, and let Dog get a good whiff of the shirt.

"Find the fella who wore this," Preacher said. "Find him!"

Dog ran into the canyon, pausing about fifty yards in to look back at Preacher, and then resuming the hunt.

Preacher swung up onto Horse's back and nodded to Two Bears.

"He's got the scent. All we have to do is follow him."

They rode into the canyon, moving fairly rapidly to keep up with Dog. Now that they were relying on Dog's sense of smell rather than trying to follow tracks, they could set a slightly faster pace.

The canyon was about fifty yards wide, with rocky walls that were too steep for a horse to climb, although a man might be able to. Although there were places, Preacher noted, where the walls had collapsed partially and horses might be able to pick their way up and down as long as they were careful.

Preacher frowned slightly as he spotted a shiny place on

a flat rock. The mark was small, barely noticeable. Preacher knew that the most likely explanation for it was that a shod hoof had nicked the rock in the fairly recent past. Blue Bull, like the rest of the Assiniboine, would have been riding an unshod pony when he came through here.

So another rider, most likely a white man, had been in the canyon recently. Preacher couldn't be sure it was today, but the evidence pointed in that direction. The antelope herd had started through the canyon, only to encounter a man on horseback. That had startled the animals into bolting back the way they had come from.

Then, Blue Bull's curiosity aroused by the behavior of the antelope, the Assiniboine warrior had ridden into the canyon as well, and . . .

Preacher couldn't finish that thought. He had no way of knowing what had happened then. Blue Bull could have run into the same hombre. There might have even been more than one man riding through the canyon.

This was Indian land, maybe not by treaty but by tradition, and the ranchers in the area had always respected that because of the long history of peace between the whites and the Assiniboine. They had never stopped white men from crossing their hunting grounds, as long as everyone treated each other with respect. It was possible some cattle had strayed up here from one of the ranches, and cowboys from that spread had come to look for the missing stock.

However, that bad feeling still lurked in Preacher's gut. It grew even stronger when he saw Dog veer toward a cluster of rocks at the base of one of those caved-in places along the canyon's left-hand wall. There was no hesitation about the big cur's movements. He went straight to the rocks and started nosing around and pawing at them.

"Your animal has lost the scent," Standing Rock said. "There is nothing there."

"We better take a closer look," Preacher said. He glanced over at Two Bears, who nodded. The chief's face was set in grim lines, and Preacher knew that his old friend had a bad feeling about this situation, too.

The search party rode over to the side of the canyon. Nothing was visible except a pile of loose, broken rocks, some of them pretty big, but the way Dog continued to paw at the stones told Preacher most of what he needed to know.

"Move those rocks," Two Bears ordered.

"But—" Standing Rock began. He fell silent when Two Bears gave him a hard look. Scowling, Standing Rock dismounted. He went to the rocks and started lifting them and tossing them aside. Several other warriors got down from their ponies and moved to help him.

They hadn't been working for very long before Standing Rock suddenly let out a startled exclamation and stepped back sharply as if he had just uncovered a rattlesnake.

Preacher leaned forward in the saddle to peer into the jumble of stone. He had a pretty good idea it wasn't a snake that Standing Rock had come across.

It was a foot.

Visible from the ankle down, the foot had a moccasin on it. The rest of the leg to which it was attached was hidden under the rocks.

The other warriors had recoiled from the grim discovery as well. Curtly, Two Bears ordered them to get back to moving the rocks. They did so with obvious reluctance.

Everybody knew what they were going to find. It didn't take long to uncover the rest of the body. It belonged to a young Assiniboine warrior. The rock slide that had covered him up had done quite a bit of damage to his features, but he was still recognizable. Standing Rock said in a voice choked with emotion, "It is Blue Bull."

"He must have been standing here when those rocks fell on him and killed him," one of the other men said.

"Why did he not get out of the way?" another man wanted to know.

"There must not have been time," Standing Rock said. "My . . . my friend . . ."

Deep creases appeared in Preacher's forehead as the mountain man frowned. He said to Two Bears, "Somethin' ain't right here. You mind if I take a closer look?"

"Go ahead," the chief said with a nod.

Preacher dismounted and approached the dead man. Standing Rock turned to face him. The warrior's stubborn expression made it clear he didn't want Preacher disturbing his friend's body. Like all the other tribes, the Assiniboine had their own rituals and customs for dealing with death.

"Standing Rock," Two Bears said. "Step aside."

"I won't do anything to dishonor Blue Bull," Preacher said to Standing Rock. "It's just that I don't think this is what it seems to be. Look at how he's layin' on his back with his head toward the wall and his feet toward the middle of the canyon."

"That means nothing," Standing Rock snapped.

"I think it does," Preacher said. "Let's say he came over here and was standin' facin' the wall for some reason. When those rocks came down on top of him, likely they would've knocked him facedown. If he heard the rocks start to fall and turned to try to run, not only would he be facedown, his head would be pointed toward the middle of the canyon."

"You cannot be sure about these things," Standing Rock insisted.

"Maybe not, but I think there's a pretty good chance I'm right. What it really looks like is that somebody dragged Blue Bull over here, then climbed up the canyon wall to start the rock slide that covered up his body."

Two Bears said, "He would have had to be unconscious or dead for that to happen."

Preacher nodded.

"Yep, more than likely. Maybe we can tell, if you let me take a good look at the body."

"He was my friend," Standing Rock said. "Stand back. I will do it."

"Sure," Preacher said. He moved one step back, but that was as far as he went. He wanted to be able to see whatever Standing Rock found.

Standing Rock knelt beside his dead friend and looked him over from head to toe.

"There are no injuries except the ones the rocks made when they fell on him," Standing Rock announced.

"Turn him over," Preacher suggested.

Standing Rock sent a hostile glance at the mountain man, but he did as Preacher said and gently took hold of Blue Bull's shoulders. Carefully, he rolled the body onto its left side.

A sharp breath hissed between Standing Rock's clenched teeth. Preacher saw what had prompted the young warrior's reaction.

A bloodstain had spread on the back of Blue Bull's shirt, just to the left of the middle of his back. In the middle of that bloodstain was a small tear in the buckskin.

"A knife did that," Preacher said. "Somebody stabbed him in the back, probably out in the middle of the canyon, and then tried to hide the body."

Two Bears said, "That would mean . . ."

"Yep," Preacher said. "This was no accident. Blue Bull was murdered."

The big man paced back and forth angrily. Despite his size, his movements had a certain dangerous, catlike quality to them. His hat was thumbed back over his blocky, rough-hewn face.

"Let me get this straight," he said. "You didn't have any choice but to kill the Indian."

"That's right, Randall," replied one of the men facing him. "He seen us. He might've gone back to his village and warned the rest of those redskins that we're up here in the hills."

The eyes of the man called Randall narrowed as he stared coldly at the two men he had sent out as scouts.

"There are several big spreads bordering the Indian land," he said. "And Two Bears doesn't mind if the punchers who ride for those ranches cut across the Assiniboine hunting grounds. You *know* that, damn it! We all do. So what in hell made you think that running into a lone warrior was going to cause a problem?"

The two men, whose names were Page and Dwyer, shuffled their feet uncomfortably. They didn't like being in dutch with the hardbitten ramrod of this gun-hung bunch that waited in the hills for nightfall.

Thirty men, along with their horses, stood around in whatever shade they could find, watching as Randall confronted the scouts. The others were every bit as rough and menacing looking as their leader.

Page had spoken up earlier. Now Dwyer said, "You weren't there, Randall. You didn't see how spooked that redskin acted. He knew somethin' was up, I tell you. Page and me did the only thing we could."

"And we covered his body up good and proper," Page added. "Nobody'll ever find him."

Randall said, "You seem mighty sure about that. You know that as soon as the rest of his people miss him, they'll come looking for him."

"They won't find him," Page insisted.

Randall wanted to say something else. He wanted to cuss the two fools up one way and down the other. Instead, he just jerked his head in a curt nod and said, "You'd better hope they don't. Finding one of their own warriors stabbed in the back is likely to spook them a lot more than running across a couple of riders would have."

Earlier, when the two men had come back from scouting the approaches to the Assiniboine village, they had brought an Indian pony with them, trailing from a rope lead held by Dwyer. When Randall had demanded to know where the animal came from, they had hemmed and hawed around for a minute and tried to say they found it, but it hadn't taken long for his cold stare to get the truth out of them.

They had run into a warrior in a canyon that cut through a ridge several miles from the Assiniboine village. The Indian kept asking questions, the scouts claimed, so Dwyer had distracted him while Page got behind him and put a knife in his back. Then they had dragged him over to the side of the canyon and caved in part of the wall on him. Chances were they were right about nobody finding the body, at least not in time to have any effect on the mission that had brought Randall and his men to this part of the territory.

With the matter settled for the time being, unsatisfactory though it might be, Randall turned and stalked away to give himself a chance to control his anger. He looked up at the sky.

In a couple of more hours, it would be dark.

And once night had fallen, he and his men could ride down out of these hills and do what they had been sent here to do. That thought put a faint smile on Randall's rugged face.

The prospect of killing always did.

SPECIAL BONUS!

*Smoke Jensen. Mountain Man. He roamed the wilderness
and was quick with a gun or a knife. The last of a breed—
one of the many brave and intrepid men who helped
tame the American frontier.*

Turn the page for Chapters One, Two, and Three of

TRAIL OF THE MOUNTAIN MAN,

one of Smoke's earliest western adventures.

Trail of the Mountain Man

by William W. Johnstone,
today's most popular western storyteller

Chapter One

As gold strikes go, this particular strike was nothing to really shout about. Oh, a lot of the precious metal was dug out, chipped free, and blasted from the earth and rock, but the mines would play out in just over a year. The town of Fontana would wither and fade from the Western scene a couple of years later.

But with the discovery of gold, a great many lives would be forever changed. Livelihoods and relationships were altered; fortunes were made and lost; lives were snuffed out and families split, with the only motive greed.

Thus Fontana was conceived only to die an unnatural death.

Dawn was breaking as the man stepped out of the cabin. He held a steaming cup of coffee in one large, callused hand. He was tall, with wide shoulders and the lean hips of the horseman. His hair was ash-blond, cropped short, and his eyes were a cold brown, rarely giving away any inner thought.

The cabin had been built well, of stone and logs. The

floor was wood. The windows held real glass. The cabin had been built to last, with a hand pump in the kitchen to bring up the water. There were curtains on the windows. The table and chairs and benches were hand-made and carved; done with patience and love.

And all about the house, inside and out, were the signs of a woman's touch.

Flowers and blooming shrubs were in colored profusion. The area around the house was trimmed and swept. Neat.

It was a high-up and lonely place, many miles from the nearest town. Below the cabin lay a valley, five miles wide and as many miles long. The land was filed on and claimed and legal with the government. It belonged to the man and his wife.

They had lived here for three years, hacking a home out of the high, lonesome wilderness. Building a future. In another year they planned on building a family. If all stayed according to plan, that is.

The man and wife had a couple hundred head of cattle, a respectable herd of horses. They worked a large garden, canning much of what they raised for the hard winters that lashed the high country.

The man and woman stayed to themselves, socializing very little. When they did visit, it was not to the home of the kingpin who claimed to run the entire area, Tilden Franklin. Rather it was to the small farmers and ranchers who dotted the country that lay beneath the high lonesome where the man and woman lived.

There was a no-name town then that was exclusively owned by Tilden Franklin. The town held a large general store, two saloons, a livery stable, and a gunsmith.

But all that was about to change.

Abruptly.

This was a land of towering mountains and lush, green

valleys, sparsely populated, and it took a special breed of men and women to endure. Many could not cope with the harshness, and they either moved on or went back to where they came from.

Those that stayed were the hardy breed.

Like Matt and Sally.

Matt was not his real name. He had not been called by his real name for so many years he never thought of it. There were those who could look at him and tell what he had once been; but this was the West, and what a man had once been did not matter. What mattered was what he was now. And all who knew Matt knew him to be a man you could ride the river with.

He had been a gunfighter. But now he rarely buckled on a short gun. Matt was not yet thirty years old and could not tell you how many men he had killed. Fifty, seventy-five, a hundred. He didn't know. And neither did anyone else.

He had been a gunfighter, and yet had never hired out his gun. Had never killed for pleasure. His reputation had come to him as naturally as his snake-like swiftness with a short gun.

He had come West with his father, and they had teamed up with an old Mountain Man named Preacher. And the Mountain Man had taken the boy in tow and begun teaching him the way of the mountains: how to survive, how to be a man, how to live where others would die.

Preacher had been present when the boy killed his first man during an Indian attack. The old Mountain Man had seen to the boy after the boy's dying father had left his son in his care. Preacher had seen to the boy's last formative years. And the old Mountain Man had known that he rode with a natural gun slick.*

*The Last Mountain Man

It was Preacher who gave the boy the name that would become legend throughout the West; the name that would be whispered around ten thousand campfires and spoken of in a thousand saloons; the name that would be spoken with the same awe as that of Bat Masterson, Ben Thompson, the Earp boys, Curly Bill.

Smoke.

Smoke's first wife had been raped and murdered, their baby son killed. Smoke had killed them all, then ridden into the town owned by the men who had sent the outlaws out and killed those men and wiped the town from the face of Idaho history.**

Smoke Jensen then did two things, one of them voluntarily. He became the most feared man in all the West, and he dropped out of sight. And then, shortly after dropping out of sight, he married Sally.

But his disappearance did nothing to slow the rumors about him; indeed, if anything, the rumors built in flavor and fever.

Smoke had been seen in Northern California. Smoke had gunned down five outlaws in Oregon. Smoke had cleaned up a town in Nevada. Since his disappearance, Smoke, so the rumors went, had done this and that and the other thing.

In reality, Smoke had not fired a gun in anger in three years.

But all that was about to change.

A dark-haired, hazel-eyed, shapely woman stepped out of the cabin to stand by her man's side. Something was troubling him, and she did not know what. But he would tell her in time.

This man and wife kept no secrets from each other. Their lives were shared in all things. No decisions were made by one without consulting the other.

** *Return of the Mountain Man*

"More coffee?" she asked.

"No, thank you. Trouble coming," he said abruptly. "I feel it in my gut."

A touch of panic washed over her. "Will we have to leave here?"

Smoke tossed the dregs of his coffee to the ground. "When hell freezes over. This is our land, our home. We built it, and we're staying."

"How do the others feel?"

"Haven't talked to them. Think I might do that today. You need anything from town?"

"No."

"You want to come along?"

She smiled and shook her head. "I have so much to do around the house. You go."

"It'll be noon tomorrow before I can get back," he reminded her.

"I'll be all right."

He was known as Matt in this part of Colorado, but at home Sally always called him Smoke. "I'll pack you some food, Smoke."

He nodded his head. "I'll saddle up."

He saddled an appaloosa, a tough mountain horse, sired by his old appaloosa, Seven, who now ran wild and free on the range in the valley Smoke and Sally claimed.

Back in the snug cabin, Smoke pulled a trunk out of a closet and opened the lid. He was conscious of Sally's eyes on him as he removed his matched 44's and laid them to one side. He removed the rubbed and oiled gun belts and laid them beside the deadly colts.

"It's come to that, Smoke?" she asked.

He sighed, squatting before the trunk. He removed several boxes of .44 ammo. "I don't know." His words were softly spoken. "But Franklin is throwing a big loop nowadays. And wants it bigger still. I was up on the Cimarron the other day—I didn't tell you 'cause I didn't want you to worry. I made sign with some Indians. Sally, it's gold."

She closed the trunk lid and sat down, facing her husband. "Here? In this area?"

"Yes. Hook Nose, the buck that spoke English, told me that many whites are coming. Like ants toward honey was his words. If it's true, Sally, it's trouble. You know Franklin claims more than a hundred and fifty thousand acres as his own. And he's always wanted this valley of ours. It's surprising to me that he hasn't made a move to take it."

Money did not impress Sally. She was a young, high-spirited woman with wealth of her own. Old money, from back in New Hampshire. In all probability, she could have bought out Tilden Franklin's holdings and still had money.

"You knew about the gold all along, didn't you, Smoke?"

"Yes," he told her. "But I don't think it's a big vein. I found part of the broken vein first year we were here. I don't want it."

"We certainly don't need the money," she reminded him.

Smoke gave her one of his rare smiles, the smile softening his face and mellowing his eyes, taking years from the young man's face. "That's right. I keep forgetting I married me a rich lady."

Together, they laughed.

Her laughter sobered as he began filling the cartridge loops with .44 rounds.

"Does part of it run through our land, Smoke?"

"Yes."

"I'll pack you extra food. I think you're going to be gone longer than you think."

"I think you're probably right. Sally? You know you have nothing to fear from the Indians. They knew Preacher and know he helped raise me. It's the white men you have to be careful of. It would take a very foolish man to bother a woman out here, but it's happened. Stay close to the house. The horses will warn you if anyone's coming. Go armed at all times. Hear me?"

"Yes, Smoke."

He leaned forward and kissed her mouth. "I taught you to shoot, and know you can. Don't hesitate to do so. The pot is boiling, Sally. We're going to have gold-hunters coming up against Franklin's gunhands. When Franklin learns of the gold, he's going to want it all. Our little no-name town is going to boom. For a time. Trouble is riding our way on a horse out of Hell. You've never seen a boomtown, Sally. I have. They're rough and mean and totally violent. They attract the good and the bad. Especially the bad. Gamblers and gunhawks and thieves and whores. We're all going to be in for a rough time of it for a while."

"We've been through some rough times before, Smoke," she said quietly.

"Not like this." He stood up, belted the familiar Colts around his lean waist, and began loading the .44's.

"Matt just died, didn't he?" she asked.

"Yes. I'm afraid so. When Smoke steps out of the shadows, Sally—and it's time, for I'm tired of being someone else—bounty hunters and kids with dreams of being the man who killed Smoke Jensen will be coming in with the rest of the trash and troublemakers. Sally, I've never been ashamed of what I was. I hunted down and destroyed those who ripped my life to shreds. I did what the law could not or would not do. I did what any real man would have done. I'm a Mountain Man, Sally. Perhaps the last of the breed. But that's what I am.

"I'm not running anymore, Sally. I want to live in peace. But if I have to fight to attain that peace . . . so be it. And," he said with a sigh, "I might as well level with you. Peyton told me last month that Franklin has made his boast about running us out of this valley."

"His wife told me, Smoke."

The young man with the hard eyes smiled. "I might have known."

She drew herself up on tiptoes and kissed him. "See you in two or three days, Smoke."

Chapter Two

"Word is out, boss," Tilden's foreman said. "It's gold, all right. And lots of it."

Tilden leaned back in his chair and looked at his foreman. "Is it fact or rumor, Clint?"

"Fact, boss. The assay office says it's rich. Real rich."

"The Sugarloaf?"

Clint shrugged his heavy shoulders. "It's a broken vein, Boss. Juts out all over the place, so I was told. Spotty. But one things for sure: all them piss-ant nesters and small spreads around the Sugarloaf is gonna have some gold on the land."

The Sugarloaf was Smoke's valley.

Tilden nodded his handsome head. "Send some of the crew into town, start stakin' out lots. Folks gonna be foggin' in here pretty quick."

"What are you gonna call the town, boss?"

"I knew me a Mex gal years back, down along the Animas. Her last name was Fontana. I always did like that name. We'll call 'er Fontana."

* * *

Tilden Franklin sat alone in his office, making plans. Grand plans, for Tilden never thought small. A big bear of a man, Tilden stood well over six feet and weighed a good two hundred and forty pounds, little of it fat. He was forty years old and in the peak of health.

He had come into this part of Colorado when he was twenty-five years old. He had carved his empire out of the wilderness. He had fought Indians and outlaws and the elements . . . and won.

And he thought of himself as king.

He had fifty hands on his spread, many of them hired as much for their ability with a gun as with a rope. And he paid his men well, both in greenbacks and in a comfortable style of living. His men rode for the brand, doing anything that Tilden asked of them, or they got out. It was that simple.

His brand was the Circle TF.

Tilden rose from his chair and paced the study of his fine home—the finest in all the area. When that Matt What's-His-Name had ridden into this part of the country—back three or four years ago—Tilden had taken an immediate dislike to the young man.

And he didn't believe Matt *was* the man's name. But Tilden didn't hold that against anyone. Man had a right to change his own name.

Still, Tilden had always had the ability to bully and intimidate other men. He had always bulled and bullied his way through any situation. Men respected and feared him.

All but that damned Matt.

Tilden remembered the first day he'd come face to face with Matt. The young man had looked at him through the coldest eyes Tilden had ever seen—a rattler's. And even though the young man had not been wearing a short gun, there had been no backup in him. None at all. He had looked right at Tilden, nodded his head, and walked on.

Tilden Franklin had had the uncomfortable and unaccustomed sensation that he had just been graded and found wanting. That, and the feeling that he had just been summarily dismissed.

By a goddamned saddle-bum, of all people!

No, Tilden corrected himself, not a saddle-bum. Matt might be many things, but he was no saddle-bum. He had to have access to money, for he had bought that whole damned valley free and clear. Bought most of it, filed on the rest of it.

And that woman of his, Sally. Just thinking of her caused Tilden to breathe short. He knew from the first day he'd seen her that he had to have her. One way or the other—and she was never far from his thoughts.

She was far and above any other woman in the area. She was a woman fit to be a king's queen. And since Tilden thought of himself as a king, it was only natural he possess a woman with queen-like qualities.

And possess her he would. It was just a matter of time.

Whether she liked it, or not. Her feelings were not important.

Three hours after leaving his cabin, Smoke rode up to the Colby spread. He halloed the house from the gate and Colby stepped out, giving him a friendly wave to come on in.

Colby's spread was a combination cattle ranch and farm, something purists in the cattle business frowned on. Colby and his family were just more of them "goddamned nesters" as far as the bigger spreads in the area were concerned. Colby had moved into the area a couple of years before Smoke and Sally, with his wife Belle, and their three kids, a girl and two boys. From Missouri, Colby was a hardworking man in his early forties. A veteran of the War Between the States, he was no stranger to guns, but was not a gunhand.

"Matt," he greeted the rider. His eyes narrowed at the sight of the twin Colts belted around Smoke's waist and tied down. "First time I ever seen you wearin' a pistol, much less two of them."

"Times change, Colby. You heard the gold news?"

"Last week. People already movin' in. You wanna come in and talk?"

"Let's do it out here. You ever seen a boomtown, Colby?"

"Can't say as I have, Matt." The man was having a difficult time keeping his eyes off the twin Colts. "Why do you ask?"

"There's gold running through this area. Not much of it— a lot of it is iron and copper pyrites—but there's enough gold to bring out the worst in men."

"I ain't no miner, Matt. What's them pyrites you said?"

"Fool's gold. But that isn't the point, Colby. When Tilden Franklin learns of the gold—if he doesn't already know— he'll move against us."

"You can't know that for sure, Matt. 'Sides, this is our land. We filed on it right with the government. He can't just come in and run us off."

The younger man looked at Colby through hard, wise eyes. "You want to risk your family's lives on that statement, Colby?"

"Who are you, Matt?" Colby asked, evading the question.

"A man who wants to be left alone. A man who has been over the mountain and across the river. And I won't be pushed off my land."

"That don't tell me what I asked, Matt. You really know how to use them guns?"

"What do you think?"

Colby's wife and kids had joined them. The two boys were well into manhood. Fifteen and sixteen years old. The girl was thirteen, but mature for her age, built up right well. Sticking out in all the right places. Adam, Bob, Velvet.

The three young people stared at the Colts. Even a fool could see that the pistols were used but well taken care of. "I don't see no marks on the handles, Mister Matt," Adam said. "That must mean you ain't never killed no one."

"Adam!" his mother said.

"Tinhorn trick, Adam," Smoke said. "No one with any sand to them cuts their kills for everyone to see."

"I bet you wouldn't say that to none of Mister Franklin's men," Velvet said.

Smoke smiled at the girl. He lifted his eyes to Colby. "I've told you what I know, Colby. You know where to find me." He swung into the saddle.

"I didn't mean no offense, Matt," the farmer-rancher said.

"None taken." Smoke reined his horse around and headed west.

Colby watched Smoke until horse and rider had disappeared from view. "Thing is," he said, as much to himself as to his family, "Matt's right. I just don't know what to do about it."

Bob said, "Them guns look . . . well, *right* on Mister Matt, Dad. I wonder who he really is."

"I don't know. But I got me a hunch we're all gonna find out sooner than we want to," he said sourly.

"This is our land," Belle said. "And no one has the right to take it from us."

Colby put his arm around her waist. "Is it worth dyin' for, Ma?"

"Yes," she said quickly.

* * *

On his ride to Steve Matlock's spread, Smoke cut the trail of dozens of riders and others on foot, all heading for Franklin's town. He could tell from the hoofprints and footprints that horses and men were heavily loaded.

Gold hunters.

Steve met him several miles from his modest cabin in the high-up country. "Matt," the man said. "What's going on around here?"

"Trouble, I'm thinking. I just left Colby's place. I couldn't get through to him."

"He's got to think on it a spell. But I don't have to be convinced. I come from the store yesterday. Heard the rumors. Tilden wants our land, and most of all, he wants the Sugarloaf."

"Among other things," Smoke said, a dry note to the statement.

"I figured you knew he had his eyes on Sally. Risky to leave her alone, Matt. Or whatever your name is," he added acknowledging the Colts in a roundabout manner.

"Tilden won't try to take Sally by force this early in the game, Steve. He'll have me out of the way first. There's some gold on your land, by the way."

"A little bit. Most of it's fool's gold. The big vein cuts north at Nolan's place, then heads straight into the mountains. Take a lot of machinery to get it out, and there ain't no way to get the equipment up there."

"People aren't going to think about that, Steve. All they'll be thinking of is gold. And they'll stomp on anyone who gets in their way."

"I stocked up on ammo. Count on me, Matt."

"I knew I could."

* * *

Smoke rode on, slowly winding downward. On his way down to No-Name Town, he stopped and talked with Peyton and Nolan. Both of them ran small herds and farmed for extra money while their herds matured.

"Yeah," Peyton said. "I heard about the gold. Goddamnit, that's all we need."

Nolan said, "Franklin has made his boast that if he can run you out, the rest of us will be easy."

Smoke's smile was not pleasant, and both the men came close to backing up. "I don't run," Smoke said.

"First time I ever seen you armed with a short gun," Peyton said. "You look . . . well, don't take this the wrong way, Matt . . . *natural* with them."

"Matt," Nolan said. "I've known you for three years and some months. I've never seen you upset. But today, you've got a burr under your blanket."

"This vein of gold is narrow and shallow, boys," Smoke said, even though both men were older than he. "Best thing could happen is if it was just left alone. But that's not going to happen." He told them about boomtowns. "There's going to be a war," he added, "and those of us who only wanted to live in peace are going to be caught up in the middle of it. And there is something else. If we don't band together, the only man who'll come out on top will be Tilden Franklin."

"He sure wants to tan your hide and tack it to his barn door, Matt," Peyton said.

"I was raised by an old Mountain Man, boys. He used to say I was born with the bark on. I reckon he was right. The last twelve–fifteen years of my life, I've only had three peaceful years, and those were spent right in this area. And if I want to continue my peaceful way of life, it looks like

I'm gonna have to fight for them. And fight I will, boys. Don't make no bets against me doing that."

Nolan looked uncomfortable. "I know it ain't none of my business, Matt, and you can tell me to go to hell if you want to. But I gotta ask. Who are you?"

"My Christian name is Jensen. An old Mountain Man named Preacher hung a nickname on me years back. Smoke."

Smoke wheeled his horse and trotted off without looking back.

Peyton grabbed his hat and flung it on the ground. "Holy Christ!" he yelled. "Smoke Jensen!"

Both men ran for their horses, to get home, tell their families that the most famous gun in the entire West had been their neighbor all this time. And more importantly, that Smoke Jensen was on *their* side.

Chapter Three

When Smoke reached the main road, running east to west before being forced to cut due south at a place called Feather Falls, he ran into a rolling, riding, walking stream of humanity. Sitting astride his horse, whom he had named Horse, Smoke cursed softly. The line must have been five hundred strong. And he knew, in two weeks, there would probably be ten times that number converging on No-Name.

"Wonderful," he muttered. Horse cocked his ears and looked back at Smoke. "Yeah, Horse. I don't like it either."

With a gentle touch of his spurs, Smoke and Horse moved out, riding at an easy trot for town.

Before he reached the crest of the hill overlooking the town, the sounds of hammering reached his ears. Reining up on the crest, Smoke sat and watched the men below, racing about, driving stakes all over the place, marking out building locations. Lines of wagons were in a row, the wagons loaded with lumber. Canvas tents were already in place, and the whiskey peddlers were dipping their home-made concoction out of barrels. Smoke knew there would be everything in that whiskey from horse droppings to snake heads.

He rode slowly down the hill and tied up at the railing in front of the general store. He stood on the boardwalk for a moment, looking at the organized madness taking place all around him.

Smoke recognized several men from out of the shouting, shoving, cursing crush.

There was Utah Slim, the gunhand from down Escalante way. The gambler Louis Longmont was busy setting up his big tent. Over there, by the big saloon tent, was Big Mamma O'Neil. Smoke knew her girls would not be far away. Big Mamma had a stable of whores and sold bad booze and ran crooked games. Smoke had seen other faces that he recognized but could not immediately put names to. They would come to him.

He turned and walked into the large general store. The owner, Beeker, was behind the counter, grinning like a cream-fed cat. No doubt he was doing a lot of business and no doubt he had jacked up his prices.

Beeker's smile changed to a frown when he noticed the low-slung Colts on Smoke. "Something, Matt?"

"Ten boxes of .44's, Beeker. That'll do for a start. I'll just look around a bit."

"I don't know if I can spare that many, Matt," Beeker said, his voice whiny.

"You can spare them." Smoke walked around the store, picking up several other items, including several pairs of britches that looked like they'd fit Sally. In all likelihood, she was going to have to do some hard riding before all this was said and done, and while it wasn't ladylike to wear men's britches and ride astride, it was something she was going to have to do.

He moved swiftly past the glass-enclosed showcase filled with women's underthings and completed his swing back to the main counter, laying his purchases on the counter. "That'll do it, Beeker."

The store owner added it up and Smoke paid the bill.

"Mighty fancy guns you wearin', Matt. Never seen you wear a short gun before. Something the matter?"

"You might say that."

"Don't let none of Tilden's boys see you with them things on. They might take 'em off you 'less you know how to use them."

Beeker did not like Smoke, and the feeling was shared. Beeker kowtowed to Tilden; Smoke did not. Beeker thought Tilden was a mighty fine man; Smoke thought Tilden to be a very obnoxious SOB.

Smoke lifted his eyes and stared at Beeker. Beeker took a step backward, those emotionless, cold brown eyes chilling him, touching the coward's heart that beat in his chest.

Smoke picked up his purchases and walked out into the spring sunlight. He stowed the gear in his saddlebags and walked across the street to the better of the two saloons. In a week there would be fifty saloons, all working twenty-four hours a day.

As he walked across the wide dirt street, his spurs jingling and his heels kicking up little dust pockets, Smoke was conscious of eyes on him. Unfriendly eyes. He stepped up onto the boardwalk and pushed through the swinging doors. Stepping to one side, giving his eyes time to adjust to the murky interior of the saloon, Smoke sized up the crowd.

The place was filled with ranchers and punchers. Some of those present were friends and friendly with Smoke. Others were sworn to the side of Tilden Franklin. Smoke walked to the end of the bar.

Smoke was dressed in black pants, red and white checkered shirt, and a low-crowned hat. Behind his left-hand Colt, he carried a long-bladed Bowie knife. He laid a coin on the bar and ordered a beer.

The place had grown very quiet.

Normally not a drinking man, Smoke did occasionally enjoy a drink of whiskey or a beer. On this day, he simply wanted to check out the mood of the people.

He nodded at a couple of ranchers. They returned the silent greeting. Smoke sipped his beer.

Across the room, seated around a poker table, were half a dozen of Tilden's men. They had ceased their game and now sat staring at Smoke. None of those present had ever seen the young man go armed before—other than carrying a rifle in his saddle boot.

The outside din was softened somewhat, but still managed to push through the walls of the saloon.

"Big doings around the area," Smoke said to no one in particular.

One of Tilden's men laughed.

Smoke looked at the man; he knew him only as Red. Red fancied himself a gunhand. Smoke knew the man had killed a drunken Mexican some years back, and had ridden the hoot-owl trail on more than one occasion. But Smoke doubted the man was as fast with a gun as he imagined.

"Private joke?" Smoke asked."

"Yeah," Red said. "And the joke is standin' at the bar, drinkin' a beer."

Smoke smiled and looked at a rancher. "Must be talking about you, Jackson."

Jackson flushed and shook his head. A Tilden man all the way, Jackson did all he could to stay out of the way of Tilden's ire.

"Oh?" Smoke said, lifting his beer mug with his left hand. "Well, then. Maybe Red's talking about you, Beaconfield."

Another Tilden man who shook in his boots at the mere mention of Tilden's name.

Beaconfield shook his head.

"I'm talkin' to you, Two-Gun!" Red shouted at Smoke.

Left and right of Smoke, the bar area quickly cleared of men.

"You'd better be real sure, Red," Smoke said softly, his words carrying through the silent saloon. "And very good."

"What the hell's that supposed to mean, nester?" Red almost yelled the question.

"It means, Red, that I didn't come in here hunting trouble. But if it comes my way, I'll handle it."

"You got a big mouth, nester."

"Back off, Matt!" a friendly rancher said hoarsely. "He'll kill you!"

Smoke's only reply was a small smile. It did not touch his eyes.

Smoke had slipped the hammer thong off his right-hand Colt before stepping into the saloon. He placed his beer mug on the bar and slowly turned to face Red.

Red stood up.

Smoke slipped the hammer thong off his left-hand gun. So confident were Red's friends that they did not move from the table.

"I'm saying it now," Smoke said. "And those of you still left alive when the smoke clears can take it back to Tilden. The Sugarloaf belongs to me. I'll kill any Circle TF rider I find on my land. Your boss has made his boast that he'll run me off my land. He's said he'll take my wife. Those words alone give me justification to kill him. But he won't face me alone. He'll send his riders to do the job. So if any of you have a mind to open the dance, let's strike up the band, boys."

Red jerked out his pistol. Smoke let him clear leather before he drew his right-hand Colt. He drew, cocked, and fired in one blindingly fast motion. The .44 slug hit Red square between his eyes and blew out the back of his head, the force of the .44 slug slamming the TF rider backward to land in a sprawl of dead, cooling meat some distance away from the table.

The other TF riders sat very still at the table, being very careful not to move their hands.

Smoke holstered his .44 in a move almost as fast as his draw. "Anybody else want to dance?"

No one did.

"Then I'll finish my beer, and I'd appreciate it if I could do so in peace."

No one had moved in the saloon. The bartender was so scared he looked like he wanted to wet his long handles.

"Pass me that bowl of eggs down here, will you, Beaconfield?" Smoke asked.

The rancher scooted the bowl of hard-boiled eggs down the bar. Smoke looked at the bartender. "Crack it and peel it for me."

The bartender dropped one egg and made a mess out of the second before he got the third one right.

"A little salt and pepper on it, please," Smoke requested.

Gas escaped from Red's cooling body.

Smoke ate his egg and finished his beer. He wiped his mouth with the back of his hand and deliberately turned his back to the table of TF riders. "Any backshooters in the bunch?" he asked.

"First man reaches for a gun, I drop them," a rancher friendly to Smoke said.

"Thanks, Mike," Smoke said.

He walked to the batwing doors, his spurs jingling. A TF rider named Singer spoke, his voice stopping Smoke. "You could have backed off, Matt."

"Not much backup in me, Singer." Smoke turned around to once more face the crowded saloon.

"I reckon not," Singer acknowledged. "But you got to know what this means."

"All it means is I killed a loud-mouthed tinhorn. Your boss wants to make something else out of it, that's his concern."

"Man ought to have it on his marker who killed him." Singer didn't let up. "Matt your first or last name?"

"Neither one. The name is Jensen. Smoke Jensen."

Singer's jaw dropped so far down Smoke thought it might hit the card table. He turned around and pushed open the doors, walking across the street to his horse. As he swung into the saddle, he was thinking. Should get real interesting around No-Name . . . real quick.

THE FIRST MOUNTAIN MAN SERIES BY
WILLIAM W. JOHNSTONE

Available Wherever Books Are Sold!

Visit our website at **www.kensingtonbooks.com**

THE MOUNTAIN MAN SERIES BY
WILLIAM W. JOHNSTONE

__The Last Mountain Man	0-8217-6856-5	**$5.99**US/**$7.99**CAN
__Return of the Mountain Man	0-7860-1296-X	**$5.99**US/**$7.99**CAN
__Trail of the Mountain Man	0-7860-1297-8	**$5.99**US/**$7.99**CAN
__Revenge of the Mountain Man	0-7860-1133-1	**$5.99**US/**$7.99**CAN
__Law of the Mountain Man	0-7860-1301-X	**$5.99**US/**$7.99**CAN
__Journey of the Mountain Man	0-7860-1302-8	**$5.99**US/**$7.99**CAN
__War of the Mountain Man	0-7860-1303-6	**$5.99**US/**$7.99**CAN
__Code of the Mountain Man	0-7860-1304-4	**$5.99**US/**$7.99**CAN
__Pursuit of the Mountain Man	0-7860-1305-2	**$5.99**US/**$7.99**CAN
__Courage of the Mountain Man	0-7860-1306-0	**$5.99**US/**$7.99**CAN
__Blood of the Mountain Man	0-7860-1307-9	**$5.99**US/**$7.99**CAN
__Fury of the Mountain Man	0-7860-1308-7	**$5.99**US/**$7.99**CAN
__Rage of the Mountain Man	0-7860-1555-1	**$5.99**US/**$7.99**CAN
__Cunning of the Mountain Man	0-7860-1512-8	**$5.99**US/**$7.99**CAN
__Power of the Mountain Man	0-7860-1530-6	**$5.99**US/**$7.99**CAN
__Spirit of the Mountain Man	0-7860-1450-4	**$5.99**US/**$7.99**CAN
__Ordeal of the Mountain Man	0-7860-1533-0	**$5.99**US/**$7.99**CAN
__Triumph of the Mountain Man	0-7860-1532-2	**$5.99**US/**$7.99**CAN
__Vengeance of the Mountain Man	0-7860-1529-2	**$5.99**US/**$7.99**CAN
__Honor of the Mountain Man	0-8217-5820-9	**$5.99**US/**$7.99**CAN
__Battle of the Mountain Man	0-8217-5925-6	**$5.99**US/**$7.99**CAN
__Pride of the Mountain Man	0-8217-6057-2	**$4.99**US/**$6.50**CAN
__Creed of the Mountain Man	0-7860-1531-4	**$5.99**US/**$7.99**CAN
__Guns of the Mountain Man	0-8217-6407-1	**$5.99**US/**$7.99**CAN
__Heart of the Mountain Man	0-8217-6618-X	**$5.99**US/**$7.99**CAN
__Justice of the Mountain Man	0-7860-1298-6	**$5.99**US/**$7.99**CAN
__Valor of the Mountain Man	0-7860-1299-4	**$5.99**US/**$7.99**CAN
__Warpath of the Mountain Man	0-7860-1330-3	**$5.99**US/**$7.99**CAN
__Trek of the Mountain Man	0-7860-1331-1	**$5.99**US/**$7.99**CAN

Available Wherever Books Are Sold!

Visit our website at **www.kensingtonbooks.com**

THE EAGLES SERIES BY
WILLIAM W. JOHNSTONE

Available Wherever Books Are Sold!

Visit our website at **www.kensingtonbooks.com**